An Angel I...

"Everything the angel tells you is truth," Aliisza said. "Every promise he makes to you will be honored. He cannot help it. It is his nature."

"That's not what I asked you," Kaanyr said. "Can you see any trickery in his offer? Have I established the parameters solidly enough? Is there anything I am missing?"

It's not what you think you see that gets you, Aliisza thought. That's only what he distracts you with. It's what you never expected that will be your undoing. And you'll deserve every last bit of misery from it, you bastard.

But Deals with Demons are Never What they Seem

THOMAS M. REID

The Empyrean Odyssey

Also by Thomas M. Reid

The Scions of Arrabar Trilogy

R.A. Salvatore's
War of the Spider Queen

FORGOTTEN REALMS

THE FRACTURED SKY

THE EMPYREAN ODYSSEY
BOOK II

THOMAS M. REID

Wizards OF THE COAST

THE EMPYREAN ODYSSEY, BOOK II
THE FRACTURED SKY

©2008 Wizards of the Coast, Inc.

Cover art by Jeff Nentrup
First Printing: November 2008

9 8 7 6 5 4 3 2 1

ISBN: 978-0-7869-4807-9
620-95981740-001-EN

U.S., CANADA,
ASIA, PACIFIC, & LATIN AMERICA
Wizards of the Coast, Inc.
P.O. Box 707
Renton, WA 98057-0707
+1-800-324-6496

EUROPEAN HEADQUARTERS
Hasbro UK Ltd
Caswell Way
Newport, Gwent NP9 0YH
GREAT BRITAIN
Save this address for your records.

Visit our web site at www.wizards.com

PROLOGUE

Kashada the Nightwraith stood very still and waited, watching a doorway from the opposite side of Helm Dwarf-friend's great hall. It was late, and only a few lanterns burned, turned low to save oil. The hall, which soared three stories high with balconies ringing it at each level, lay shrouded in shadows. Kashada would not be seen among them.

A wisp of a girl in a nightshirt entered the hall from that far doorway. Though the other figure also stayed among the shadows, Kashada could see her plainly. It was Ansa, the Dwarf-friend's lover. The girl padded across the hall in Kashada's direction. Her shoulder-length curls bounced gently in a most provocative way as her hips swayed a tiny bit more than necessary.

Kashada grinned to herself in the darkness of her hiding place. Tramp, she thought. Dwarf-friend likes them saucy.

As the young woman passed the great table and its high-backed chairs, Kashada settled a bit deeper into her own shadows, comforted by their cloaking darkness. She brought a spell to mind, a simple trick that would allow her to become a shadow herself should Ansa hesitate and perhaps sense her presence there. Despite her seeming innocence, the girl was anything but, and Kashada the Veiled One would not risk ruining Zasian Menz's plan by getting caught spying.

Ansa reached a passage leading from the great hall and proceeded down it. As she disappeared from view, Kashada slipped from her hiding place and followed silently after. The shadow-garbed woman reached the hallway and peeked around the corner: the girl stood a few paces away, her back to Kashada. At the far end of the hall, Zasian strode toward them from Helm Dwarf-friend's private chambers. It seemed to Kashada that Ansa cringed. Perhaps Ansa did not wish to be seen, but it was clearly too late.

Kashada watched as Zasian strode toward Ansa and stopped directly in front of her. "Look at me, child," he said, and he reached out to lift her chin with his finger.

The girl shivered at the man's touch, and Kashada had to stifle a chuckle. It was not a shudder of timidity, but of lust. She wants to bed him, too! the Veiled One thought, amused.

If Zasian noticed, he did not react to it. "You know you shouldn't be out here," he said, "especially not dressed as you are."

The man continued his admonishment, but Kashada stopped listening. She used the time to study the girl, scrutinizing every detail. She would need to duplicate Ansa's image as perfectly as possible when the time came. The nightshirt did little to hide the younger girl's shape, and Kashada noted the plump curves with a mixture of appreciation and jealousy.

It has been far too long since I truly looked that . . . firm, the woman mused.

As Zasian continued to speak, he pulled a pendant from his pocket. He strolled around Ansa, explaining many things to her, but Kashada ignored him. She focused on the face, the green eyes, the dimples. She established every last feature firmly in her mind's eye. It would need to be perfect to fool Dwarf-friend.

When she was certain she could become Ansa in every way, Kashada turned her attention to Zasian's words once more. "Get yourself out of sight, and don't let me catch you out like this again." His tone was stern, and he pointed down the hall.

"Yes, my lord," the girl said, and she turned and practically ran from him.

When Ansa had vanished through another door, Zasian turned to where Kashada hid. He did not look directly at her, but let his gaze sweep back and forth along the hall. "Well?" he asked, walking slowly, scanning the shadows. "Did you see enough?"

Kashada shimmered into view, letting the darkest of the shadows slide from her. She made a gesture and spoke a soft word, manipulating other bits of shadow. They swirled around her, clinging to her in wisps, changing her appearance. In a matter of heartbeats she was no longer Kashada the Nightwraith. Instead, she stood before Zasian as the girl in the nightshirt.

"Yes, my lord," Kashada said, shifting her voice to mimic Ansa's. She giggled softly.

Zasian frowned and began to circle her, inspecting her form. Kashada followed him with her eyes, shifting her weight and cocking one hip to the side as she had seen Ansa do. She felt his gaze and, despite herself, she felt a tiny shiver run through her.

"It will serve," the man said, sounding unimpressed. He returned to stand in front of her.

Kashada grimaced. *You* do a better job, she thought.

"You understand what must happen?" Zasian asked.

Kashada glared at him. "We have discussed this many times, priest," she said. "I am no novice at these intrigues."

"Nevertheless," Zasian replied, lifting his nose in a haughty manner, "I must be certain. Cyric will brook no failures on your part."

"Nor will Shar stand for any on yours," Kashada shot back. "Do not presume to lecture me, Menz. I know my task, *and* my burden. You just make certain you fulfill your end of this bargain."

Zasian studied Kashada's face for a moment, then gave her a curt nod. "Very well," he said. "Remain hidden and wait for the others to arrive. It may take time before we can begin."

Kashada smiled in mocking sweetness at Zasian. He cocked his head to one side, frowning again, but before he could say anything more, she stepped back into the deeper shadows and vanished.

The priest of Cyric shrugged and walked away, moving toward another wing of the Master's Hall.

❖ ❖ ❖ ❖ ❖ ❖ ❖ ❖ ❖

Time passed slowly, but Kashada had the patience to endure it. She had spent more than a few nights cloaked in darkness and silence, waiting. Events would unfold when they were ready, not when she desired. Secrets and betrayals were most effective when left to simmer.

After a while, Zasian returned with three others following him. Two men and a woman crept along the hall. The first, a short, stocky fellow in a leather jerkin, wore an array of small blades on numerous belts draped across his body. He had a satchel slung over one shoulder with a weighted net dangling half out of it. Behind him strode a woman, a warrior in heavy mail and brandishing a mace. A taller, thin man brought up the rear, a wand clutched in his hand as his loose trousers and shirt billowed out behind him. Kashada remained hidden and watched as the entourage walked by.

Kashada bristled when the woman passed her position. The Sharran could feel the cloying, sickening radiance of holy power waft from the warrior and knew she bowed to Torm without even needing to see the badge upon her armor. The sensation turned her stomach.

The priestess of Torm slowed a half-step, wrinkling her nose as though she smelled something distasteful.

The Nightwraith shrank back, deeper into the shadows that hid her, and held her breath.

The armored woman turned from side to side as though listening and looking for something. Behind her, the arcanist tapped her shoulder and urged her forward. She frowned and gazed absently around for a heartbeat or two longer, then she nodded and continued.

Kashada exhaled in relief.

At the end of the hall the prowlers paused before the door leading into Helm Dwarf-friend's chambers. Zasian gestured and said something too quiet for Kashada to hear. The shorter of the two men vanished. A moment later, the other male made a gesture and a red-framed doorway of energy appeared before him. The man stepped through and then he, too, vanished, the doorway winking out behind him. Finally, the woman raised her mace and shoved herself through the door. Zasian remained, watching.

Kashada stole from her hiding place and slipped down the

hall toward him, darting from shadow to shadow.

No sounds issued from within the chamber beyond the door. Whatever was happening, someone had made sure through some means, magical or otherwise, that it didn't rouse the rest of the hall.

When she drew close, Kashada paused. She watched the priest, waiting for a sign. Zasian turned toward her and nodded.

With a flick of her fingers, Kashada's body melted into the darkness and she found herself in a shadowy mirror-world of the one she had departed. The features were all there, identical in size, shape, and placement, only different. Everything looked less solid to the woman's eye, and the colors appeared washed out, gray and dull. Only the shadows themselves seemed real, somehow more physically firm than the surfaces upon which they were cast.

No versions of Zasian or anyone else stood within that hall.

Kashada paid no mind to the surreal quality of the place. With practiced ease, she flowed along the shadows, coming up to and then passing through the wall separating the hall from the chamber beyond, the one she knew served as Helm Dwarf-friend's bedchamber. She found the room to be in a similar condition to the passageway behind her. Shadow versions of all the furnishings sat arranged within the confines of the chamber, but of the Master of the Hall, there was no sign.

Kashada moved to a darkened corner and undid the magic of her spell. Instantly, reality returned to normal, and the light of hated Selûne shining through the slats of the shutters revealed the mounded form of someone in the bed. Kashada stood unmoving for a moment, watching the sleeping figure while listening for any signs of disturbance from the chamber beyond the door. Nothing emanated from that place, and Helm Dwarf-friend slept soundly.

Smiling, Kashada crawled into bed beside the man and snuggled up against him. Helm snorted once and rolled toward her, one thick arm coming to rest draped across her waist.

Kashada waited.

A deep thunderous rumble tossed the room around, and Kashada nearly pitched from the bed. She gave a little shriek as Helm cursed and sat up.

"What was that, lover?" Kashada asked, her voice disguised as Ansa's. She huddled close to the man at her side and tried to sound frightened.

"By the Lady's horn, I don't know!" he rumbled, flailing to free himself from the bedcovers. "I'm going to find out, though." He drew up his trousers. "Stay here," he added, turning to look at Kashada. "I'll be back soon."

"Very well," Kashada replied, pulling the covers around herself. "Hurry, lover."

Helm gave her a quick smile and a wink before yanking his shirt over his head and heading out the door. In the chamber beyond, a commotion arose. Kashada watched as Helm reached the door and yanked it open. The man took one stride through and drew up abruptly just as a blazing white light filled the chamber from some source out of Kashada's line of sight.

Kashada heard several gasps, and someone murmured, "Blessed angels!" It was not difficult for her to cower in the sheets and wait as she had been told. She did not want to come face to face with a holy being. The thought turned her stomach.

Take the fool alu and be gone, Kashada thought. Don't come sniffing in here.

She heard a voice ring out. "By Lord Tyr's justice, we claim this fiend for our own purposes." Its tone was thunderous, charged with power. "Do any among you offer reason we should not?"

Some faint murmuring reverberated from the chamber, but none dissented against the speaker.

"Very well," the being continued. "Then this one shall not trouble you again."

Kashada blinked. The blazing light was gone.

Helm turned and looked to Kashada. He nodded once, satisfied that she was safe, then slammed the door. She could hear him, his voice muffled through the portal, demanding to know what in the everlasting Hells was going on.

❖ ❖ ❖ ❖ ❖ ❖ ❖ ❖ ❖

It took the rest of the night to sort everything out.

By morning, Helm Dwarf-friend was convinced that the city had come under attack, and that his own life had been targeted by a fiendish creature who had attempted to disguise herself as Ansa. His seneschal Zasian, acting on reliable information, had brought a team to the Master's chambers just in the nick of time. The alu had been defeated, and angels in the service of Tyr had taken her away for judgment.

Helm was exhausted when he finally returned to his chambers the following evening. Ansa was there, of course, ready to soothe his tired muscles with her soft, delicate body. She tended to him with all the care and warmth of a young, vibrant lover, and the Master of the Hall did not suspect a thing. When he was asleep not long after, Kashada smiled to herself.

Soon it would be time to raise her secret temple to Shar, within the very heart of Sundabar. And when she was ready, Kashada would bring the Dark Goddess's revenge upon all the North.

CHAPTER ONE

The wind howled and buffeted Zasian, and he fought against it. Learning to fly in dragon form was harder than coercing magical energies to aid him in flight. The priest struggled to familiarize himself with subtle shifts in frame. He practiced flexing muscles he never imagined possessing before. It was not easy.

He had to work all the harder because of the distractions. The wind certainly made things more difficult, but that was a mere inconvenience, an occasional jarring shift that he could account for and dismiss. A gust or down shear might startle him, but it would not ruin him.

He felt some residual queasiness from the mushrooms Aliisza had introduced into the dragon's system, too. The occasional rumble or twitch deep in his belly led him to suspect that they were not completely purged. He hoped they would not become a greater problem.

The dragon fighting to regain control of his own body was far more dangerous. Zasian could feel the being's rage, sense the overwhelming power tucked away, pounding futilely against the dweomers he had erected to contain him. Though he trusted that the magic was strong enough to withstand the raw fury of the dragon, he had to be careful not to succumb to his crafty wit.

That's not quite right, the dragon would say. *You're too stiff with the tail. You must let it glide, not twitch. If you'll allow me, I'll demonstrate.*

But of course Zasian would not relinquish control, even for an instant. To do so would mean death for him. Still, he admired the beast's efforts, his desire to live. Despite the panic the dragon must have felt from not being in control, he whispered, suggested, always so reasonable, so helpful.

I understand your fear, dragon, Zasian said, *but your efforts are wasted. I know your mind better than you do. My course is set. I know the inevitability of what must happen. You cannot undo this.* The dragon grew quiet, and Zasian could feel his fear grow.

He ignored the beast, and the journey continued.

Eventually, the dragon renewed his efforts, but Zasian was prepared. He fought the dragon with the same growing ease with which he battled the unfamiliar shape and muscles.

A searing pain filled the priest's abdomen, and for a startled breath or two he feared that it was the dragon, finally finding some crack in his prison, at last reaching out with some energy to stab at Zasian's presence from within. But the dragon seemed just as surprised as he, and before the beast could take advantage of the priest's confusion, Zasian had his guard up again.

But he was going to be sick.

Damned mushrooms, Zasian thought. *I must land.* He began to look everywhere below him, desperate for a safe haven. Another sharp, white-hot pain shot through the priest, and his fear of injury and falling to his death overcame his cautious hesitation. Even if there were any cursed celestials nearby, he would just have to risk it.

The priest spied a smallish bit of land, an uprooted, inverted mountain bobbing and weaving in the tempestuous winds. It slipped in and out of view several times, obscured by the racing, roiling clouds, but Zasian kept his bearing true and half-flew, half-tumbled to its upper surface.

Another sharp agony rammed into his gut as he flopped onto the open space atop the nodule of rock. A handful of scrawny trees whipped around in the fierce breezes, but at least they offered him some cover from unwanted eyes.

Not that anything would be out and about, trying to fly through this, Zasian thought.

He marveled again that the House of the Triad was in such an uproar. It was not known for anything other than idyllic weather, but Cyric's efforts to drive a wedge between Tyr and Helm must have been going better than expected. Zasian almost laughed, imagining the natives' consternation and panic over the disruption to their beloved paradise. A chortle almost escaped his wyrmish maw, but yet another shooting pain turned the sound into a grunt of anguish.

He really was going to be sick.

Zasian was fully in the act of retching something up, struggling to control both the writhing, twitching body and the sentience that wanted it back, when he realized the cause of his distress.

Something was coming through the portal.

Just as he and Kaanyr had crossed into the heavenly plane, another creature was making its way into the House by means of the efreeti sultan's favorite pet.

He and the half-fiend had been followed.

In a brief moment of panic, Zasian worried that whatever was inside him knew he was vulnerable and would attempt to slay him from within. In that heartbeat of alarm, he almost lost his wits, almost allowed the dragon to regain a foothold. But he felt the surge of the dragon's attack and braced himself enough to stem the assault.

Then he coughed once and vomited the interloper free.

Myshik Morueme went sprawling upon the tall grasses at Zasian's clawed feet.

❖ ❖ ❖ ❖ ❖ ❖ ❖ ❖

"Justice is not some gaudy cloak," the angel standing opposite Tauran insisted, "worn only when it suits us and later cast aside as unfashionable!" The bronze-skinned deva fanned his white wings in agitation and punctuated his final, harsh words by jabbing his finger into the air. His dark eyes, which matched his short, dark hair, blazed with ire.

The two majestic archons that had arrived at the storm dragon's lair with him stood with their great wings unfurled. They perched on the balls of their feet and watched the proceedings with wary gazes. Except for the feathered appendages, they appeared sublimely human in many ways, but they towered half again as tall as the angel they flanked, who himself stood head and shoulders higher than Aliisza.

The alu saw Tauran's hands clench. He stood confronting his counterpart, his back to her, an unlikely champion in her eyes, shielding Aliisza and her two half-fiend companions from the other angel's ire. "Nor is it a cudgel, existing solely to pummel everything within reach, my old friend," he said, his voice softer but hinting at anger just the same.

That was it, Aliisza realized. An old friend. She

remembered the celestial from her first day within the House of the Triad. Tauran had named him Micus then.

At any other time, Aliisza might have marveled at her good fortune, serving as witness to two angels bickering. It was not often that celestial beings disagreed so vehemently, and rarer still that they did so in front of others. Despite the privilege, Aliisza did not celebrate her luck. A warm, intense radiance surrounded the two angels, a glow of divine power that pained the alu to her demonic core. She blinked repeatedly, wanting to look away, but she forced her gaze to remain fixed upon them.

Her very life depended on the outcome.

"Not all justice is equal, Micus," Tauran said in more gentle tones. "You more than most should understand that."

The other deva's eyes narrowed in accusation. "You sound like one of Helm's apologists. Are you straying, my friend? Have you lost your way? Tyr's Court has no more room within it for a wavering, stumbling soul than it does for the likes of these craven wretches."

Beside her, Kaanyr Vhok, Aliisza's lover and commander, issued a low growl and reached for Burnblood, the enchanted blade sheathed at his left hip. The cambion's mouth curled in a faint sneer. His olive skin and white hair held a peculiar tint in the combined light of the strange, surreal chamber in which they stood and the purplish storm beyond its open-air periphery.

At Kaanyr's threatening move, the two celestial creatures flanking Micus grew restless. Their forearms transformed into long, formidable blades that blazed with fire. The cool, damp air of the templelike chamber rippled with the heat. Muted thunder rumbled within the endless storm that roiled beyond the edges of the marbled floor, echoing the strained emotions within.

Though Aliisza often considered Kaanyr's good looks and roguish attitudes irresistible, at that moment her simmering anger with the half-fiend made him come off as more churlish than charming.

Playing the indignant, entitled boor again, Aliisza thought.

She reached out to Kaanyr to halt his petulant behavior, but Kael was already there, placing a restraining hand on his sword arm. Aliisza's half-fiend, half-drow son leaned near Vhok's ear and whispered something. The cambion's eyebrows arched up in surprise and anger, but he stayed his hand before shrugging off Kael's grasp. That charcoal-skinned face never changed expression. Kael stepped back again, clasping his hands together atop the greatsword he held point down before himself.

At a soft word from Micus, the archons relaxed slightly, and the flaming swords winked out, becoming forearms once more.

Aliisza wondered how her son had come by such a blade, as well as the glimmering plate armor that adorned his body. He had donned it shortly after she had awakened, during the moments between Tauran's cryptic plea and Micus's unexpected arrival.

So much had happened in those few moments. Aliisza had been surprised to awaken at all, for tempting a celestial storm dragon to swallow her whole had seemed an addle-brained course at best. Doing so to rescue a lover who had tricked her into the convoluted scheme in the first place was pure idiocy. Even afterward, she had expected Tauran to condemn her for her acts, but instead he had asked for their help. None of it made any sense, and Micus and his twin bodyguards had arrived before Tauran could explain anything further.

So many questions, Aliisza thought, turning her attention toward Tauran once more. *And he's the only one with answers.*

Tauran spoke, answering Micus's question. "I stray no more than any open-minded member of the Court," he said. "Though I may be a loyal servant of Tyr, were I to refuse to examine all sides of a debate out of blind loyalty, I would be a poor one." Aliisza saw Micus bristle, but he said nothing as Tauran continued. "Though Helm and Tyr disagree, each of their arguments must have some merit. When their feud has ended, I fully expect there will be compromise, with parts taken from each to make the whole. Until then, I show respect to all parties by refraining from premature judgments."

"Perhaps your wisdom is unmatched in such troubling times," Micus admitted—grudgingly, it seemed to Aliisza, "but Tyr's law on this matter is clear and not subject to interpretation. These . . . these *intruders,*" he said, gesturing at Aliisza and Vhok, his distaste punctuating every word he spoke, "have broken those laws by their very presence here! Justice is absolute in this case, and there is no room for debate. Were Helm able to perform his duties properly, you and I would not even have need to discuss this. Justice already would have been meted out."

"And yet he cannot," Tauran countered, "and I suggest that it is by corrupt design. I dare not speak more here, but I ask you to trust me. Extenuating circumstances exist with regard to their intrusion and should be weighed before judgment is rendered. Let their story be heard, Micus."

The other deva grimaced. "I've known you and called you friend from time immemorial, Tauran, but I think you tread in dangerous places now. I fear your wisdom is lacking in this instance, but because you have asked it of me, I give you my trust. I pray you do not suffer for it."

With that, the deva gave a curt nod in the direction of the three half-fiends and turned away. With one graceful leap, he took flight, launching himself out into the raging storm beyond the perimeter of the mystical place where the rest of them stood. The other two creatures, as if sensing his intentions, kicked themselves aloft in mirrored motion, following behind Micus. The trio disappeared into the churning, purple clouds.

The moment the three interlopers had gone, Kaanyr spun to stare Kael down. "Don't you ever lay a hand on me again, you son of a mongrel. I will slice it from your arm if you do."

The half-drow blinked his garnet-hued eyes once and said in an even tone, "Please try. So much good would come of ridding the world of you. I welcome the opportunity."

"Kael," Tauran said, moving between them. "Vhok still has a part to play in this. Reign in your killing lust for the moment, please."

The half-drow stepped away and returned his attention to adjusting the straps of his armor.

"And you," Tauran continued, turning to face the cambion, "you would do well to remember to hold your temper in check while visiting the Court of Tyr. Don't make it more difficult than it already is for me to maintain your status as a guest here. Until we can convince them otherwise, most citizens of the Court, like Micus, will perceive you as an invader."

Kaanyr scowled. " 'We'? I have no intention of convincing anyone of anything. That's your game, not mine. When you were bargaining with Micus, you forgot to consult with the bargaining chip. I never agreed to go anywhere with you or tell anyone my 'story.' "

Tauran nodded. "Of course. Forgive me. I should not have presumed." He turned and began to pace, clasping his hands behind his back in a studious manner. "Based on your stance, then, I trust that you would prefer to be considered a deadly intruder to be slain on sight. Is that correct? Please let me know in no uncertain terms how you wish to be treated, so that I might inform the folk of the realm. Once they hear of your unwelcome entry into our Court, they most likely will be lining up for the chance to slay you." He turned back to Vhok and gave the half-fiend a level stare. "So? What say you? Bargaining chip or outlaw? The choice is yours."

Vhok's eyes narrowed, and Aliisza saw his hand twitch, hovering over Burnblood. When Tauran didn't react, Kaanyr relaxed his posture and folded his arms across his chest. "Entice me," he said with that same smug sneer Aliisza was growing tired of. "What do you have to offer me besides your supposed protection from harm, in return for my cooperation?"

"Why, your freedom to return home, of course," Tauran replied with all sincerity. "The portal through which you traveled here has flown away, it would seem, and you will not get far hunting for another." Vhok's expression changed only subtly, but Aliisza could tell he was admitting to the veracity of the angel's comment. "All I ask for in return is that you travel with me back to the Court and explain in exacting detail everything you know about Zasian, his intentions . . . all of it."

Kaanyr scowled at the mention of the priest's name. "Not as much as I believed, obviously," the cambion muttered half to himself. "His deception was thorough." Vhok straightened again. "But your offer is not strong enough to convince me to admit as much before a court of sniveling wretches such as yourself." He stepped closer to Aliisza. "I think we'd rather take our chances finding our own way home, without aid from you."

Aliisza sidestepped away from Kaanyr and turned to face him. "Remember what you just said about bargaining chips, and the follies of not consulting with them?" she asked.

Vhok's face darkened in anger. "You would betray me for this . . . this *angel*?" he snarled, waving his hand toward Tauran dismissively. "That is not the Aliisza I know. Perhaps Zasian's spells of shielding did not work as well as he promised. The simpering celestial's magical coercion has changed you after all." The cambion adopted a dismayed expression. "He lied about everything else, why should I have expected him to be truthful in this?"

Aliisza ignored Kaanyr's shallow tactic. "He's not the only liar," she shot back, letting that simmering anger erupt at last. "You deceived me, you bastard," she said, shoving her chin up a bit in defiance. "You let him weave spells upon me, let me become hunted and caught, let me suffer an angel's 'healing ministrations,' all for your own gain! You put my child, a child I didn't even realize I bore, in danger!" She gestured toward Kael, who had stopped studiously ignoring the whole proceeding and was now watching the two fight with an implacable stare.

Kaanyr snorted in derision. "A child that was not mine!" he said. "The moment I'm out of your sight, you're tumbling between the sheets with a drow wizard and who knows what else!"

Aliisza rolled her eyes. "Don't play indignant with me," she said with equal coldness. "You've shared many another maiden's bed in your time, too. We both know that we do what we do. It's beside the point." The alu waved her hand to dismiss his argument. "You thought the child was yours when you hatched this scheme. You believed you were sending your own son into harm's way, and me along with him, for your personal gain."

"It worked, didn't it?" Kaanyr asked. "You and I are both standing here, at the other end of the journey, aren't we? Why are you whimpering about it?"

"I'm not," the alu retorted through clenched teeth. His ability to change the argument around never failed to annoy her. "As I said, we do what we do, and I shouldn't expect anything different from you." She stepped back, joining with Tauran and Kael, leaving the cambion by himself. "Just don't expect me to 'take my chances' with you when there are better offers on the table."

And don't expect me to leave my son just because he's not your child, she silently added.

Kaanyr stood glaring at the alu for a long moment, as if sizing her up. Finally, shaking his head almost in disgust, he shrugged. "Very well," he said, turning to Tauran. "Let's negotiate."

"My offer still stands," the angel said. "Your freedom to return home in exchange for your testimony before an assemblage of high members of the Court. Everything you can recall concerning Zasian in exchange for free passage from this place with your health intact."

"A fine bargain for most, I'm sure," Kaanyr replied, folding his arms across his chest once more and beginning to pace, "but I require something more."

"The reason you came here in the first place," Tauran said. "It must be a great prize, if you were willing to risk your lover, your child, and your own life in order to claim it."

Kaanyr nodded. "Indeed. And I will have it before I return to claim Sundabar as my own. But it is a trifling thing for you to grant, I think, and thus not something that should cost overly much." He drew a deep breath and said in the most casual, off-hand way, "I wish to bathe in the Lifespring, to partake of its influences."

"I see," Tauran said, sounding doubtful.

"As I said, a simple request, easily granted. And in exchange, I will happily provide you and your assemblage the most exacting, detailed tale of Zasian Menz I can muster."

Tauran shook his head. "Alas, it cannot be, Vhok, for that is a sacred pool, and you are not worthy to enjoy its soothing, healing embrace. It is, after all, the very potency of godhood."

"I will have its energies," Kaanyr said. "Even if I must slay every one of you stinking, self-righteous poofs to get to it."

The sharp ring of sword on marble was the only indication to Aliisza that Kael had moved, but almost instantly he was standing between Vhok and the other two. "Me first," he said, assuming a defensive stance. "Whenever you're ready."

Kaanyr pulled Burnblood free and dropped into a crouch of his own. "I see you inherited your father's bluster," the cambion said, beginning to circle. "And it seems you are also destined to inherit his method of demise—at the hands of demons." He feinted a strike at Kael's leading knee, but the half-drow slid his much larger blade into place to block the blow with a mere flick of his wrists.

Later, Aliisza would find it difficult to recall the word that Tauran muttered. The instant after he did so, however, a thundering, concussive roar and a blinding flash of light slammed against her, knocking her to the marble floor in a daze. As the world around her tilted askew, she curled into a fetal ball and clamped her hands over her ears, fighting to regain her equilibrium and sight.

As the ringing and afterimage of searing whiteness faded from her ears and eyes, the alu rose onto her knees and looked around. She saw Kaanyr sprawled nearby, his arms clamped around his own head. Burnblood lay unattended a few paces away. Then he, too, sat up, blinking and rubbing at his eyes.

"Enough," Tauran said. "You try my patience."

Beside the angel, Kael had returned to his stoic stance, greatsword point down before him. He seemed none the worse for wear from Tauran's powerful magic.

"If you wish to die trying to gain access to the Lifespring, I will not try to discourage you from it. But that was just a taste of what I and my kind can inflict upon you here within the Court, Vhok. Do not consider yourself so potent that we all would fall helplessly before your blade."

Kaanyr grimaced but said nothing.

"If such a quest is so important to you, then at least hear me out before you begin your ill-conceived rampage. I propose an expansion of our bargain. You desire to claim the powers of the Lifespring for your own. Though rare is the instance when outsiders are permitted to draw on its essences, such an act is not unheard of. In such dire circumstances as these, I believe I can bring it to fruition for you."

Kaanyr cocked his head to one side, considering. "I'm listening," he said quietly.

Tauran continued. "The price you will pay is steep. You must earn this blessing, Vhok. You must redeem yourself in some fashion, not only for your trespasses against the Court of Tyr, but for your very base nature itself. Only by serving me for a time that I choose and in a task I designate do you fulfill your end of this bargain. In exchange for that service, I will persuade the Court to permit you full access to the Lifespring."

"What type of service? What duration? I will not agree to vagaries, angel. Your terms must be explicit. I will not succumb to trickery."

Aliisza had to turn her face away to keep from letting Kaanyr see her smile. So he thinks, she thought. How little he knows.

"You must aid me in stopping whatever scheme Zasian Menz, priest of Cyric, plots within this realm. You must assist me in hunting him down, capturing him, and putting a stop to his machinations."

"That could take but a few hours or tendays on end!" Vhok exclaimed. "I do not have the luxury of limitless time to devote to this."

"Then you have no accord with me," Tauran replied with cold finality. "That is the price you must pay for claiming the benefits of the Lifespring. And know this, Vhok. I will bind you to this service once you agree to it of your own free will. You will be coerced to comply with your end of the bargain."

Vhok rubbed his chin with his hand. "What if Zasian succeeds with whatever scheme he has developed before we catch him? What if he accomplishes his plot and returns to Toril before we can put a halt to it?"

"If we come to a point where your services are no longer beneficial, I will release you from your servitude and permit you to return unharried to your home, but you will not so much as set eyes on the Lifespring in that case."

There was a long silence then, as the angel and the cambion eyed one another, each waiting for the other to flinch, to falter and give the other the final upper hand.

"Think of it this way," Kael spoke at last. "He offers you a chance at revenge against your betrayer. I know your kind, Vhok. You'd like nothing more than to hunt Menz down and ruin his plans. That's what you do, isn't it? Disrupt and depredate?" It was the first time Aliisza had seen Kael smile. It was Pharaun's smug smirk, and it unnerved her.

Kaanyr mused a moment longer, then turned to Aliisza. "Walk with me," he said, and he took her by the elbow and led her away. They followed the edge of the pool of water, passing through the mist that wafted from its surface until they were almost out of sight of the other two. Aliisza began to wonder if Kaanyr had deemed their chances higher if they simply fled right then. She cast a glance back, at Kael in particular. She was not yet ready to abandon her son, despite the strange nature of his behavior. Whatever his upbringing, he was still her child.

"What do you think of the idiot's offer?" Kaanyr asked as he stopped and turned her to face him. "You've dealt with him before. How cagey is he being? What tricks will he try to play upon us?"

Oh, no, Aliisza thought. You must run this gauntlet on your own, just as you forced me to do. Aloud she asked, "What's so important about this bath?" It had better be damned exhilarating, she thought, to send me through all I've endured just to get yourself here. "What is this Lifespring you keep speaking of?"

"It is a wellspring of golden waters that brims with the energy and power of godhood. Though it would not make me a god, it would grant me the power to rule like I have never had before. With that magic at my command, I could enter Sundabar not as a mere conqueror but as a beloved leader, a sovereign worth worshiping. The people would cast out Helm Dwarf-friend, pull him from his throne, and kneel before me in adoration, never wondering why at all."

Aliisza looked upon Kaanyr's face, so full of rapturous,

fervent conviction, and had to keep from shuddering. His pre-occupation with unseating the Master of the Hall of Sundabar had gone beyond sensible. He was edging close to the abyss of unreason.

So be it, she thought. "Everything he will tell you is truth. Every promise he makes to you will be honored. He cannot help it. It is his nature."

"That's not what I asked you. Can you see any trickery in his offer? Have I established the parameters solidly enough? Is there anything I am missing?"

It's not what you think you see that gets you, she thought. That's only what he distracts you with. It's what you never expected that will be your undoing. And you'll deserve every last bit of misery from it, you bastard. "Only that the timing is so vague. All the impetus is on you to help catch Zasian quickly. Succeed admirably, and you gain all that you seek. Falter or fail, and your prize becomes less and less valuable."

"Yes," Kaanyr replied, stroking his chin again. "And though the angel has every impetus to accomplish this quickly—at least based on his comments to Micus—your whelp has every reason to interfere, to watch me fail spectacularly. In truth, he might already be instructed to trip me up, just at my moment of glory. We can't have that," the cambion said with a chuckle. "I'll just have to make sure that sabotage is prohibited in the contract."

With that, he turned and strode back toward the other two, leaving Aliisza without so much as a thank you. The alu stared daggers into his back then followed after him. She couldn't wait to see how Tauran yanked the rug from beneath Kaanyr.

"You have my solemn word," Tauran was saying as Aliisza rejoined the group, "that neither Kael nor I will do anything to thwart you from completing your duties, nor will we urge anyone else in the service of the Triad to do so. If you succeed in helping us stop Zasian, you will have nothing but our gratitude."

"And the right to immerse myself in the Lifespring," Kaanyr added.

"Yes," Tauran said.

"Which *will* grant me the legendary powers it is renowned for. I will gain preternatural leadership qualities. All mortals who look upon me will wish to worship at my feet."

"I cannot promise that each and every one of them will be enslaved to your charms, but your influence and charisma will be august."

"And the freedom after that to return to Sundabar and claim its throne, with no interference from you or anyone else within this realm."

"You may leave here unmolested at that time, but once you return to your home, how you choose to wield your newfound powers and the Court's reaction to it are beyond the scope of this agreement."

"Good enough," Kaanyr said. "I accept."

Tauran nodded and closed his eyes, as if in prayer. When he opened his eyes again, Aliisza wondered if he had woven the coercive magic upon Kaanyr. "It is done," he said. "You are now bound to serve me until your appointed task is complete."

The cambion frowned as the angel turned to the alu.

"And you?" Tauran asked.

Aliisza shrugged. "I have no need to bathe in the Lifespring," she said, smiling in bemusement. "I see no reason to agree to anything other than what you offered me before. In exchange for what I know of Zasian—which is quite little, actually—I am free to return to Toril."

Kaanyr gaped at her for several seconds. In return, she smiled at him. "How does it feel?" she asked in her sweetest, most innocent voice.

"You treacherous, conniving little—"

"Help us anyway." It was Kael who had spoken, and he looked at his mother with a strange expression.

Aliisza wasn't certain what it conveyed.

"Why?" she asked, a sense of caution sweeping over her. "What's in it for me?"

"The chance you wanted before, back in the garden," the half-drow replied. "The chance to know me." Aliisza wasn't sure how to respond. It was almost as if he were baiting her. "If you return to Toril, to your home, that will be it. Whatever chance you have of showing me your maternal love will be lost to you. *I* will be lost to you."

Aliisza peered into those garnet eyes and felt a deep pain in the core of her being. Despite the notion that her transformation into a being of goodness had all been a lie, a deceit of Tauran's from which Zasian's magic had shielded her, there was still some truth in that message of selflessness. If she walked away, no matter how much fun it would be to spite Kaanyr, she would never see her son again.

"Very well," she said in a small voice. "I will remain here and help you." Then she quickly added, "But of my own volition. I do not submit to any magical coercion, Tauran," she said, giving Kaanyr another smug smile. He only glared at her in return.

"As you wish," the angel said in answer. "You serve of your own free will. But know this; should you interfere with my efforts at some point in the future, I will also have no compunction against dealing with you." There was a hint of something dangerous in the deva's tone as he said that.

Aliisza nodded.

"Now then," Tauran said, "it's time to explain to you all that has happened since you escaped the garden. Incidentally, because of the nature of the portal you traversed to get here, time has flowed quite differently for you two than for Kael and me. Twelve years have passed since the day you entered the storm dragon's maw."

Kaanyr's howl of anguish and betrayal made Aliisza clamp her hands over her ears.

CHAPTER TWO

Zasian reared back from the half-dragon sprawled before him. The priest expected the whelp of Clan Morueme to attack him the moment he became lucid, but Myshik only writhed upon the grass in obvious pain.

He burns, Zasian realized. Already, terrible lesions had formed on the bluish skin, ugly and red. Some had begun to fester, becoming yellow pustules. Vhok and Aliisza had had the benefit of the water, he remembered. The foul bile from the dragon's innards did not punish them as severely.

Myshik groaned and tried to wipe away the caustic fluids from the storm dragon's stomach that coated him, but each touch made him twitch and recoil. Zasian merely watched for a moment, wondering what had possessed the creature to follow him and the cambion through the portal. He's either a fool or totally devoted to his cause, the priest decided. Either way, I cannot have him interfering.

Zasian rose up, prepared to lash at Myshik with a rake of his claws. He would rend the draconic hobgoblin into pieces and be done with him. But Myshik saw the movement and sprawled forward onto his stomach as if in supplication.

"Master," he said, almost plaintively, "heal me and I am yours to command."

Zasian halted his impending strike. "Serve me?" he asked. He had not thought of such a possibility. "Why would you choose to serve me now, after. . . ." Suddenly, he realized that Myshik did not recognize him as the priest accompanying Vhok. The half-hobgoblin only perceived him as a great storm dragon.

"I am lost in this place, and you are kin," Myshik said, looking up. "Why would I not? All I ask is that you reward me for my faithful service, that I may some day return to my clan a hero." He grimaced in pain.

Zasian wanted to smile. Yes, he thought, I'll reward you. But before I destroy you, perhaps I can make some use of you after all.

"Why are you here?" he demanded, letting the deep, rumbling voice of the storm dragon wash over Myshik. "How did you come to be inside me?"

"I—I followed someone," the draconic hobgoblin replied, sounding uncertain. "The foe of my sire, a greedy fiend." Myshik paused, grimacing. When the suffering lessened, he continued. "He and another entered a most peculiar passage, perhaps a portal to this place. Did any others arrive as I did?"

"Why do you seek this fiend?" Zasian asked, letting his borrowed voice continue to boom. "What interest does he hold for you?"

"It is my uncle's bidding that I slay this fiend. Back where I come from, he and his army encroach upon my clan's territory. If I were to defeat him and return home with proof of the deed, I would be honored among my kind."

Zasian considered a moment. "Very well," he said, "I will

accept your servitude. Our purposes might not be so crossed, it would seem."

Do you know the efreeti saying that the enemy of my enemy is my friend? Zasian wondered. But he kept his identity to himself.

The priest contemplated how best to heal the creature abasing himself before him. Between the battle within the sultan's palace and the unexpected fight with the angel and his sidekick upon arriving on the plane, Zasian had exhausted the majority of his divine magic. After fleeing from the deva, he had needed the rest of it to treat his own wounds. He had nothing left to give, at least for the moment.

Besides, he thought, I don't want to give too much away about myself. He wouldn't suspect a dragon of such divine power as I have, so why tip my hand? Zasian had an idea.

"Can you travel?" he asked Myshik.

The hobgoblin nodded.

"Then I will bear you to a place where you can bathe in the very energy of the gods. The waters I know of will cleanse you of any taints and poisons, scour away your wounds, and fill you with the power to aid me as only a suitable servant should. In return for this boon, I expect you to hold to this bargain we make here. If you break our agreement, I will hunt you down and destroy you. Is that understood?"

Myshik nodded. "I so swear it."

Without further deliberation, Zasian scooped the draconic creature up and hoisted him into the air. Once aloft, he began beating his powerful wings, flying into the howling wind, taking them both toward the heart of the House of the Triad.

❖ ❖ ❖ ❖ ❖ ❖ ❖ ❖ ❖

"We can't stay out here in this!" Tauran screamed, but Aliisza could barely hear him. The chill, biting wind stole his words away as it lashed the four travelers. Stinging sleet pelted them as they descended through gray, roiling clouds, making the alu squint. When a particularly vicious gust pummeled her, Aliisza went tumbling and nearly lost sight of her companions.

This can't be right, Aliisza thought, struggling to straighten herself. We should have left those storms behind by now.

Nearby, Kaanyr also fought to remain aloft. The howling gale buffeted him, spinning him like desiccated leaves churned up from the forest floor. His cloak whipped around his body, periodically enveloping his head. He yanked it free and pushed onward, seemingly oblivious to the stinging pellets of ice.

Through it all, the cambion never stopped scowling.

It's his own fault, Aliisza thought, flapping her own wings with furious strokes to close the distance between herself and Tauran. She had to stay close enough to avoid losing sight of the deva, but not so close that they might collide because of the storm. He's so bull-headed lately.

The cambion had screamed and ranted at the other three for several long moments after Tauran's shocking revelation. Stunned herself, Aliisza hardly noticed his reaction at the time.

Twelve years? she had thought. How is that possible?

But Tauran had been forthright, and Kaanyr realized that he had been duped, had been played despite all his careful scrutiny of his deal with the angel. He had yanked Burnblood free, but even with all the rage spilling from him, the cambion was unable to strike at any of them. The magical coercion that Tauran had woven into the bargain prevented Vhok from interfering with the objectives or its participants. Aliisza realized only later that her decision to aid in the quest had spared her from Kaanyr's attack.

Not that he hadn't tried, she remembered. In his moment of unreasoning outrage, she had seen the burning hatred in his eyes, watched as the muscles corded in his neck from the strain of wanting to kill her then and there. For whatever reasons, real or imagined, he blamed her for his predicament.

He let himself fall into Tauran's trap, I had nothing to do with it. Well, that's not exactly true, she admitted, feeling a rather uncomfortable emotion.

It surprised the alu that she could experience such a debilitating thing as guilt. In the past, she had always blamed such silly frailties on the human side of her and then promptly buried them, but she found herself reluctant to tamp down her own emotions at that moment. Perhaps the time spent in Tauran's care had affected her more than she might have liked.

Never mind, she told herself. *Just keep up!*

Tauran was saying something and gesturing downward, but Aliisza could not hear the angel's words. Nonetheless, she nodded and tried to follow, her flight made clumsy in the gale.

Just beyond Tauran, Aliisza could barely make out Kael's form. Her son was also fighting the wind, working to fly where the deva directed. Wings that had sprouted from his boots bore him, and though to the alu's eye they seemed incapable of effectively bearing the half-drow, they served their purpose well enough. He seemed at ease, following his mentor as if he had trained for it most of his life.

He has, Aliisza reminded herself, reflecting on the angel's unwelcome news from yet another perspective. *He's spent a dozen more years following Tauran around.*

That thought made the alu profoundly sad and jealous all at once. Her mind had a hard time accepting the idea that she had been trapped within the storm dragon's gullet for more than a decade. It had seemed like mere moments to her and Kaanyr.

I had already lost his childhood, Aliisza lamented, *and now this.*

During all that time, Kael had grown up under Tauran's care, studying with the angel and embracing the teachings of the gods who dwelt within the House of the Triad. Tauran had been given so many years of Kael's life to mold and sculpt, making him a being of goodness and light.

And now he's some soldier devoted to Torm, Aliisza thought, feeling the sadness and resentment wash over her again. *A divine champion, chasing after Tauran and all the fool causes he embraces. And I missed the chance to let him see the truth.*

Aliisza vowed to change that. She promised herself that she would unmake what Tauran had crafted in her absence. Though she wasn't sure how, she would not go down without a fight. Kael was her son, not the angel's.

A burst of wind rocked Aliisza again, dragging her from her thoughts and resolutions. Tauran had surged far ahead, with Kael close behind him, and she and Kaanyr had lagged behind, she lost in her contemplations and he fighting his cloak. The angel and the champion vanished within the thick mists of the nearest cloud. Fearing that she would lose them, Aliisza went into a dive to try and catch up. Angling her body and folding her arms and wings in tight, she descended like an arrow. She tried to ignore the flecks of ice that stung her face, squinting for some sign of Tauran and Kael.

She plummeted into the cloud and lost all sense of depth

or direction. The disorientation lasted only a moment before she was out the other side. Below her stretched the vast panorama of the plane, with its myriad floating masses of land, all of them uprooted clumps of earth with raw, jagged undersides. She spotted Tauran and Kael too, not so far ahead as she had feared. They drifted toward a particularly large island of rock, one that sported several ridges with a hollow in the center, like some mountain valley surrounded by aged, weathered peaks.

A forest dominated the terrain, and as she drew closer, the alu could see that many of the trees were mighty elder things, akin to the tallest specimens she had seen in the ancient forests of Toril. Even so, the wind lashed at their branches, sending the crowns of the great trees whipping back and forth in the maelstrom. Aliisza also noted that a thin veneer of white had begun to accumulate upon the massive floating mass, swirling sleet and snow pellets combining with a glaze of outright frost.

Tauran led the way into a small meadow in the midst of the ancient trees. He came to rest near the center of the clearing but immediately moved off to one side, seeking shelter beneath the bowers and trunks. Aliisza fought the swirling, slashing wind and managed to follow him down. The moment her feet touched solid ground, she huddled against the blasts of frigid air and trotted after the angel. Kaanyr and Kael followed close behind.

Once within the relative protection of the forest, Tauran found an outcropping of stone that jutted up like a canted fist. He moved into the lee of the rock, wedging himself close against it. Aliisza and Kael joined him, and soon they huddled together out of the worst of the weather. Kaanyr stood out a few paces, paying no mind to the stinging sleet and snow.

"We'll rest here a moment," the angel said, breathing heavily, "before we continue on."

Aliisza nodded gratefully and struggled to catch her breath. "What is this?" she asked after a time, gesturing all around them vaguely. "What's happening?"

Tauran grimaced. "Upheaval. Catastrophe. Turmoil," he said.

"Speak plain, deva," Kaanyr snapped. "What does that mean?"

"He means," Kael interjected before Tauran could speak, "that this is what happens when the gods quarrel."

Tauran nodded. "Yes. Tyr and Helm are having an argument. They are both very angry, and their anger has spilled out to engulf all of the House."

"What's their quarrel?" Aliisza asked, surprised to see such vehemence made manifest. "Micus hinted at a disagreement, but this?" She gestured again. It was as if the deities were ripping the cosmos apart.

"The minds of the gods are difficult to fathom," Tauran answered. "Perhaps the solars who attend them know more, but even they aren't divulging much. All we know is that it has to do with Ilmater's departure, and Tyr's choice to replace him within the Triad."

Kaanyr snorted. "What a waste of time," he said, rolling his eyes, "fretting over the loss of *that* martyred idiot. The weakest, most pathetic—"

The cambion's words were cut short as Kael shifted his position to level his greatsword at him. "Do not speak of the Crying God in such an irreverent manner."

Vhok returned the glare and reached for his own blade, but Tauran growled, a deep, reverberating sound that froze everyone in place.

"Enough!" he screamed. "I will not tolerate these constant displays of bravado! Kael, our bargain with the half-fiend does not preclude him from expressing his opinions. If he chooses not to honor Ilmater as you might, that is his business. Leave him be."

Kael frowned and opened his mouth as if to argue, but then seemed to think better of it. With a single, curt nod, he withdrew his blade and leaned against the outcropping, arms folded across his armored chest.

"And you," Tauran said, addressing Kaanyr. "You will not so easily wriggle free of your obligation. The *geas* upon you may permit you to defend yourself should we attack you, but it will take more than taunts and veiled insults to expend our patience. Your energy would be much better served in aiding us than trying to trick us. We are not easily duped."

Kaanyr glowered for a moment then broke into a smile. It was the first time in quite some while that Aliisza could remember the cambion doing so. "Now that I know how much it galls you to suffer my remarks, you may rest assured that they will come thick and often. I will never be your lackey, deva."

Tauran stared levelly at Kaanyr for several moments. His face remained neutral, with the exception of one corner of his mouth twitching. Then he shrugged. "It will change nothing."

"So why did Ilmater depart?" Aliisza asked. "And whom did Tyr choose?"

"Tymora," Kael answered, pushing himself away from the rock to stare out past Kaanyr into the swirling weather. Aliisza wasn't certain if there was disapproval in the half-drow's voice or not.

Tauran nodded. "Yes, Tymora," he said. "Ilmater went to

Sune's embrace and now dwells with her in Brightwater. Many believe Tyr holds similar feelings for Tymora and has asked her to come to him for the same reasons."

Kaanyr snorted again. "So everyone is sharing someone's bed. Hardly seems a worthy reason for raising such a storm," he said.

"There are those who believe Siamorphe would make a better choice," Tauran replied, "including Helm. The Watcher, for whatever reason, has chosen to make his feelings known. Somehow, he sees it as his duty to challenge Tyr's decision."

Aliisza sighed. "And thus their followers argue, debating the merits of each god's position."

Tauran nodded. "Such is the way of the gods sometimes," he said. "Despite your condescension, our lives are not so different from your own. There is strife in all things. We simply choose to resolve it differently."

Kaanyr chuckled. "Yes, casting a deadly squall across the entire plane is definitely a more noble and righteous means of resolving things," he said. "You should be proud."

Aliisza noted Tauran's lips purse in anger, but the deva didn't reply.

"Tell me," Kaanyr asked, "are you looking forward to victory? Will it feel good to point out to all of Helm's followers after the fact that yours was the superior position? Or maybe you're worried about backing the losing side? Maybe there's a little fear gnawing at you that *you'll* be the one scorned and ridiculed."

Tauran's expression darkened.

"Yes, I can see it," Kaanyr continued, "a hint of something less than wholesome. Deep down, you secretly know you're either going to be very satisfied or thoroughly ashamed. And no matter which way things are decided, you'll be forevermore scarred with the flaw of imperfection. No more glorious white light surrounding you, angel. No more air of righteous smugness that you are beyond reproach. I've changed my mind about all this." He gestured beyond their coarse shelter. "I *want* to stick around, just to see you fall."

Kael turned and stepped between his mentor and Vhok, facing the deva. "His words are pointless," the half-drow said. "Ignore his lies." Unlike before, when he had seemed so eager to punish the cambion for his irreverence, Kael's demeanor was stoic, pointedly ignoring Vhok.

He's recognizing how Kaanyr is trying to bait them, Aliisza realized. He's starting to see how manipulative and devious Kaanyr can be. The alu had long considered that one of her lover's more endearing qualities, but at that moment, she also felt a swelling of pride course through her for her son. Perhaps he's not as naïve and idealistic as I thought.

"We have other issues to consider," Kael said, drawing Tauran's attention away from Vhok's taunts. "It will be nightfall soon, and we'll never reach the Court in this storm. We must either find or build better shelter here."

"No," Tauran replied. "We won't stay here."

"But the storm grows worse," the half-drow argued. "We can't attempt to reach the Court until things improve."

"There is a village on the far side of the valley," Tauran answered, pointing toward the middle of the island of rock. "We can reach it on foot. We'll go there and wait out the storm."

Kael nodded in acceptance, and the quartet set out. Tauran led the way while the half-drow brought up the rear. Aliisza watched as Kaanyr struggled futilely against the magical bonds, but after a moment's exertion he was plodding along behind the angel. Aliisza took up a position beside him, risking his wrath in order to speak with him.

"How long do you intend to fight this?" she asked him—softly so the other two could not hear.

"What do you care?" Kaanyr snapped at her. "You can fly away home any time it suits you. If you find my struggles unpleasant, you don't have to remain and watch them."

"I chose to stay," she said, "for more than just him." She jerked her head once back behind the two of them.

"Truly?" Kaanyr asked, his voice mocking. "You have room in your heart for more than your precious son? I find that difficult to believe. He is, after all, so perfect, a creature of goodness and noble upbringing."

"So is it him you hate, because he isn't yours? Or is it me? Either way, it's pathetic. If it's him, why do you care? He was nothing more than a tool to you before, when he was the means of getting me into this place. And as for me, you didn't seem to have a problem throwing me into Pharaun's or Helm Dwarf-friend's bed when it benefited you. You cannot have it both ways, Kaanyr."

The cambion was silent, and when Aliisza risked a glance at his face, he seemed deep in thought.

"What's done is done, you always say, lover. So now I ask: Am I not still yours?" She slipped into that old familiar sultry purr and began to saunter. "Do you not desire me still?"

"You betrayed me to his trap," Kaanyr replied, scowling. "You think I'd take you into my bed now?"

Aliisza's eyes narrowed coldly. "You betrayed yourself," she spat. "You became so consumed with conquering that city, so preoccupied with unseating Helm Dwarf-friend, that you forgot your caution and abandoned your cleverness. You were willing to sacrifice everything"—she paused, giving him a pointed stare—"*everything* you had for that dubious prize. So do not scold me of betrayal."

They trudged on in silence for a moment more, then Aliisza continued. "Besides, Tauran took nothing from you that Zasian did not already steal. He merely forced you to do something about it on his terms rather than your own. Though I don't blame you for despising him, you ought to be thankful for the chance to work with him to undo that damnable priest. Think of it as an unexpected advantage."

Kaanyr looked at her for several long moments, his eyes boring intensely into her own. "Do not expect me to enjoy it," he said at last. "And do not think I care one whit for either of their lives. Whatever you may think of them, I do not share in it."

Aliisza laughed. "You think I've suddenly developed delusions of a conscience? You think I'm so different? Zasian did his work well, my love! All of that sickly sweet caring and sacrifice business was just a game. When all is said and done, I still serve one person only." Me, she silently added.

"We shall see," Kaanyr replied.

❖ ❖ ❖ ❖ ❖ ❖ ❖ ❖

The group continued on in silence after that, following the path Tauran blazed through the ancient trees. Aliisza caught herself marveling at their majesty, and she was thankful for the protection they provided from the blustering wind. Beyond their tops, out of sight and muffled through their foliage, she could hear deep rumbles, as of almost continuous thunder.

Soon after, the alu realized they had begun following an actual path. It was narrow, little more than a game trail, but it led down into the center of a great valley. Occasionally, Aliisza caught a glimpse through breaks in the forest of a great open space in the middle of the depression. Though it was hard to tell with the swirling snow and sleet, she believed she caught sight of buildings, too. They were getting closer.

When they neared the edge of the clearing, Aliisza first noted it by the increase in the wind. Tauran led them out of the trees, still following the path, which did indeed take them toward a small gathering of simple cottages clustered together. The alu caught the faint whiff of smoke and thought she could hear a startled scream.

When Tauran sprinted forward, she knew it had not been her imagination. As one, the four of them rushed into the village. More screams erupted from among the cottages, and then Aliisza could see the flames of a fire spreading along a rooftop.

Tauran surged forward, but Kaanyr drew up suddenly, staring at the sky. "Gods and devils," he breathed.

Kael nearly ran into the cambion from behind. "Go!" he shouted. "There are folk in trouble!"

But Kaanyr did not move. Instead, he only pointed skyward, and both Kael and Aliisza turned to stare.

Another great island of land filled the sky and grew larger as it tumbled toward them.

CHAPTER THREE

Kaanyr stood rooted to the spot, staring at the massive rock island tumbling slowly, inexorably, toward them. His sense of depth seemed askew to him. The great edifice appeared large and dangerously close, yet the haze of swarming, wind-whipped clouds still partially obscured it, revealing how far away and vast it truly was. His mind couldn't reconcile the disparity between the two.

As Aliisza and Kael ran forward, chasing after Tauran, Kaanyr shouted, "We have to get clear!"

Kael stopped and turned back, motioning for the cambion to follow. "No! We must save these people!" He shouted to be heard in the whistling wind.

Kaanyr refused to budge. "That's not part of the bargain!" he shouted back. "I agreed to help you stop Zasian, not rescue peasants!"

Kael grimaced only slightly. "For all we know, Zasian did this!"

And there it was. The half-drow had planted the seed. Kaanyr's whole world shifted. Moments previous, he could have freely risen aloft, taken to the air to escape the doom that threatened them. Once the concept had been tied to Zasian's machinations, though, the cambion could no more flee than he could sprout fins and swim through stone.

Bastard, Kaanyr fumed.

Even as he imagined ways to rend the half-drow, he found himself trotting forward, preparing to lend a hand.

Tauran reached the outskirts of the simple village and threaded his way through the outlying cottages and disappeared between them, heading toward the fire. Aliisza darted after him with Kael at her heels. Kaanyr shook his head in consternation and followed them. Once past the outer ring of homes, he could see that a longhouse near the center square had caught fire. The flames, fanned by the crazed winds, had become a great, swirling column, engulfing the building and threatening others nearby.

A crowd of folk, humans by the look of them, had gathered. Many just stood watching helplessly as others tried to douse the flames with buckets of water. Tauran moved among the fire brigade and frantically gestured with his hands. At first, Kaanyr thought the angel was telling them to get away from the conflagration. He quickly realized his mistake when a cascade of water tumbled from nowhere upon the flames. Though the divinely summoned water diminished the fire, it was not enough. Already, smoke poured off a nearby barn.

Gods and devils, the cambion silently swore. Forget the fire! Get these cretins out of here!

Aliisza reached Tauran and Kaanyr could see her grab him by the shoulder. The alu had shifted her form slightly, looking completely human, though she had not changed her features. She spun the angel around and pointed into the sky at the drifting crag that approached. Kaanyr reached them just as Tauran's eyes grew wide in disbelief. Kaanyr glanced at the huge bulwark again and saw that it was on a trajectory to pass right over them, on a course to strike the far side of the mass of earth upon which they stood.

It missed us, he thought, relieved.

"We must get these folk to safety!" the angel shouted. "Hurry!"

Kaanyr looked at Tauran, confused. "It won't strike here!" he replied, pointing downward, at his feet. "It's going over there," he said, pointing into the distance. "The hamlet is safe."

Tauran shook his head. "It doesn't matter. Once they collide, this whole island will be rocked to its core. It might begin to shift sideways, or worse yet, shatter and crumble apart beneath our feet. We have to get them off!" He gestured at the folk around them.

"That's a fool's errand, and you know it!" Kaanyr said, shaking his head. "Let's just be about our business. Surely catching Zasian is more important than dealing with these lackeys."

The villagers, their attention drawn away from the fire and toward the looming threat of the great mass of rock, began to panic. A few screamed while others raced around, running everywhere at once. A couple jostled Kaanyr as they fled.

Tauran pursed his lips. "No," he said firmly, "we must help them. I can't force you to assist me, but—"

"I already convinced him that Zasian could be behind this!" Kael interjected, shouting to be heard over the roar of the flames and the screams of the villagers. "He might have created it as a distraction for something else!"

Tauran nodded as if warming to the idea. "Yes, perhaps," he said. "We may need to investigate this fire, question these folk. You are bound, Vhok. Help them!"

Kaanyr narrowed his eyes in fury. "What the Hells do

you want from me?" he yelled at the angel. "I'm no good to you dead!"

"Gather the folk in the meadow outside of town," Tauran said to Kael. "Keep them there until I return. I'm going for more help." With that, he took to the air and hovered there a moment. "Citizens!" he shouted, his voice magically amplified and echoing across the village above the sound of the wind and flames. "Stay calm! My companions and I will aid you, but you must do as we ask. Follow their directions, and I will return soon!" He looked down at Kaanyr and gave the cambion a pointed look. "Do it," he said. Then he whirled, beat his wings furiously, and soared off into the storm-tossed sky.

"Cursed angels!" Kaanyr shouted after the rapidly diminishing figure. "So blasted arrogant!"

"Just get them—" Kael said, but a deafening rumble cut his words off. The ground pitched beneath their feet, knocking them both down.

The two islands collided.

Kaanyr felt the shock waves as tons of rock ground together. The earth buckled and shifted. The force of the collision sent trees flying. Soil shot into the air and then, caught in the wind, began swirling and darkening the sky like some terrible black rain.

"By the Blind One!" Kael bellowed, scrambling to gather himself. "Watch it!" He leaped toward Kaanyr, grabbing the cambion and yanking him to one side.

Where Vhok had been sprawled a moment before, the remains of a chimney attached to the longhouse came crashing down, sending shards of stone and dirt everywhere. The bits of debris stung Kaanyr's face and eyes. The longhouse, already mostly an inferno, collapsed a heartbeat later. The implosion sent a shower of sparks up and outward, pelting those nearby with embers and spreading thick, black smoke everywhere. The screams of burned folk rose in pitch and intensity.

Kaanyr looked at Kael for a moment, torn between his disdain and a grudging appreciation for the half-drow's effort to rescue him. But the holy warrior was already on his feet, moving off to shout instructions to the people and heal the wounded.

"Kaanyr!" It was Aliisza shouting from across open ground. The cambion looked in her direction and saw her near a collapsed dwelling. She was kneeling as though she had been peering into the interior of the structure. When she caught his eye, the alu motioned frantically for him to come to her.

Vhok scrambled to his feet and moved toward Aliisza even as the ground rumbled and shuddered again beneath him. Already, the cambion could sense a change. It was tilting. Tauran had been right; the collision was slowly upending the whole island.

"What?" he demanded, reaching the half-fiend. He squatted next to her. "What is it?" he asked, staring where she peered.

"I think there's someone trapped in there," Aliisza said, pointing. "I thought I heard a scream just as it began to fall."

"Probably already dead," Kaanyr said, rising. He reached down to take Aliisza by the arm. "Nothing more to do here," he added. "Come."

"Wait!" Aliisza said, resisting his tug. "I can hear crying. I think it's a baby."

Damnation, Kaanyr silently groused. Everywhere she turns, she thinks she sees a child that needs her. That fool angel *has* addled her brain. "Are you sure?" he asked doubtfully. "I don't hear anything."

"Just help me," Aliisza insisted, grabbing hold of a timber

that jutted from the wreckage of the home. She tried to hoist it up, but it didn't budge.

Sighing, Kaanyr took hold of the timber. Together, they lifted. The pile of ruined dwelling shifted slightly, but they couldn't move anything. "No use," Kaanyr gasped as he eased the piece of lumber back down. "Too heavy."

"Hold on," Aliisza said, reaching into a hidden pocket within her armor. She pulled something out. Before Kaanyr could see it, she brushed it against him and muttered an arcane phrase. He felt a surge of raw power course through him and knew she had enhanced his strength. She quickly did the same to herself. "Try again," she said.

Shrugging, Kaanyr grabbed hold of the timber and heaved. Aliisza joined him. Together, they forced the length of wood upward, shifting the pile of destroyed home with it.

As the hoisted lumber reached its apex, Kaanyr could see a hollow space near the center. A girl of perhaps fourteen summers lay sprawled there, a bloody gash across one cheek. A smaller child, little more than a baby, squirmed beside her. It appeared unharmed.

"Can you hold it?" Aliisza asked. "Keep it off me!"

Before Kaanyr could even answer, she released the timber and darted into the remains of the dwelling.

The cambion grunted at the increased burden and felt his muscles quiver with the strain of it. "Hurry!" he grunted at the alu, who was kneeling down next to the injured girl. "Quickly, Aliisza!"

"I'm trying!" she replied. "She's stuck under something."

Vhok shifted his feet and tried to get a better grip on the timber. He managed to get his shoulder under it and brace it, but he knew he could not remain there long. It was simply too heavy.

Just like her, the cambion fumed. Never one to let the facts get in the way of her bull-headed intentions. At least *that* hasn't changed.

Kaanyr could sense the land continue to tilt, and with it, the weight of the debris shifted and grew heavier, over-whelming him. His arms, already shaking with exertion, began to burn. "Now, Aliisza! I'm losing it!"

"I can almost . . ." she said, her voice muffled, but Kaanyr couldn't hear the rest. His legs quivered like jelly, and despite his ferocious will, the timber, and everything above it, began to collapse atop her. "Aliisza!" he grunted. "Get out!"

But the alu did not emerge from beneath the dwelling, and with a snarl of frustration and dismay, Kaanyr lost his grip on the wood.

It slammed to the earth with a deep thud.

❖ ❖ ❖ ❖ ❖ ❖ ❖ ❖

Behind the thick underbrush at the top of the three-sided open grotto Myshik knelt and peered through the foliage at the guards below. He counted four of them, hound-headed creatures standing easy but alert. They hung near the back of the secluded area, beneath the overhang that surrounded the open pit. Each of them kept a sword strapped to his or her back.

The draconic hobgoblin tightened his grip on his axe and waited. He felt good, eager for the coming battle. His whole body quivered with anticipation and energy, the residual effect of his healing dip in the magical waters of the Lifespring. Tekthyrios had borne him to a desolate, craggy spot high in the sky of the mystical place and eased him into the spring-fed pool.

The effect had been immediate and profound. All of the half-hobgoblin's wounds and scars faded in a matter of moments. Vitality and strength filled his whole being, but along with that enchanting healing had come a taint, a sick feeling of *something* that made Myshik's stomach churn. It left an odd taste in his mouth and a faint ache in his bones. He fretted over its effects for a while, but eventually dismissed them as minor irritants compared to the wonderful rejuvenation he'd experienced.

Tekthyrios had bathed in the soothing pool too and seemed to luxuriate in its magnificent effects as well. When they had both had their fill, the dragon took hold of Myshik and rose aloft once more. They set out for a new destination, and along the way, the dragon explained his plan, and the half-hobgoblin's role in it.

Myshik tingled with excitement and anticipation.

The forest around him was unusually quiet. He knew that the storms raging all through the House had not abated, but the great woodland surrounding him kept the worst of the wind at bay. He could still hear it roaring through the crowns of the massive trees, but it was a muted sound—distant, eerie. It had helped mask his approach to the edge of the pit.

The **C**-shaped pit was almost perfectly curved, a sort of sinkhole that had formed along a ridge of hard stone. Eons of water spilling into the basin had hollowed it out, carving it bit by bit, even cutting into the walls so that they curved inward, leaving an overhang around the perimeter of the place. At several points along the semicircle to Myshik's left, the trickle of waterfalls spilled over the side and splashed into a pool that took up most of the floor. Water escaped from the pool out the open side of the basin, to the half-dragon's right.

Myshik could hear the guards' voices drift toward him,

but their words were too soft to decipher. He watched them as they conversed. The dog-creatures exuded an aura of calmness, yet they never seemed to grow listless or distracted from watching their surroundings. He wondered how long they had been posted there, guarding that cave.

One of the four, a female with white fur and stubby, triangular ears, stood up straighter and sniffed the air. She looked apprehensive, and Myshik grew very still as her eyes scanned the bushes where he had chosen to conceal himself. The other three grew more alert too, and one of them spoke sharply. In response, she pointed in Myshik's direction. Her companions turned their attention his way, and for a moment, the half-hobgoblin thought he might have to launch his attack early.

Now, Tekthyrios's voice echoed in Myshik's mind.

Smiling, Myshik rose up to his full height and stepped forward, plummeting off the edge of the rim and into the pit. He unfurled his wings and glided downward, angling his descent so that he would swoop in toward the nearest guard.

She let out a warning growl and yanked her sword free. She took a defensive stance and waited for Myshik to get within reach. Her companions fanned out to either side, their blades also drawn. He could see the grim determination in their eyes.

"You may not pass," the guard said, speaking in perfect Draconic.

Here we go, the half-dragon thought as he glided into range.

"Turn back or be destr—"

The guard's words vanished in a thunderous boom as Myshik emitted a great blast of lightning and engulfed her. He saw the other three grunt in pain at the searing burst of light. They spun away, covering their faces with their arms.

Though she cringed in blindness from the unexpected assault, the female guard looked otherwise unmarked.

Resistant, Myshik realized. Would have been good to know.

In the moment it took for the guards' eyesight to return, Myshik pulled back his axe, aiming at the closest guard's neck.

A shout of warning from one of the other hound-creatures caused Myshik's target to start. She tried to spin away as Myshik reached her, but the alarm came too late. The half-dragon swung his axe around in a huge, sweeping arc and cut into the guard's shoulder and neck. The magic of the axe thundered.

The guard gave a short, shrill yelp as the blow knocked her sideways. She tumbled head over heels and went sprawling into the shallow water of the pool. It began to turn crimson. She did not move again.

Another of the guards gave a howl of dismay and lunged at Myshik, swinging his sword in a wide arc. Myshik leaped backward to evade the weapon. He landed lightly on his feet, brought his axe into play, and the fight was on.

The three remaining guards circled the draconic hob-goblin, mouths agape as they eyed him with anger. Myshik spun in place, expecting a coordinated attack. He knew he couldn't overextend or fall for feints, so he kept his blade defensive, waiting for that first sudden burst.

He was not disappointed.

The trio moved elegantly, together, leaping in to slash at their foe. As the half-dragon shifted to evade the first strike, two more came at him lightning quick. Though the guards' swords were bulky and slow, they handled them well. He deflected the first two swipes, but the third was too fast. The edge of the sword raked across his shoulder, cutting through his thick leather armor.

Myshik snarled, but he let the pain wash over him. He focused on it.

It infuriated him.

Another struck at Myshik, followed by another. He roared in defiance and swatted the attacks away with his axe. The weapon felt almost weightless in his hands. It took no more effort to wield than if it were a hollow stick. He bellowed again, challenging the guards, and rushed at one of them.

The hound creature faltered and stumbled back a step. The other two closed in behind Myshik, but he didn't care. All his fury, all his hatred, he poured into the thought of destroying that one foe retreating from him. He closed the distance, one, two, three steps through the shallow water of the pool. All the while, he yanked and hacked with his axe, pummeling the guard's defenses, battering the sword out of the way.

Myshik could see the strength waning from his enemy, could see the grim determination in his eyes turn to worry, then outright fear. Myshik never relented, even when he felt the faint stroke of a sword across his back, striking one of his wings. Another step forward and he had the guard down on his knees, scrambling to keep his sword high enough to block Myshik's relentless axe strikes.

On the third blow, Myshik's axe cleaved the sword in twain and kept going, splitting the hound creature's skull. The explosive thunder that accompanied the strike rendered the guard nearly unrecognizable.

The half-dragon barely sensed a slice across the back of his knee. His leg weakened. Rather than allow it to give way, Myshik channeled even more anger into himself. He spun, refusing to show any sign of the injury, and chose another target.

The two remaining dog creatures pressed the attack, and Myshik saw that their swords were bloodied. Absently, he decided it must be his blood.

He didn't care.

Pressing the fight at the guard on his left, Myshik assaulted anew. He used quick, powerful strokes with his axe to bludgeon his foe's defenses, shifting his attention only long enough to ward off the worst of the other guard's attacks. As before, his rage and focus overwhelmed his enemy. The guard staggered from his ferocious strikes, and when he went down to one knee in exhaustion, Myshik stepped in for the killing blow.

Before he could finish off his opponent, a brilliant illumination filled the half-dragon's field of vision. A presence had arrived, glowing with power, and Myshik flinched despite himself. The being hovered above the kneeling guard, a creature of silvery white. It gazed sternly down at Myshik with golden eyes, a massive greatsword clasped in its hands.

"You who have defiled this place and slain my guards, your end is nigh," it said, and its voice filled the pit, shook the walls, and sent ripples dancing across the water. It drew its sword back to strike, and Myshik cowered.

A shadow passed over them.

The magnificent and terrible creature faltered and turned its gaze skyward. Myshik smiled to himself as the massive form of the storm dragon, Tekthyrios, slammed into the angel. The white-skinned creature went spinning backward, its sword lost. It struck hard against the wall of the pit and sagged downward.

The two guards, who had stepped back to give the solar room to mete out its justice, stood frozen in place, staring at their fallen savior.

Tekthyrios wheeled and settled into the middle of the pool. The storm dragon nearly filled the open area. The guards quavered before the beast. Terror filled their expressions.

Myshik hefted his axe and struck. He heard the familiar concussive thump as he connected, and the head of one of the guards tumbled away. Its body flopped down into the shallow water.

The dragon roared at the angel and slashed out with his claws. The keen appendages were as long and thick as Myshik's legs and as sharp as the finest swordmaster's blades. Blood spattered the entire grotto. The dragon struck again and again, and the solar screamed in pain.

Myshik ignored the battle. Though his rage and strength were waning, he had one last guard to deal with. The hound creature, his eyes filled with dread, backed away, then turned to run.

He managed three steps before Tekthyrios's tail slammed against him. The force of the blow sent the archon sailing across the open pit to crash against the far wall. As he slid down and settled onto the damp earth at the water's edge, his eyes rolled back in his head and his tongue lolled from his mouth.

"Well done, my friend," Tekthyrios boomed. "Well done, indeed."

Myshik bowed in acknowledgment, and the act nearly made him faint. Woozy from injuries, he felt each gash and broken bone keenly as his rage faded. He sank down to his knees, panting.

"I fear I have spent myself," he said. "My strength is gone."

The great dragon stepped close to him and reached a clawed foot out. Placing that appendage gently against Myshik's back, Tekthyrios muttered a prayer, not in Draconic but in a language the half-hobgoblin did not recognize.

Myshik felt energy flow into him, restoring his vigor and easing his injuries. When the dragon completed the spell, Myshik stood straight and tall again, refreshed.

"Now," Tekthyrios said, "let's see if we can retrieve my prize."

❖ ❖ ❖ ❖ ❖ ❖ ❖ ❖

Aliisza struggled to shift the stone block that trapped the young girl's foot, but she couldn't do it. Despite her magically enhanced strength, the alu could get very little leverage. The weight of other debris atop the stone compounded the difficulty.

"Hurry!" Kaanyr growled. "Quickly, Aliisza!"

"I'm trying," she answered, reaching for a thick length of wood to use to pry the stone upward. "She's stuck under something."

The girl stared fearfully at Aliisza as the alu wedged her makeshift lever under the rock. Beside her, a small child, a little boy of only a couple of summers, cried, his tears making glistening tracks in the dust on his face. Aliisza shoved on the lever and saw the stone budge the slightest bit, but she was at the wrong angle to bring her full weight to bear.

"Now, Aliisza! I'm losing it!" Kaanyr shouted, and she could see the crushing weight overhead beginning to sag.

She shifted position to try again. "I can almost get her," she said, but the shadow of the debris hanging over her head grew darker.

It was collapsing.

"Aliisza!" Kaanyr shouted, his voice muted. "Get out!"

No time, the alu realized.

Reacting on instinct, Aliisza uttered an arcane phrase. A red, shimmering doorway appeared horizontally beneath the half-fiend and her two charges. As one, they fell through the portal just as the pile of ruined dwelling slammed down.

The other end of the magical doorway dumped the trio onto the grass a few paces behind Kaanyr. As she fell through, Aliisza flung herself to one side so as not to land atop the children. She hit the ground hard, knocking the wind from her lungs. She lay next to the girl and sobbing child for several moments, trying to suck in air.

At last, Aliisza caught her breath enough to sit up. Kael had joined Kaanyr and the two were attempting to hoist the pile of wreckage aloft once more, but the tilting ground was making the task more difficult. The slope caused more and more of the weight of the pile to lean forward, directly opposing their efforts.

The alu was mildly surprised to see the two of them working together, almost frantic to rescue her. It was strangely comforting.

"Kaanyr! Kael!" the alu called, rising to her feet. The duo stopped their efforts and turned toward her. Aliisza saw relief in both their faces.

Concern? she wondered, unused to such on her behalf. Where did that come from?

Beside her, the girl stood up and scooped up the younger boy. She appeared ready to bolt, but Aliisza took her hand. The squeezing grip that met hers was tight. She remembered another time and place, and a pair of children playing in a walled garden. She had helped, then.

"Where's your family?" the alu asked, looking down at the girl. "Where can we find them?"

The girl didn't say anything, but she pointed in the direction of the open field beyond the village.

Kaanyr and Kael joined them, both panting heavily. "You're quick," Vhok said between gasps, a hint of admiration in his words. "I thought we'd lost you."

"It takes more than a falling building to stop me," Aliisza answered.

Kael said nothing, but he eyed the two children that Aliisza had in tow and gave her an appraising stare. He nodded.

The ground rumbled beneath the group's feet and began to pitch and buck again. Aliisza fought the urge to assume her natural form and rise upon her wings to escape the unsteady ground. Instead, she grabbed hold of the girl's arm to help hold her steady.

"We have to get out of here," she said, looking at both Kaanyr and Kael. "Where's Tauran?"

Kael opened his mouth to answer her, but his eyes grew wide as he spotted something over Aliisza's shoulder. "There!" he shouted, showing a hint of a smile.

All of them turned to look where Kael pointed. A handful of angelic creatures hovered over the open field. Tauran was among them, along with several of the larger, more silvery creatures who had sat in judgment at Aliisza's trial. It felt very long ago to the alu, but a feeling of dread still washed over her at the memory.

The angels had opened some kind of glowing, pearlescent portal and were motioning and guiding the villagers through. The folk crowded around the magical doorway, pushing to get through to safety as their island home shook and rocked, tilting farther and farther to one side.

The angle had grown sharp enough that Aliisza found herself digging her heels into the soil to keep from sliding. They didn't have much time left.

Tauran spotted them and flew over. "Is this the last of them?" he asked, motioning toward the young girl and her smaller companion. "Is anyone else still here?"

Aliisza shrugged, but beside her, Kael shook his head. "We're the last," he said. "Everyone else is already over there." He indicated the portal with a jerk of his head.

"Then let's go," the angel said, grabbing the girl and boy in his arms and hugging them close. "This whole place is falling apart."

Even as he spoke, a series of horrific, ear-shattering pops and booms reverberated around them, and great crevices formed in the rock. Massive shards of stone sliced upward as other chunks crumbled and fell, leaving gaping fissures. The ground became a morass of fragmented, churning stone, some parts caving in as others surged skyward. The remaining buildings of the village shivered and crumpled.

The young girl screamed, and Tauran shoved himself into the air and fanned his wings wide. He carried his two charges aloft, with Kaanyr, Kael, and Aliisza all close behind.

"To the portal!" the angel shouted to be heard over the roaring wind and shattering stone.

The four fliers winged their way toward the opening watched over by a pair of majestic solars. The gateway no longer rested upon solid ground, but instead hovered in the open air. Tauran shot through the portal first, and the rest followed him. As Aliisza reached the mouth of the doorway, she paused and turned back to gaze at what was left of the great floating island.

It had fallen far beneath them by that point, nothing

more than a cascade of tumbling rock, soil, and vegetation. It disappeared into a thick layer of cloud that spread out below them.

She wondered if anything sat below the falling detritus. For a brief moment, she thought of actually soaring after it, just to make sure. Then she realized what she was contemplating and shook some sense back into herself.

Someone else's problem, she told herself. You've done enough rescuing for one day.

Turning back to the doorway, she darted through, and the two solars followed close behind.

CHAPTER FOUR

Myshik found the descent through the earth unsettling. It wasn't the magic itself; his draconic heritage had made him used to that. No, he did not mind most preternatural exercises. But sliding through solid rock was something new.

The half-dragon felt neither substantial nor ethereal. He couldn't find a word that quite described it. Regardless, the spell that Tekthyrios had employed was strange.

It's as though the rock slides through *me,* he decided.

Once the celestial guards had been dispatched, the storm dragon had instructed Myshik to enter the cave and seek an inscribed circle upon the ground. The symbol was easy to spot, and once Myshik stood within it, Tekthyrios engaged the magic.

The half-dragon began to sink into the ground immediately, as though it had turned to quicksand. But it did not suffocate him, and once over the initial fear, Myshik found the journey fascinating.

He descended for several moments then suddenly found himself falling through a white void. He engaged his wings on instinct, struck the bottom of the vacancy without much force, and settled easily into a crouch. Myshik tried to peer around, but a bright, pearlescent glow surrounded him, and he was forced to squint as his eyes adjusted. At last, the draconic hobgoblin's vision returned, and he could examine his surroundings.

Another figure drew his attention. It lay huddled near his feet, unmoving. It faced away from him, so he could not discern the nature of the creature, other than to note that it was a humanoid dressed in a simple brown robe and had long, rather unhealthy hair.

Myshik felt over his shoulder for the handle of his axe to reassure himself, then he began to examine the place.

He discovered that he stood at the bottom of a perfect sphere, and the glow of light seemed to radiate from the walls, indeed the entire inner surface of the room. The chamber was not very large, perhaps only ten paces in diameter. Utterly devoid of any furnishings or features, it would have proven to be a rather mind-numbing prison, should he have found himself trapped there.

A cursed existence, the half-hobgoblin thought, glancing again at the figure.

Is she there? the storm dragon's voice inquired, bouncing around in Myshik's head as his father's and uncle's once had.

Yes, he answered. *She?*

Indeed, came the reply. *Wake her, but do it gently. She has been there a long time and may not know what to make of a visitor, especially one of your . . . um, countenance.*

As you wish. Myshik stepped closer to the figure.

Fighting the urge to grip his axe, the half-dragon knelt down beside the figure. He reached one clawed hand out and tapped the woman once, softly, on the shoulder.

She did not budge.

Myshik tapped again, then he took hold of her shoulders and shook her.

With a shriek, the woman rose up lightning fast, turning with fingers outstretched. She lunged at Myshik, who fell back involuntarily from her unexpected onslaught.

Her wrinkled and pale face framed eyes as black as midnight that burned with hatred, or perhaps insanity. Her gray hair hung in long, limp clumps around her face and nearly down to her waist. Her breath smelled foul, and Myshik could see only a few cracked, yellowed teeth as she sucked in air for another scream.

She came at him where he had sprawled, hands outstretched to throttle him or claw his eyes out. He let her momentum carry her forward, over his own body, then used his feet to propel her past himself. She soared beyond him and struck the sloping side of the sphere with a gasp and a thud.

She's enraged! the half-dragon said as he clambered to his feet. *Wants to rend me! How do I stop her without maiming her?*

There was a soft laugh in his head not of his own mind's making. *She is harder to maim than you might imagine,* came the answer. *Speak to her. Call her name. Kashada.*

Myshik turned to face the crazed woman and saw her gathering herself for another charge. Her face contorted in rage or fear, and her eyes glazed with it. The half-dragon doubted she would make sense of his words.

"Kashada!" he called out. "I am not here to hurt you!"

The woman shrieked and rushed at him, her fingers bent into the shape of claws. She reached for his face, his eyes, but the draconic hobgoblin leaped high and used his wings to gain even more elevation. Her pell-mell charge overbalanced her, and she stumbled into a heap against the opposite slope of the sphere.

Myshik dropped deftly to the surface once more. "Kashada!" he said, more forcefully. "Hear me! I have come to take you from this prison! Let me help you!"

Kashada whirled, staggered like a drunken thing, and glared at her would-be rescuer. "Shadows!" she screamed at him. "There are no shadows!" She swayed where she stood and began to sob, clenching her eyes shut in misery.

Her mind is lost, Myshik thought, projecting to Tekthyrios. *She has no reason left. She screams of there being no shadows.*

Of course! Tekthyrios said. *How clever. Myshik, you must create a shadow for her. You can restore her mind if you can show her a shadow. Do it!*

The half-dragon scowled, looking around the sphere. He had not noticed it before, but with light glowing from the entire inner surface, no shadows were cast anywhere. He could see no way to shield any area from the light.

Kashada howled, a forlorn wailing that reminded Myshik of the jackals in the great desert of Anauroch, singing to the moon at night. She kept her eyes closed, uninterested in attacking him further.

A thought struck Myshik. Working quickly, he removed his cloak and draped it upon the lowest point of the sphere, essentially the floor. He reached into an inner pocket and pulled out an oblong bundle. Unwrapping it, the half-dragon produced a glowing, prism-shaped white crystal twice as thick as his thumb and as long as his hand. He knelt down upon his cloak and held the crystal over it. He placed his other hand between the glow of the crystal and the dark cloth of the cloak. A faint shadow formed there.

"Kashada," Myshik called. "Look, a shadow."

The crone's eyes flew open, and she ceased her wailing. She stared at Myshik for a moment, cocking her head from side to side like some predatory bird. Then she spied the light in his hands, and the patch of darkness he had created. She shrieked in delight and rushed forward. Myshik flinched, expecting her to strike at him again, but instead she knelt down, cooing softly.

"Darker," she demanded, still staring at the shadow. "It must be darker. Make it darker!" she finished with a scream.

Myshik frowned, uncertain. Then inspiration struck. He rose to his feet again and loomed over the crystal, blocking as much of the sphere's light as he could with his body.

The shadow of his hand upon the cloak deepened.

"Yes!" Kashada shouted in triumph. Her voice had changed. It was stronger, less shrill. "You've done it!" Then the woman lunged forward and dived at the hand-shaped area of darkness.

Before Myshik's eyes, she melted into the shadow and vanished.

❖ ❖ ❖ ❖ ❖ ❖ ❖ ❖

Tauran rested upon his favorite protrusion of stone, high above the Lifespring. He sat a pace away from the edge, leaning back against a towering pinnacle of rock pointed skyward like a poniard. A tumbling waterfall roared next to him, emerging from a cleft in the cliff face and plunging over the side of the protrusion, out of sight.

"We should be inside!" Micus said, shouting to be heard. The other angel sat next to Tauran, huddled against the spire of rock, trying to avoid of the worst of the wind. "Why in the Hells are we out here in this?"

Tauran ignored his friend and crawled toward the end of the protrusion. The howling, lashing storms whipped the spray from the churning torrent, peppering him with a fine, cool mist. The dampness made the stone beneath his hands and feet slick. The wind tore at his tunic as if it wanted to rip him from the precipice and carry him away. Ignoring the gale, Tauran reached the edge and peered over.

It was a long drop.

The spire behind him rose as the tallest, most impossibly thin peak in a high, sharp ridge of jagged, jutting stone. The ridge formed a deep basin surrounding the Lifespring on three sides. Most days, the waters shimmered in golden sunlight, a tranquil pool of divine healing magic. That day, they churned and frothed in a blue-gray maelstrom covered in whitecaps.

Tauran could barely see the distant shore, where the water spilled over a lower lip of the ridge to other basins even farther below. Remnants of clouds, shredded and reformed by the whipping wind, slashed across his view, giving the whole plane an eerie, translucent look.

Tauran crawled back to his friend. "Do you remember the first time you asked me about diving off here?" he asked Micus. "Right before I began teaching you how to do it?"

The other angel frowned but nodded. "Yes," he replied. "Right before we tried to save that marilith's child. What of it?"

"Do you remember what you asked me that day?"

Micus shook his head. "Something about why you did it. But it was a long time ago."

Tauran nodded. "That's right. I told you that I did it to remind me that the easiest path is not always the right one, and that I must remain vigilant against complacency. Right?"

"I suppose so," Micus answered, his face filled with doubt. Then his eyes widened. "You're not actually planning to—you must be mad!"

Tauran held his hand up, gesturing for his old friend to relax. "No," he said. "I'm not mad. No diving for either of us today."

Micus sagged back in relief. "Good," he said. "Because if you tried, then I'd *know* you had lost your way."

"That's just it, though," Tauran said. "I feel like what I face right now, with Aliisza and Vhok, is just like diving off this precipice. The easy thing would be to remit them to the High Council, let them lock the fiends away, and move on to other things."

"Sounds like a fine plan to me," Micus said dryly. "And the one I'm advising you to go with."

"But don't you see? That's the easy path. It's the safe path. I don't think it's the right path." Please understand me, old friend, he thought. You of all my companions might recognize what I'm trying to say.

Micus was silent for a moment, then said, "Sometimes, we need others, wiser than ourselves, to tell us which path to follow. Sometimes, like young children, we try to climb over boulders in the road, rather than go around them. Why does *every* path have to be hard?"

"They don't," Tauran admitted. Tyr knows I wish *this* one weren't so hard. "But diving off these rocks was supposed to remind me to stay vigilant against growing complacent. That means recognizing when the harder route is the right one."

Micus sat without speaking for another moment. "It sounds as though you've already made up your mind, Tauran," he said at last. "You've already decided what you're going to do, and nothing I say will change your decision."

"Perhaps," Tauran said. Yes, he admitted to himself. I have.

"Then what do you want from me?" Micus asked. "What purpose can I possibly serve by sitting out here in this wretched storm?"

I need you to believe in me, Tauran thought. I need you to tell me that I'm not trying to dive off this cliff right now. Because that's what this feels like. "I just wanted you to understand that I'm clear headed, steady in my faith," he said aloud. "I just wanted you to know that I believe in my heart that something is profoundly wrong with the universe right now, and I can see it, even where others cannot."

"Tauran," Micus said. His voice was odd, almost warning his friend. "I can't support what I don't believe in. We have existed with Tyr's laws for millennia, and they have served all who dwell within this realm quite well. Right now, at this moment, when so much else is in turmoil, is the very time to uphold them. That is how they endure, how we survive."

"I know," Tauran said, suddenly feeling very tired.

"You want to bend one rule, and then another, and another. You claim that it's because you see some catastrophe on the horizon, and you intend to stop it, but what if the very catastrophe you envision is the result of your own misguided transgressions? What if some calamity does befall the House, and it all could have been avoided if you had just adhered to the rules?"

Tauran held his hands up in despair. "It is always possible," he admitted. "I cannot foresee the outcomes any better than you." That's why I feel like I'm standing on the edge of this maelstrom, ready to throw myself over. "But every way I look at this, I see the same thing. Every part of my body just feels that I am right."

It was Micus's turn to throw his hands up. "We are not creatures of gut instincts and intuitive guesswork, Tauran. Watching you place so much emphasis on 'feelings' troubles me more than anything. As far as I'm concerned, the path is clear. There is no deliberation necessary. The law is the law, and we are bound to abide by it."

Tauran nodded, staring at the wet rock before him. "I understand," he said. He felt a great sadness wash over him. "You would handle this differently. I had hoped you would see my viewpoint, had hoped that all these years of diving together from this point had allowed us to share some common insight. I guess it is not to be."

Micus reached out and placed his hand upon Tauran's arm. "I'm sorry, my friend. I do see the value in what you taught me, but vigilance can only carry one so far. Powers much greater than ourselves have both the wisdom and insight to guide the rest of us, and we have the wisdom—and the responsibility—to be guided. If you doubt, turn to Tyr. He is mysterious, but he will not lead you astray."

Tauran smiled. How can you be so sure? he thought. "I hope you are right," he said.

Micus rose up onto his knees. "Do not stay out here much longer, my friend," he said. "This storm seems to grow worse by the moment."

"I won't," Tauran promised. "See you in a while."

Micus stood and launched himself into the tempest. Fighting the winds, he flew off, leaving his friend alone to contemplate.

Tauran frowned as he watched the other angel grow small before vanishing within a cloud bank. The storm *is* going to get worse, he thought. Much, much worse.

Micus had not been gone long when another angel arrived

at Tauran's ledge. She swooped up from below and hovered for a heartbeat or two, then she settled in the spot where Micus had stood only a moment before. She reached out to steady herself against the buffeting winds.

Tauran started at her arrival, then he smiled and stood. "Eirwyn!" he said. "I hate it when you do that."

"Oh, you do not!" she replied. "You're very glad to see me, and you know it."

She looked older than Tauran, her bronze skin criss-crossed with wrinkles. Her merry eyes twinkled with genuine friendship as she smiled. Her long, flowing hair hung down in a single braid over one shoulder. It gleamed silver in the cloudy day.

She went straight to Tauran. "You look very tired," she said, embracing him.

I am tired, he thought. Bone weary, as the mortals say. "I'm better now that you're here," he said. "What's brought you?"

The elder deva adapted a look of mock indignation. "Why, Tauran! You wound me! Think you so little of my divination skills that you would doubt my ability to know when and where I am needed?"

Tauran laughed, gladness filling him for a moment. "You divined that I would be here?" he asked.

"No, I did not expect to find you here," she answered. "I merely augured that I would be needed here, at this time. As usual, I was right." She hugged him again, then pulled back to stare the angel squarely in the face. "What troubles you?" she asked.

Tauran looked away and felt the full weight of his worries. "I don't know," he said, watching the storm-tossed clouds roil around the two of them. "I fear that I am losing my way, Eirwyn," he said, returning to gaze earnestly at her. "No one seems to see what I see, the menace that seems to be gathering in the House. Not even Micus shows any grasp of the threats I fear."

Eirwyn sighed. "This feud between Tyr and Helm has upset the balance. The sooner they settle it, the better off we'll all be."

For a moment, they sat together unspeaking, with only the roar of wind and waterfall filling their ears. The moment stretched out, became a bit uncomfortable. Tauran wanted to share more, but he fretted that he was about to cross a threshold from which he could not return.

"You can tell me, Tauran," Eirwyn said at last. "It won't hurt my feelings. We've been friends too long to let this feud come between us."

If only it were that benign, Tauran thought. He smiled slightly. "It's actually the opposite," he said. He drew a deep breath before proceeding. "I believe Tyr has lost his reason."

Eirwyn drew her head back a bit when she heard the angel's words. She scrutinized him for several heartbeats, until he began to fear that he had misjudged her. *I thought she would understand better than most. But maybe—*

"That's a dangerous thing you say, Tauran," the elder deva said. "Most within the House—or at least the Court—would not take kindly to hearing those words."

"Believe me," Tauran said, "I know. I dare not blaspheme that way in front of"—he cast a quick glance in Eyrwin's direction—"anyone less sympathetic to the notion." He saw her smile slightly then. "But I believe it," he continued, "and furthermore, I think I can prove that Cyric has his hand in it."

Eirwyn gave a small gasp. "You don't really have a good grasp for building support for your ideas, do you?"

Tauran's chuckle felt mirthless. "It would seem not," he

said. "And yet, I'm about to go before the High Council and argue that very thing."

"Tauran!" she said, admonishing him. "I don't think that's wise."

Tauran sighed. "Perhaps," he said. "But if I'm correct and do nothing, then I fear I have committed the greater crime. The risk I take in revealing my suspicions pales in comparison to the repercussions if I am right."

"What leads you to believe this?" she asked.

Tauran explained what he knew of Aliisza, Vhok, and Zasian.

When he was done, Eirwyn sat very still. Finally, she rose to her feet. "What you claim is very serious, Tauran. But my divinations did not lead me here to talk you out of your plan. Of that I am confident."

Tauran stared up at her, waiting to see what she would say next. What he thought he had lost in Micus, he hoped against hope he had gained in Eirwyn.

"I am going to meditate on this," she said. "And when I have more information, I will seek you out again. Perhaps I have a part to play in this."

"Thank you," Tauran said, rising to face her. "You've given me renewed strength to see this through."

Eirwyn held up her hands to forestall his gratitude. "I cannot promise that I will be able to offer you much," she said, "but I will do what I can."

"That is all that I can ask," Tauran replied. He hugged her then, thankful for her friendship.

When he stepped back, her gaze bore into him. "Be very careful, Tauran," she said. "You will make many enemies revealing these theories. The High Council of Tyr is a dangerous entity to rile."

Tauran nodded. "I know," he said. Then he drew a deep breath. "But I am due to appear before them any moment, so I must go. Thank you again."

Eirwyn smiled and vanished. A moment later, Tauran departed too.

Neither of them had noticed the lantern archon flitting nearby, hiding beneath the protrusion upon which they sat. Having heard the entire conversion, it vanished, too, hurrying with a heavy heart to report to Micus of Tauran's treachery against Tyr.

❖ ❖ ❖ ❖ ❖ ❖ ❖ ❖

Aliisza sat on the bed and wished Kaanyr would stop pacing. The cambion had been at it since the two of them had been brought to her chambers—at least, she assumed they were hers. It felt as if only a day or so had passed since she had last been there, and she had to keep reminding herself it had been eleven years. She wondered if anyone else had spent time here. That thought mildly annoyed her.

What's the matter with me? she thought, growing more agitated. I'm acting like I *want* to stay here.

On the contrary, the moment two of the dog-headed creatures had escorted the pair to her chambers while Tauran and Kael departed to attend to other matters, Aliisza had grown restless. Certainly, the foreboding sensation of being trapped again unsettled her. But the alu knew it was more than that.

Tauran and Kael's departure had stirred feelings of . . . regret.

I didn't want them to leave, Aliisza realized. Am I so loath to face Kaanyr alone? Or is there more to it?

"I've been going about this all wrong," Kaanyr said, disrupting her thoughts. "I've been fighting this the whole time. I should know better."

"Fighting what?" she asked, thankful that he had deigned to come out of his brooding to speak to her.

"The angel's hold over me. His plans. All of it."

"Yes," she said.

Kaanyr stopped pacing and turned to look at her. "What is that supposed to mean?" he asked, scowling. "You never just agree with me lately."

"Only because you've been making no sense lately," she countered. "You have been acting the fool, revealing your every emotion, reacting instead of scheming. You have not been the Kaanyr Vhok I thought I knew." Does that Kaanyr Vhok even exist? she wondered.

The cambion stood and stared at her for a long time. His eyes bored into hers, roamed up and down her body, lingering appreciatively in certain places. She had assumed her true form when they had returned to her chambers, but he hadn't noticed before right then. For the first time in a very long time, Kaanyr seemed . . .

Hungry, Aliisza decided. She actually began to blush beneath that gaze.

Kaanyr seemed to shake himself out of his carnal stupor. "I'm not the only one behaving oddly," he said. He turned and sat upon a cushioned chair on the far side of the room. "You are not yourself, either."

Aliisza caught herself feeling a bit jealous that Kaanyr had managed to stroll away so easily. She didn't want the moment to end quite like that.

"Who's to blame for that?" she asked, feeling the tiniest bit petulant. "Who arranged for me to become trapped here, under the tutelage of an angel? What did you expect would happen?"

"Zasian assured me that his protective spells would ward you from any true change." Vhok's voice was quiet. "Did he lie about that, too?"

Aliisza thought for a long moment before answering. "No," she said at last. "But he didn't tell you the truth, either. What he did—the spells that he wove over me to shield me from Tauran's influence—wasn't so much a protective mask as it was a . . . reversion."

Kaanyr cocked his head to one side. "Explain," he demanded.

"He didn't cast a spell that would shield me from something Tauran forced on me. He cast a spell that would change me back at the end."

"So the angel's damnable tricks took hold?" Kaanyr narrowed his eyes and scowled.

"That's just it," Aliisza said, feeling uneasy. She wasn't sure if she wanted to admit her next words to herself, much less to Kaanyr. "There were no tricks, my love. He only showed me a perspective."

"Perspective about what?"

"About the nature of goodness. It's not so easy to explain. I'm not sure I understand it myself."

"I'm not sure I want to," Kaanyr countered, waving her away.

"Oh, but you will hear what I say!" Aliisza shouted, angry at his flippant dismissal. "You are the one who subjected me to it, so you are damn well going to hear me out!"

Kaanyr glowered at the alu, but he finally nodded once, almost imperceptibly. "Because it's you," he said.

A flood of old emotions rushed through Aliisza, but she

pushed them away and continued. "I came to understand that I could give myself up, make myself vulnerable, and allow myself to care about others before myself," she said. "I learned to surrender to caring, because it can come back tenfold, if you let it. I know it doesn't make any sense to you, because you did not go through what I did, but trust me, there can be times when the benefit you reap is worth the price you pay."

She could tell by the look on Kaanyr's face that he either didn't understand what she was talking about or didn't care to. She pushed on without letting him interrupt.

"I think Zasian understood what would happen to me and simply lied to you. He might have told you that Tauran's efforts would involve coercion or divine trickery, but that's not how it happened. I came to those conclusions on my own. All Zasian did was plant a trigger that would remind me of who I was before—snap me out of it, if you will."

Kaanyr pursed his lips in thought. "So, where do things stand for you now?" he asked. "Whose side are you on?"

"That's just it," Aliisza said, rising from the bed to begin pacing. She had to choose her next words very carefully. "I'm not on anyone's side."

"So you believe this nonsense that the angel spouts?" The cambion's voice dripped with disgust. "Or else you claim to in order to torment me."

"No!" Aliisza said, turning to face him. She clenched her hands, feeling helpless to explain. "Not like that," she said, but her voice was faint. She knew Kaanyr wouldn't believe her. She didn't believe the words herself.

The reward you reap is worth the price you pay.

"I love four men," she said at last, blurting it out before she could think about it.

Kaanyr raised one eyebrow. He looked almost bemused. "That's just not a word I hear from your lips, lover," he said, then, when he realized his own irony, added, "at least not used in that way."

Aliisza almost chuckled. He thought her notion of being in love was stranger than the fact that she shared it among four men. "I love each of you in a very different way," she said, "and I will not demean any of it by trying to explain them all to you."

"How noble of you," he countered. That sardonic tone was back.

"But know that you are one of them," she said, staring him straight in the eye. "Despite everything that has happened, despite all that you have done to me, I am still yours, lover." She almost felt herself slip into that provocative, purring tone of voice. She resisted it.

Kaanyr smirked. "You have a strange way of showing it," he said. "Most of my lovers don't trick me into entering sub-servient arrangements with angels."

Aliisza smiled sheepishly in spite of her pounding heart. "I know," she said. "I was angry with you. I wanted to punish you."

Kaanyr raised that single eyebrow again. "Punish me?" he asked. "I don't take too kindly to punishment," he said. "From anyone," he added. His voice carried a dangerous edge to it.

Aliisza did allow herself to slip into that familiar role of temptress then. She sauntered over to Kaanyr. "Perhaps," she said, and she was almost surprised at how smoky her voice had become, "but I do." She closed the distance until she was standing directly in front of him. She cocked her hips to one side and rested her hands on them. "Aliisza's been a good girl," she said softly. "Make her bad again."

She held her breath, wondering if it would work.

Kaanyr sat very still, though the alu could see the muscles of his neck working as he swallowed several times. She knew she was getting to him.

"Why are you still here?" he asked, his own voice soft. "You can flee whenever you want. So why remain, be that angel's lackey?"

Aliisza cast a glance toward the open balcony, saw the roiling storms beyond the opening, and returned her gaze to the cambion's face. *Don't think I haven't thought about it,* she thought. *Almost every second since we got tossed back in here.* "Because I want to stay with you," she answered, and it was the truth.

Kaanyr nodded. "And who are the other three?" he asked.

Aliisza fought not to show her fear. *What will you do when I tell you?* she wondered. She took a deep breath. "One, I love like a mother. One, like a daughter. And one no longer even lives," she said. "But the only one that matters right now, I love in the most mischievous way possible."

Kaanyr smiled then and reached for Aliisza at last.

CHAPTER FIVE

"But this is a matter of honor!" Tauran argued, his voice rising. It echoed throughout the hemispherical chamber, reverberating back against Kael as he and the deva stood before the Council. Its members sat arrayed in a semicircle, nine solars in all. Each one rested upon a thronelike chair arranged on a raised, curved dais around half the chamber. Kael never liked having to peer upward to face the members. Their silvery faces and golden eyes were inscrutable, and it always left him with the feeling of being on trial.

Perhaps we *are* on trial, he thought. The whole House has lost its senses. They've never questioned Tauran like this before.

Somewhere beyond the chamber, muted rumbles reverberated from the growing chaos sweeping the plane. Kael could feel the power of the storms in the stones beneath his feet. The entire Court of Tyr shook with the energy of the gods' argument.

So much anger, Kael thought, dismayed. So much energy wasted. Surely they should be— No. Do not think that way.

Do not try to fathom the depths of the gods, he told himself. Serve them well.

Tauran continued. "I made a bargain with the two of them, and I gave them my word."

"That may be," said the High Councilor, sitting in the very middle of the assemblage. "But in this instance, it might not have been yours to give. There is much occurring here that we do not yet understand, and you risk not only your own reputation within the Court, but the well-being of many that dwell within the House."

"They agreed to be bound by obligation," he said, as if that answered all the Councilors' doubts. Kael suspected it did not, and he wondered why. What has Tauran ever done to make you doubt? he wondered, frustrated.

"One of them agreed, Tauran, not both," the High Councilor said. "The cambion is an easy read. He is as manipulative and cunning as he is corrupt, and he will cause you trouble. She, on the other hand, is an unknown factor in all of this, and she has already violated numerous laws as our guest."

Tauran nodded and spread his hands in supplication. "I cannot defend all of Aliisza's actions to this point, Councilors, but I can also see how our influences have begun to affect her. She has behaved with more compassion than even I would have imagined. She risked injury to herself in order to save a pair of young petitioners in that village today. I believe she has started down a path to redemption."

Kael frowned while listening to Tauran describe Aliisza's selfless act. Redemption? That did not fit the image of her in his mind. Would she have saved them without the protection of your bargain? he wondered.

"This is the third time you have come before us concerning

this being, Tauran," another of the Councilors said, her feathered wings fluttering behind her to show her impatience. "Each time before, you have asked us to accept your wisdom, to trust you in these matters, despite our better judgment. In both cases, events did not play out as you expected."

Kael saw Tauran shift from foot to foot, saw the deva's own wings flutter in agitation. He had never seen the angelic creature seem so . . . *ruffled* before. They're not buying it either, he realized. Maybe trying to sell everyone on her good points isn't the best way. Torm knows it's hard for *me* to see her good side. But you know her better than anyone here, he thought. Convince them so we can go.

"Now you stand before us again, pleading for more leeway," she continued. "It is not a pattern that lends itself much to confidence and optimism on our part."

Tauran spread his hands again. "As I have said before this court in the past, I believe our best hope of gaining her trust and ultimately turning her to a path of goodness is to give her some room, some freedom. We must allow her to feel her way through this on her own."

"Such a course is risky."

"My plan involves more risk, to be sure, but I believe the greater rewards are worth it. The less we interfere, the more likely it is that she will embrace this new outlook. The more we restrict her, attempt to confine her actions to that narrow path, the more she will resist and turn against us."

The High Council was quiet for a long moment. Kael wondered if they were silently conversing or merely thinking. The half-drow caught himself wanting to pace and had to force himself to remain still.

He could see both points of the debate. On the one hand, Aliisza was willful and impudent. She was not bound to serve anyone and could wreak havoc on Tauran's schemes at any inopportune moment. And Kael detested the idea of relying on immoral fiends, full-blooded or not, in order to hunt down Zasian. The holy power of Tyr and Torm should be enough!

On the other, Tauran's arguments about the extraordinary nature of the circumstances made for compelling testimony. Members of the Triad were arguing, fighting even, and the entire Court seemed paralyzed, unable to come to any consensus on what to do. All the gatherings, all the proceedings—where little more than debate ever occurred—were growing tiring and irksome. The loyal champion of Torm wanted action.

Even if it means being near her? he asked. As if to answer, Kael felt a strange, uncomfortable sense of curiosity invade his thoughts. He did want to be near her. *Why?* he wondered, struggling to understand such strange emotions. *You have Tauran already. What else do you need?* Kael thought again of Aliisza risking herself to save those two children. *Would she have done that for me?* a tiny part of him wondered. *No,* he decided, trying to push that thought away. *You only want her near to prove to yourself once and for all that she was the uncaring fiend you've always imagined,* he scolded himself. *And you cannot let that jeopardize Tauran's plans. You have duties.*

Still, the image of his mother lingered.

"Here is my fear in all this," the High Councilor said at last. "That you—and we—are being manipulated by these fiends in ways that we do not yet understand, and we will be filled with regret when we do, when it's too late. You yourself have admitted to such once already, the second time you stood before us, after the alu escaped your custody."

Several murmurs of agreement arose from the other

Councilors gathered there. Kael scanned them all, studied their faces, and saw nothing but grim countenances and disapproval. They reflected Kael's own suspicions. Vhok, Aliisza, and Zasian had pulled off a most extraordinary trick in order to breach the House's defenses.

"I have little doubt that you believe you are fit to repulse such subterfuge," the High Councilor continued, "but these beings—these invaders—are clever. Even now, they may be continuing a plot they hatched long ago, designed to take advantage of your willingness to give them leeway. It is in our nature to offer forgiveness, redemption. Such generosity, though natural and good, can be taken advantage of."

"I am well aware of the risks, Councilor," Tauran answered, staring down at the polished stones of the floor. "But I am also well aware of Vhok's and Aliisza's motivations. I, perhaps better than you, know what they want, what they seek. Not what they claim to want, but what they truly desire. I, unlike you, am in the field, confronting such beings. I deal with them, know their cunning firsthand. I have already used such knowledge to gain their cooperation. It will aid me in keeping my wits going forward, I assure you."

The Councilors stirred, shifting or murmuring among themselves, but none of them confronted Tauran on that point.

Kael nodded slightly to himself. Yes, he thought. We can use them to our advantage, instead of the other way around.

"Perhaps you'd care to explain how you knew right where to find the half-fiends?" came a voice from behind the pair of them.

Kael recognized the voice before he even turned around. He closed his eyes and stifled a groan. No! he fretted. Tauran almost had them won over. Why now?

"Micus," Tauran said, turning to face the newcomer. "What are you doing here?"

"Making certain the Council knows all the facts about your theories, Tauran. They need to understand just how erratically you've been behaving of late. I'm here to make sure they do."

"Micus, I already told you, we—"

"Tell *them*," the other deva interrupted, pointing at the members of the Council. "They are the ones you need to convince. I have already made up my mind."

Tauran stared at his friend for a long moment. It seemed to Kael that he debated something, but whatever was on the angel's mind, he did not share it. Instead, he turned back to face the members of the Council. They all remained silent, waiting expectantly.

"As you are well aware," the deva began, "it's been more than a decade since we—since I—lost track of Aliisza the alu. Her escape was remarkable, leaving her son, Kael, trapped in her body for the duration. He managed to adapt, learning to use her body's innate magic in order to alter his physical form to his own, more familiar guise. Despite his heritage, you all know him now as a devout and loyal servant of Torm, a champion in combat, and a noble companion."

The angel paused and looked over at Kael, who only nodded once in appreciation. Privately, though, the half-drow beamed. It had been a profound struggle to learn to exist in another's body, a half-fiend's body, and he was pleased with himself, just a little, not only that he had succeeded, but that others had noticed.

Tauran continued. "For reasons that neither of us can explain as of yet, Kael experienced an odd sensation earlier this day, a sudden and strange connection with his mother.

Whether that link was due to their blood relationship to one another or some astral bond between Aliisza and her body—or perhaps both—it was strong enough and focused enough that Kael was convinced he knew where she was. The pair of us set out at once to locate her."

At that point, the Councilors began murmuring among themselves again. Tauran waited patiently while they absorbed what he had described, but Kael glanced over at Micus, who frowned.

"Is this as Tauran has described?" the High Councilor asked, and it took Kael another moment before he realized the solar was speaking to him.

He blinked, trying to find his voice. The solars had never called on him before.

"Yes, High Councilor," the half-drow replied. "I have no explanation for it, but it was unmistakable, and the sensation led me unerringly to her." He looked at Micus and asked, "Is that so hard to accept?"

The scowling deva shook his head. "Only in that it seems less plausible than the prospect that you two have known where Aliisza was all along and merely went to join her at an appointed time and place."

Kael gaped at Micus while the chamber erupted in a dizzying cacophony of incredulous debate. To the half-drow, it seemed as though half the Councilors argued for an immediate investigation into Tauran's activities while the other half decried his unfair persecution. Tauran said nothing, but he, too, turned to look at his old friend with a sorrowful expression.

When the High Councilor had at last restored quiet, he turned back to Micus. "Please provide some evidence for your accusations, Micus."

Micus bowed his head, as if the words he was about to impart pained him greatly. "Before I proceed, let me be blunt. It brings me no pleasure to disclose these points. Tauran is my friend, and I have observed him on countless occasions carrying out his duties with both supreme devotion and suitable aplomb. His energy seemed tireless, his dedication unquestionable."

Then why are you turning on him, you backstabbing bastard? Kael wondered.

"But that merely makes his recent erratic behavior all the more noticeable," Micus continued. "I have observed, to my great chagrin, that Tauran has begun to question many of his values, as well as those of the House. He has chosen courses of action that fly in the face of our established procedures and policies. He has enabled the criminal activity of intruders into our realm through both dubious deed and cowardly inaction. In short, I fear that his morality has been compromised, and he has thrown in with these half-fiends he purports to supervise. For what purpose, I do not know, but I fear my friend has turned."

More murmuring arose, but the High Councilor silenced them quickly. "Please proceed with your evidence, Micus," the solar instructed.

Micus nodded. "Of course. In addition to this questionable explanation of how Tauran and Kael came to find the alu and this new intruder—this cambion—I submit Tauran's insistence of late on debating the merits of Tyr's righteousness in the conflict with Helm."

A few murmurs of disapproval issued from the Council. Kael wasn't certain whether they were directed at Micus or at what Micus had said.

"Tauran has called into question Tyr's wisdom. I have listened to him say it."

Kael couldn't stand how Micus was skewing Tauran's words. He stepped forward. "He only insists that Helm must have very good reasons for his side of the debate, and that we should reserve our judgment until the two gods have settled their feud. Esteemed Councilors, examining every side of an argument with an open mind is a far cry from conspiracy against the House."

For once, no sound at all issued from within the chamber. All sets of golden eyes had turned to stare coldly at the half-drow, their displeasure plain. But Kael refused to back down. He stared back, waiting for someone, anyone, to challenge the point. In the background, muted thunder rumbled again, and the floor vibrated with it.

"I'm sorry, Councilors, forgive his impudence," Micus said. "Kael is as loyal and devout a student as any deva could ask for, but his allegiance calls his neutrality into question. His perspective on this issue wavers from the truth considerably."

Kael seethed and opened his mouth to argue further, but Tauran placed a restraining hand on the half-drow's arm. When Kael caught his mentor's glance, the angel shook his head almost imperceptibly. You're not helping, was the message. Kael sighed and nodded, and Tauran released his grip.

The High Councilor spoke. "Your accusations are grave, Micus, and despite his impudence, Kael is correct. Engaging in such debate is not a crime against Tyr's law. I hope you have something more substantial to tell us to back up your claims."

Micus frowned, and Kael had to clench his jaw to keep from grinning at the angel.

"Of course, High Councilor. What I intend to submit next brings me no joy to share. In fact, it shames me to admit. But I truly want only to ensure that Tauran cannot deceive you—if that is in fact his intention—and to avert his own ruination." The other angel turned to look directly at his counterpart. His next words were clearly intended for his fellow deva. "Despite what he must think, I seek only to save him from himself and bring him back into Tyr's embrace. If I am proven incorrect, and Tauran has engaged in no real wrongdoing, then I will beg his—and this Council's—forgiveness."

A long moment of silence stretched out as the two angels studied one another. Finally, Kael saw Tauran nod, just once, the tiniest bit. An acknowledgment of his continued friendship, the half-drow supposed.

He has more charity than I, Kael thought. I couldn't be quite so generous after such a besmirching.

Micus nodded. "I overheard a conversation today," he said, "between Tauran and a servant of Helm."

Tauran gasped, and Kael jerked his eyes in the angel's direction. Tauran stared at Micus with a look of both dismay and betrayal. "You spied on me?"

Micus ignored him. "As you can see, he does not deny it. Yes, I enlisted the assistance of a lantern archon today, and I heard, with my own ears, Tauran suggest that Tyr's judgment in certain matters pertaining to the membership of the Triad is questionable, and that perhaps he is unfit to dispense a ruling on the matter. Tauran has actually claimed that Helm might be correct in challenging the Maimed One."

More murmuring issued from the Council, but the High Councilor silenced it with a loud query. "What say you to these charges, Tauran?"

The angel stepped forward, peering up in the direction of the solar. "I don't deny it," he said without a hint of shame or regret. "I do believe that Tyr's wisdom has failed him."

The murmuring returned and rose in volume to outright dismay.

"And this," Tauran continued, "is why I believe we desperately need the half-fiends' help." The noise level increased. Tauran raised his hands, asking for patience. "This destructive argument that roils throughout our home, this bitter feud between beloved Tyr and noble Helm"—more than one solar frowned at that appellation—"is not the conduct suited to two benevolent and wise deities."

The murmuring grew louder, and one Councilor rose to her feet, incensed at the deva's words. "You overstep your bounds, Tauran!" she shouted. "It is not your place to presume to know the wisdom of Tyr!"

"Perhaps," Tauran countered, raising his own voice to be heard, "but no one else seems willing to question these events. I believe this crass debate has been contrived, engineered by those who would see the House brought low."

Even more dissent filled the chamber as the members of the Council all began talking at once. Kael sensed the anger in their demeanors, and it shocked him to see the stoic solars, always inscrutable, exhibiting such passion.

They are frightened, he realized. What could scare a solar? he wondered, growing more uneasy with each passing moment.

A particularly deep and rumbling disturbance shook the chamber. The champion of Torm had to take a step to steady himself as the floor pitched. He saw the much more graceful angels spread their wings to compensate for the undulating foundations. The rumble subsided, and with it, the solars' berating of Tauran.

See? Kael wanted to shout. That's what scares you. You know he speaks the truth.

"I sense some malevolent manipulation behind this"—Tauran paused, waving one hand vaguely around himself—"this furious dispute between them. Whatever their disagreement—and I do not profess to understand the ways of the gods—but whatever their disagreement, it strikes me as unduly vehement and bitter. This is not the behavior of the immortals I have served. Furthermore, our disparaging treatment of Helm's loyal servants is not in keeping with what I know in my heart to be just and fair. The same holds true, I suspect, for you. It is not who we are, Councilors." The deva scanned the room once, locking gazes with each member of the Council, before he proceeded. "I witnessed events today that have convinced me that Cyric has a hand in Tyr and Helm's disagreement. I think Vhok and Aliisza were unwittingly caught up in the Liar's machinations, and they can help me find out if I'm right."

"No!" shouted one of the solars.

"The impertinence!" yelled another.

Kael could not remember a time when he had witnessed the powerful creatures in such emotional disarray. They clearly found the entire prospect of their own god stumbling in his judgment too much to bear. For the first time, he feared what they might do to Tauran to counteract their own uncertainty.

"Blasphemy!" Micus shouted. "He is unfit for his station! He has fallen in league with fiends and aims to assist them in a foul plot!"

Kael took a single step toward Micus, his face a snarl of hatred. *He's been your friend forever!* the half-drow thought. *How dare you smear his name, you bastard! You don't deserve his friendship.*

Micus saw the movement and gestured. "As you can see,"

he said, raising his voice to be heard, "even his pupil has been tainted. It pains me to see, but what should we expect from the offspring of such dubious stock? Tauran has failed in that effort, too."

There was more outrage among the Council, but Kael could barely hear it. He was too busy fighting to get past Tauran to reach Micus. He didn't remember drawing his weapon, but somehow the sword was in his hands.

Tauran held Kael by one arm, straining to keep the half-drow from striking the other angel. "Control yourself!" he shouted. "You do us no favors by unleashing your wrath!"

Micus stood a few paces back, on the balls of his feet, as though prepared to combat the champion of Torm should he manage to break free from Tauran's grasp. His expression was one of grim regret.

The chamber continued its uproar.

Kael finally relinquished and stared at the floor, shamed. Tauran was right; his own actions were just as much of a betrayal as anything Micus had concocted. "Forgive me, Tauran," he murmured.

The deva made a faint gesture of dismissal. We'll speak of it later, was the message.

The High Councilor called for quiet once more, but it took him shouting, "Silence!" in a thunderous, commanding tone before all became calm again.

"In light of the evidence," the High Councilor said in a tone that suggested he would brook no further outbursts, "coupled with my own grave concerns about the intentions of these fiends in our midst, you are hereby ordered to your quarters until further notice, while an inquiry is launched into your behavior. That applies to both of you," he added, pointing to Kael.

The half-drow bowed his head, remorse filling him, both at his own improper actions in the face of the Council and at their knee-jerk reactions.

"And what of Aliisza and Vhok?" Tauran asked, his tone neutral. "What is to become of them?"

Kael could hardly imagine the effort it took his mentor to remain so calm in the face of such betrayal.

"They are intruders, High Councilor," Micus argued. "Both of them. Aliisza violated the terms of her stay with us when she fled in her son's body, and her efforts to assist Vhok's intrusion condemns her equally."

"Indeed," the solar said. "For now they will be required to remain under guard, until this inquiry can sort everything out. I put you in charge of their care, Micus. Make certain that they do not—"

Kael was knocked from his feet as the hemispherical chamber lurched violently to one side. He stumbled to his knees and slid across the rapidly tilting floor. He heard the concerned shouts of the angels, deva and solar alike, all around him. The half-drow righted himself and took to the air, using the magic of his winged boots.

The chamber shook again, and a great, deafening peal of cracking stone pulsed through it. Kael clamped his hands over his ears and peered around, seeking the source of the noise. The majority of the white, glowing dome had shattered overhead. A multitude of jagged shards of the strange, glassy material rained down upon the occupants. Lashing wind howled through the opening and whipped the myriad fragments around in a deadly storm.

Kael flinched away and hid his face. He prayed to Torm that his armor would shield him from the worst of the flying debris. The half-drow felt the shards pelt him, crashing against the metal outfit. The sound was horrendous, a cacophony of tinkling and breaking, like poorly made chimes. The swirling material stung every bit of exposed flesh.

Suddenly, the storm was over. The wind still howled, but the maelstrom of broken, jagged debris had vanished. Kael risked a look around and saw everyone else in the chamber doing the same. Tauran and Micus were both bloodied in many places, their white garments stained red. They eyed each other and the members of the Council. The solars had been left unscathed, and the High Councilor held his hand aloft in a finished gesture.

He put a stop to it, Kael decided. Banished the shards with his divine power.

The roar of another deep-throated rumble coursed through the chamber from beyond its ruined walls, and the world shook again. Kael stared upward through the gaping hole in the ceiling and gasped.

The view was surreal, something from a nightmare.

The very sky had fractured. Some of it was night, studded with stars, while in other places the red glow of sunset or the wispy white of clouds shone through. Every bit of it drifted and tumbled, like individual windows peering into other worlds or pieces of a broken and scattering image, a stained glass window burst from its frame.

Another rumble shook the world, and the hemisphere ripped in half.

The solars vanished, winked out like fireflies on a summer night. Micus disappeared too, leaving only Tauran and Kael hovering in the middle of the destruction.

As the chamber separated and began to fall away to either side of him, Kael felt the storm's full force. It lashed against him from every direction, sending him spinning. His boots were useless. He flailed, terrified that he would be dashed against some remnant of the world, crushed between massive blocks of whirling, spinning stone and earth. It was the end of all things, he was certain.

Tauran grabbed hold of Kael. The half-drow flinched, then was thankful for the anchor point. The angel drew him close and wrapped his wings around the armored warrior in a protective embrace. "Hold still!" he shouted over the incessant roar of the wind, and Kael did so, trying to become small within the feathered barrier. He felt his ears pop as something around him shifted, and he squeezed his eyes shut.

There was blessed quiet.

The half-drow felt the two of them settle onto something hard, and Tauran stepped away, leaving Kael standing on his own. He opened his eyes and peered around.

The two of them stood within the columned temple of the storm dragon, where he and Tauran had discovered Aliisza, Vhok, and Zasian.

Kael realized he was holding his breath, and he let it out with a gushing sigh. The sound of water dripping blended with the faint roar of the storms raging beyond the walls of the temple.

"What happened?" he asked, turning to stare out at the cloud tops. They roiled as always, crackling with flashes of lightning.

"It's Helm," Tauran said, and the tone of his voice scared Kael like nothing else before.

He spun to confront his mentor.

The angel's face wore such a look of despair and sorrow that it nearly made Kael drop to the floor and weep. "What?" he whispered, terrified of the answer. "What happened to him?"

Tauran drew a deep, shuddering breath before answering. "He's fallen in battle. Tyr has slain him."

❖ ❖ ❖ ❖ ❖ ❖ ❖ ❖

Myshik feared being left within that sphere. He would suppose later that it was only a brief time, but while he was within, it lasted an eternity. Kashada had vanished, leaving him in solitude, and all he could think of was being trapped, with nothing but light on every side. He remembered the woman's craze-filled eyes and shuddered.

Tekthyrios! he called. *She has fled! Return me to the surface!*

The storm dragon did not answer, and Myshik fought his rising panic. The idea that he had been duped by the great wyrm was unbearable. *Tekthyrios!*

Easy, small one, the dragon finally answered. *She is here, with me, but still uncertain of herself. Let me calm her, and then I will bring you back up. A little patience!*

Myshik did not respond. He stared around the extent of the sphere. Without shadows, the half-dragon found it hard to maintain a sense of the size of the place, but in his barely contained panic, he was certain it was growing smaller. He was on the verge of screaming at the storm dragon again when he began to rise through the air, up into the highest point of the sphere and beyond. That same sensation of the stone and earth sliding through him was much more welcome the second time.

At last he stood on the surface, within the small grotto. Tekthyrios sat there next to a beautiful, mysterious creature. Myshik supposed it was Kashada, though she was nothing like he had seen of her within the sphere.

A tall, lithe woman stared at him from behind a hood and veil made of equal parts black cloth and shadows. Her eyes, once so feverish with dementia, studied him with keen interest. As black as midnight, they bored into his very core. For a long moment, Myshik noticed nothing else, but finally he managed to tear his gaze away from hers and see the rest of her.

She was swathed in tight-fitting black clothes, reminiscent of an assassin's garb. They, like the hood and veil, danced with shadows. The ensemble made Myshik's eyes hurt, and when he glanced away, she seemed to vanish several times. Forcing himself to keep her firmly in view, the hobgoblin studied the rest of her newfound gear. A belt kept several sheathed daggers handy at her waist, and he noted two more protruding from the tops of her soft black boots. She stood on the balls of her feet, light and delicate, ready to spring in any direction.

"Myshik," Tekthyrios said from beside the mysterious woman. "This is Kashada."

Without waiting for the half-dragon to say anything, Kashada bowed with a deep flourish. "My thanks for your part in my rescue," she said. Her voice was soft, throaty, little more than a sultry whisper. "That . . . place"—and she seemed to shudder, though Myshik wasn't certain he saw it clearly—"was unbearable."

"I only spent a moment there, and I can imagine," the hobgoblin replied. Then he turned to Tekthyrios. "Now that we have rescued your prize, what are your intentions?"

Tekthyrios laughed, a deep rumble that reverberated through the grotto. "She is but the first of many, my eager little half-dragon," he said, fanning his wings. "There are much bigger prizes awaiting us. But we must bide our time for a bit, wait for the sign to come."

Myshik cocked his head to one side. "What sign?" he asked.

A sudden roar filled the sky above, and all three flinched from it. The draconic hobgoblin risked a glance upward and saw what he imagined the end of the world might look like. The clouds had turned to ash and flame in some places, and to pulsing, throbbing, sickly green in others. In between, like great fractures in the foundation stone of a massive keep, jagged stretches of midnight sky gleamed through.

A howling wind rushed through the trees overhead, stripping the leaves from their branches and uprooting many of them. The winds swirled and sent a spray of water from the nearby falls. The force of the wind knocked the three companions flat. They even shoved Tekthyrios downward from the crush of the violent blast. Myshik cowered and imagined being scoured from the small floating island. Only the protective walls of the grotto had saved him. The thought of spinning out into the maelstrom made him blanch.

"There we go," Tekthyrios said. "The sign has come. Helm is dead at last." He rose up onto his feet again. "Gather close, you two. We have a journey to make."

Myshik shifted his gaze between the dragon and Kashada, stunned at the news. Helm, dead? Can this be?

From behind her veil, Kashada's eyes glowed. Without any fear at all, she approached the huge storm dragon and allowed him to grasp her in his foreclaw. As Tekthyrios lifted her into the air, she gave one small, throaty laugh. "All praise to the Dark Goddess. It has begun."

Myshik began to dread that he had gotten himself into the middle of such a tangled mess. Whatever Vhok had been chasing, the barbaric hobgoblin could not imagine that it involved the plots of gods. But his father's instructions had been clear. He would see the task through, no matter what. Bring honor to the clan, he reminded himself.

Shrugging in acceptance of his fate, Myshik allowed Tekthyrios to take hold of him as well.

The storm dragon rose up to his full height. "Come, my little thieves. We have a prize to steal, and a god to steal it from!"

With that, he launched himself skyward.

CHAPTER SIX

Aliisza started awake. A feeling of worry washed over her, though about what, she couldn't figure. Something wasn't right.

She glanced at Kaanyr, still sleeping beside her. He appeared at ease, peaceful, unaware of any danger.

The alu slipped from the covers and dressed, listening for any sounds that might indicate a threat. She fingered Pharaun's ring and scanned the room with its magical energy, seeking anything out of the ordinary. She detected scattered and powerful images, part of the existence and amenities of the room, but nothing threatened her.

The feeling wouldn't go away.

She crossed the floor to the door leading out and pressed her ear against it. There was only silence beyond. She sighed, wondering if her nerves were just a trick of her imagination.

Too long wary of bad dreams, she decided.

Trying to relax, Aliisza turned and headed to the balcony. The storm still raged beyond it, though why it didn't penetrate the interior of the room, she could not say. Nothing actively blocked it, but nonetheless it was as if she watched it through a heavy window or scrying glass. The light was odd, disconcerting. She stepped closer, taking in more of the sky.

Clouds tumbled around, both above and below. They seemed to boil, and lightning raced through them, crackling with purple and green. The storm obscured everything, though Aliisza knew from past experience there was little else out there to view. No land spread out below the great white-stoned city known as Tyr's Court. No top or bottom defined the endless space that stretched beyond where she stood.

Just about to turn back to her bed and her lover, Aliisza felt it. A soft rumble and a quivering vibrated in the stone beneath her feet. It was faint, almost imperceptible, but she had no doubt it was real. The energy to make the mountain rumble would have to be great indeed, and with that realization, Aliisza knew something dire was happening.

"Kaanyr, wake up," she called, still staring out at the furious sky. When he did not answer, Aliisza turned and strode across the chamber with a purpose born of fear. "Kaanyr!" she said again, shaking his shoulder.

"Hmm? What?" he asked, rubbing his eyes. "What's wrong with you?" he snarled, rolling over and trying to yank the covers tighter around himself. "You wear a fellow out, then won't let him sleep."

"Something's wrong. The whole place is shaking. Can you feel it?"

Kaanyr sat up, looking at her. "I've known you long enough not to question *that* tone," he said. His voice was gentler, almost concerned.

As she returned to the balcony, he rolled out of bed and slipped into his clothes, then he came to join her. "What is it?" he asked, holding her shoulders and pressing in close from behind. "What do you feel?"

"The Court," she said. "It's shaking, vibrating. Can't you feel it through the floor?"

Kaanyr stood still and quiet for a moment.

Aliisza felt it again, a soft rumble, as though far below her a part of the rock was cracking or crumbling away. "There, did you feel that?"

"No, lover, I didn—"

Both of them pitched off their feet and went sprawling across the room as a vicious quake rocked the place.

Aliisza landed on her shoulder. She rolled to ease the impact and wound up crumpled against the base of the large tiled basin where she had once bathed in perfectly heated water and scented oils. She rapped her head against the stone and winced.

"Gods and devils, I felt *that!*" Kaanyr grunted from somewhere on the far side of the room. "What the blazes is going on?"

Aliisza found herself earnestly wishing Tauran were there. "Let's find out," she said, trying to rise. Another forceful heave threw her off balance, and she hit the floor once more. When she recovered her balance, she realized the room was no longer level. In fact, it was slowly tilting.

"We must flee!" she cried, scrambling to Kaanyr. "We cannot stay here!"

"I cannot go," the cambion said, his voice low. "The angel's magic binds me here."

"No," Aliisza said softly, dismayed. She remember all too well a time when she wanted more than anything to launch herself from the balustrade of that balcony, to soar free in the open sky outside, beyond the Court. The magical coercion she had agreed to then had held her there, had prevented her from acting on her thoughts. It had nearly driven her to madness.

"There has to be a way to get around it," she said, thinking aloud. "Self-preservation has to count for something."

"Don't you think I've been trying to make that work?" the cambion said, almost snarling. Whatever fleeting moments of gentle affection he had shown during their carnal pleasures vanished in his frustration at his predicament. She sensed that he still blamed her, at least in part, for her role in his ensnarement. "Just go," he said. "Go find out what's tearing the place apart. Find the angel, if you can."

Aliisza looked at Kaanyr for a moment, trying to get a read on his intentions. His face was clouded with anger and fear, but he seemed earnest. She felt a new sense of respect for him pass through her. Respect, and something familiar and tender. "Very well," she said, spinning back toward the door. "I'll return as soon as—"

A knock came at the portal, cutting her off. She reached for the handle and yanked it open, ready to chastise Tauran for his part in leaving Kaanyr trapped within the chamber, but the words died in her throat.

Micus stood there, accompanied by two of the hound-headed creatures—or archons, as Aliisza had learned. "You two must come with me at once," he ordered. "The High Council has questions."

Aliisza shook her head and backed away.

"No," she said. "Where is Tauran? He should be the one to come for us."

Micus took her retreat as an invitation to enter the room. He stepped through the doorway and the archons followed. "Tauran has been relieved of his responsibility for you," the angel said. He made a gesture to the creatures behind him, and the pair vanished, reappearing just inside the balcony, blocking that egress. "The High Council has put me in charge of your well-being, and I have questions. Now come with me."

Behind her, Kaanyr snarled. She turned in time to see him draw his enchanted scepter from the loop on his belt and drop into a crouch. He took a couple of steps toward Micus.

"You're sealing your own fate, demon," Micus said, pulling his own mace free. "I'll send you to oblivion and be pleased to be rid of you. Tauran's coddling of the likes of you sickens me."

Aliisza tried to step between Kaanyr and the deva. "Stop it!" she shouted. She directed the outburst mostly at her lover, but it was intended for both of them. "That's not going to help!"

"The Hells with helping," Kaanyr growled. "I struck my bargain with one angel and one angel only."

Out of the corner of her eye, Aliisza saw one of the archons step closer, loosening his sword. She groaned, unsure how to get all of them to stand down.

"Vhok!" a voice bellowed. "Back away! Do not confront Micus!"

Aliisza's heart leaped in joy at the sound. She turned in the direction of the voice and saw Tauran, with Kael at his side, standing in the hallway. Tauran stepped in as Micus glanced back over his shoulder. Kaanyr snarled in frustration as he retreated, backing up and replacing his weapon in its belt loop. Aliisza could see in his expression that the cambion fought with all his will to resist the command, but it was futile.

"I knew you would come here," Micus said to Tauran, turning and stepping back so that no one could maneuver behind him. He also made a subtle motion to the approaching archon, who nodded and stepped back to rejoin his companion by the balcony. "In fact, I almost expected you to be here already, trying to help them escape."

"Micus," Tauran said, his tone plaintive. "You can't really intend to carry out the High Council's instructions, can you? We have to find out what has caused this tragedy!"

"That's precisely what I intend to do. The High Council will sort this out. It is not for us to question. But I knew you would go against them and try to stop me, because you have lost all sense of propriety, Tauran. You can't even see how off balance you have become." Micus's own words sounded sorrowful to Aliisza. "You must surrender to me. I can't let you run off with them, not now. The Council has spoken."

Tauran shook his head. "But Cyric is out there, somewhere, making all this happen! If we don't stop him, if we don't catch Zasian and end his scheme, this whole terrible catastrophe is just going to get worse!"

"That all may be," Micus said, coming to stand close to Tauran and placing both his hands on his counterpart's shoulders. "But that is not for us to deal with. The High Council heard the charges and your explanation, and they found it wanting. You're breaking your oaths by disregarding their commands, my friend. I can't let you ruin yourself over this."

Aliisza snorted in disgust. "I don't know what the Hells you are talking about with this High Council, Micus, but you ought to listen to him. Zasian is out there, and he's up to something. We can help you find out what."

The angel turned to glare at her over his shoulder. "You'd like nothing better than that, wouldn't you, fiend? We should just let you and your rutting partner here run free across the House, bringing all your clever schemes to fruition, is that it? Well, I've got news for you. The days of you two despoiling our sacred home are at an end." He turned back to Tauran. "Now, if you have any desire at all to stay in the

Council's good graces, instruct this foul trespasser to come along without any trouble."

Tauran shook his head again. "No, Micus. I can't just stand aside and let you take them to their doom. I gave my word."

"Your word is not fit to give! You've violated everything you stand for, Tauran. Now see reason."

Tauran gazed at Micus a moment longer, then sighed, looking resigned, and hung his head. "Vhok . . ." he said.

To the Hells with this, Aliisza thought, feeling old self-preserving emotions rise up within her. Time to go my own way.

But the alu hesitated. She felt rooted to the spot, unwilling to leave Kaanyr behind. Or Tauran, or Kael, she realized. The price you pay for love, she thought in dismay, remembering Tauran's teachings. She tried to shake off those new, vulnerable feelings. Blast them all! she silently admonished. I'm not under any oath! And Micus is a mule-headed fool!

Aliisza still hadn't made up her mind when Tauran completed his command. "Micus and his two companions are not to be killed, but they are preventing you from aiding me."

Aliisza's stare flew to Tauran in disbelief. Behind him, Kael grinned and stepped deeper into the room.

Micus gasped. "Are you mad?" he demanded. "You'll be—"

The angel's next words were cut off by a warning shout from one of the archons. "Beware!" he said, fumbling for his sword.

But Kaanyr, already straining to get at Micus, reacted swiftly once freed. He had his scepter back in his hands in the blink of an eye. The cambion took two rapid strides forward and walloped Micus across the back of the head. A concussive thump accompanied the strike, and Micus grunted in shock and pain and sank down to one knee.

"Vhok!" Tauran shouted, dismay clear on his face at watching his former friend struck so viciously.

"He'll live," the cambion replied, turning toward the balcony. "Let's get out of here before he realizes it." He took a step toward the two archons blocking his way, swishing his mace back and forth with a malevolent grin on his face.

Aliisza smiled and pulled her own sword free. "Nice to have the old you back," she said, stepping beside him to face the hound-headed creatures. Kael moved to join them as well.

"No!" Tauran said from behind them. "We go out this way!" As the angel finished his statement, a shimmering blur of a wall sprang up between the combatants, blocking the archons off from the rest of the chamber. Aliisza saw that the humming barrier consisted of dozens of razor-sharp blades, small knives and daggers, spinning and whirling. "We're leaving. Now!" Tauran commanded.

Kaanyr snarled in frustration, eager to get at the archons, but with a huff he stepped back and turned to follow the deva. Kael nodded once at the two creatures before he, too, spun on one foot and dashed to the door leading out.

Aliisza risked a quick glance down at Micus, who was clutching his head with both hands. In the time it took the alu to look away from the archons, they disappeared from beyond the wall and reappeared on the near side. They rushed at her, blades raised. She cursed her foolishness and scampered backward, muttering the words of a spell. She made a quick sign in the air with one hand and backed through the doorway. A dense fog filled the chamber, obscuring her foes, and her from them.

Then she turned and sprinted after her companions.

❖ ❖ ❖ ❖ ❖ ❖ ❖ ❖ ❖

The storm dragon hovered above a small clearing within the mist-filled woods for a moment then dropped through the opening in the canopy. He settled to the forest floor and released his two companions. Kashada slipped free of his grasp and found herself standing on soft, spongy ground. She stepped away and turned to look back at her companions. Myshik bulled his way free of the dragon's foreclaw, all rippling muscle and stocky resolution.

Around the trio, the strange forest remained still. The howling storms and bizarre, color-streaked sky of before were gone. In their place, a pall had settled over the plane, a gray, misty world that whispered of dreary winters along a jagged coast. The damp weather permeated the odd trees and muffled distant sounds.

The trees, exotic in shape in their own right, became even more peculiar when viewed through the veil of mist. They took on twisted, warped forms half hidden behind curtains of gauzy light. They challenged the senses, thrusting from the ground at odd angles. The ground, too, varied from that of most forest floors. It surface, uneven and coarse, undulated into the distance like some ancient giant thing's cracked and weathered skin.

A bird cawed not too far away, but the fog stifled its cry. Somewhere deeper in the distance, Kashada detected a muted conversation. The words were much too soft to make out.

"Remember," Zasian said quietly in the deep, rich tones of the storm dragon's voice, "this is not a fight we need to win, nor do we even want to try. The object is to distract them long enough for you to slip past and enter the caves. Are we clear?"

Kashada nodded. Myshik scowled in displeasure, as if the concepts of deception and subterfuge were the most unnatural things in the world. His attitude made plain his constant desire to fight, to prove his mettle and prowess.

Kashada chuckled inwardly. *He will learn in time,* the shadow-mystic thought.

"Where do these caverns lead?" Myshik demanded, almost sounding petulant. "Why are we going there? Will they lead us to Vhok?"

Kashada again questioned Zasian's decision to keep the half-dragon around. Myshik was barbaric, filled with battle-lust and always craving treasure. She had said as much at her rescue, suggesting that she and the Cyricist simply leave the creature within her prison sphere. But Zasian had refused, claiming to hate wasting resources. He argued that he could imagine a host of different situations where having the winged hobgoblin around would be useful.

Kashada wondered if the priest would come to regret his decision in time.

"They lead to another place," Zasian answered, "where there is much wealth for you to claim in the name of your clan."

Myshik's eyes brightened considerably at the mention of potential riches. "If that is so, then I care little for where we go."

"I thought so," Zasian said.

The priest looked to Kashada.

She nodded, letting him know that she was ready.

"You both know what to do," he said. "Begin."

The pair turned and left him then, moving deeper into the misty woods.

Kashada led the way, listening for the sounds of the faint conversation she had detected a moment before. She cast a simple spell as she walked, one that permitted her to tread upon the shadows as if they were solid surfaces. The magic quelled the noise of her passing and she glided along, reveling in her freedom.

I spent too long in that damnable sphere, she thought, shuddering. The Dark Goddess herself would hardly have fared better in such a stretch of time.

Beside the woman, Myshik strode with solid, purposeful steps, yet his footfalls remained soft.

So, Kashada mused, he does know the value of subtlety. Perhaps he will be of some use after all.

At one point, the woman caught a sound and held her hand up to signal Myshik to halt. She stood very still, listening. The voices she had detected before were stronger, though still too distant to make out words. They were moving in the right direction.

Kashada knelt down next to the half-hobgoblin to discuss their plan. "Remember," the mystic said as they rose and prepared to separate, "our signal must be strong so that Tekthyrios will hear it. But do not get too caught up in the fight. The idea is to fool them and send them running about in confusion, not go toe to toe with them. Understand?"

Myshik's red eyes squinted at her and he smirked. "I am not a fool," he said sourly. "The cunning as well as the strength of a dragon flows through my veins. I know my purpose."

Kashada smiled, though she knew the barbarian could not see it behind her veil. "Very well," she said. "See you on the other side." She turned to go then, stepping lightly through the undergrowth and leaving the half-dragon to carry out his own part of the scheme.

Kashada kept the voices to her right as she circled around to the left. She wished that Zasian had been willing to wait until nightfall to conduct their plan. So many more shadows to work with. He's waited twelve years for this, she thought. What's the hurry now?

A few more steps carried Kashada to a low ridge. Beyond it, on the far side of a trail winding through the woods, a trio of figures rested upon a fallen log. She noted their slender, coppery features and woodland clothing and nodded in satisfaction. Elves.

A patrol, she decided, and far from home.

They sat huddled in discussion, but she noted that they kept a vigilant eye on each direction of the trail. Though they sat, they held their postures erect, wary. They were watching their surroundings carefully.

A bit spooked, are we? Kashada thought. This will be fun.

The shadow-mystic studied the environs near the three elves and selected an area of gloom directly beneath them, where the shadow of the log against the ground was deepest. She focused her mind and let her fingers dance a delicate pattern in the air. She felt the energy of her magic connect with the shadow and watched as it began to move.

The shadow wriggled and expanded. It grew darker and spread.

One of the elves noticed the effect and gave a startled shout. The three of them leaped from their seats and backed away.

The shadow rose from the ground, deepening until it had become black as midnight. It changed shape and divided until four blobs of darkness separated themselves from one another. The blobs lengthened and crouched as the three elf scouts pulled their swords free and went into defensive stances. One of them put a horn to his lips and blew a long, plaintive note.

Calling for reinforcements, Kashada realized. Good. Myshik is bound to hear that. Can Zasian?

The blobs became feline in shape, lithe hunting cats on the prowl. One of the unearthly beasts let out a yowl, a haunting cry that made the three elves shiver.

One of the scouts lunged at the shadow-cat closest to it, but the magical beast shifted to the side, dodging the blow. The cat leaped at its attacker as if it were pouncing on a rabbit.

The elf screamed and fell back as the shadow engulfed him. The other cats rushed at his companions. The group became a swarming, chaotic fracas. Snarling cats tumbled, bit, and raked at the elves while the scouts frantically sliced back at them.

Kashada waited and watched, listening to the raucous sounds of battle.

A shout from her left caught the mystic's attention. She glanced in that direction and spied four more elf scouts rushing through the forest, following the trail. They reached their beset brethren and joined the fight.

Excellent, Kashada thought, and she crept away, moving to swing wide of the elves' position and get around them, heading toward the cave where she and Myshik were to meet Zasian.

She reached a point where she was certain she was out of sight of the roiling fight behind her and started walking faster. She had taken perhaps half a dozen steps when a figure popped into view directly ahead of her.

Like the others, the figure had pointed ears, angular features, and a slender build, but unlike them, she wore a delicate set of plate mail and stood with a noble bearing. A radiant aura surrounded her. Kashada squinted at the bright light and faltered to a stop.

"What trouble are you causing in my woods, witch?" the woman asked, brandishing an incandescent sword.

❖ ❖ ❖ ❖ ❖ ❖ ❖ ❖ ❖

Zasian waited for the sign that his two minions had begun their attack. Tekthyrios stirred, struggling against his cerebral bondage again. The effort to keep the dragon's consciousness contained had become almost an afterthought to Zasian. He had mastered the art of it quickly, and despite a few instances of sudden, sneaky efforts to catch him off guard, the storm dragon had ceased trying.

But as he waited, Zasian idly toyed with Tekthyrios, taunting the storm dragon with the knowledge of what was about to happen. When the creature at last understood the priest's plan and his own fate, he began anew the effort to break free of his captivity.

No, Zasian whispered to the dragon. *I need your skin a little while longer.*

Tekthyrios did not answer, but he continued to hammer at the barrier blocking him from control of his body.

There's nothing you can do about it, Zasian conveyed.

Perhaps, the storm dragon replied, surprising the priest. *But you will not escape quite so easily as you think.*

Are you certain? Zasian asked. *Who will tell them what has become of us? You? What will they do even if they figure it out? Come after us? By the time anyone finds you here, we will be long gone.*

Nonetheless, the dragon projected, *yours will come due.*

I think not, Zasian replied. *The Black Sun's plot is unfolding nicely.*

And I am safely a part of it, Zasian thought privately.

How many can make that claim? Others may believe they serve the Prince of Lies, but few truly understand the depth and breadth of his schemes. Sooner or later, Cyric's going to succeed at something magnificently terrible. Where better to be standing when the world comes crashing down than at his right hand?

A shout of alarm in the distance brought Zasian out of his ponderings. The attack had begun.

Time to get to work.

CHAPTER
SEVEN

Y ou did what was necessary," Kael said. His voice echoed within the eerie silence of the storm dragon's temple, along with the faint but steady dripping of water in the distance. "It's the right choice in your heart. That is most important." The holy warrior knelt next to Tauran, who sat crosslegged with his chin resting on his hands, staring at the floor.

"Perhaps," the angel replied, his voice glum. "But I broke Tyr's law. I disregarded the High Council's direct orders. I am a criminal."

Kaanyr, reclining next to Aliisza a short distance from the two, snorted. "Yes, he's the scourge of the cosmos," the cambion said with a chuckle.

"Be quiet," Aliisza scolded. "He turned on his own kind to rescue you from a very unpleasant fate. Whatever else you may think of Tauran, you at least owe him a little gratitude for that."

"I wouldn't be in such a situation in the first place if it weren't for him," Kaanyr replied. "It was his idea to parade us before all the angels in the heavens. What did he think would happen?"

"I don't think he expected them to turn on him," Aliisza said. "He feels betrayed right now." *And I know that feeling all too well,* the alu silently added.

"Well, he'd better get over this and stop his moping," Kaanyr said. "It won't take Micus and the rest of them long to hunt us down. This isn't a safe place for us to remain."

Aliisza nodded, but she didn't answer. She was thinking about what Tauran had revealed in his plaintive conversation with Micus. He had used the words "tragedy" and "catastrophe." She glanced out at the churning sky beyond the edges of the temple. The clouds around the sacred dwelling of the storm dragon still billowed and tumbled, obscuring her sight, but at least they didn't roil with sickly color and jagged lightning quite as much as before.

Aliisza recalled the fractured sky heaving overhead as they had fled the great marbled city. The whole mountain upon which the Court rested had heaved beneath their feet. Everywhere they ran, the inhabitants were in a panic. She saw many of them crumpled, sobbing, while others merely wore ashen, grim expressions.

Something terrible has happened, she realized. *Something that threatens to tear apart the very fabric of the House of the Triad's existence. And Tauran is convinced that Zasian is responsible for it.*

Eventually, the horrid chaos that had engulfed the plane and shook the Court to its foundations had abated. A level of calm returned that permitted the quartet of fugitives to escape. Aliisza had no doubt that they would not have survived in the open sky otherwise.

The alu rose to her feet and walked to where Tauran and Kael sat, each in silent contemplation. She squatted before the angel and gazed at him. His expression was sorrowful to behold. He seemed to bear the weight of the world on his shoulders and knew he was on the verge of dropping it.

"What happened?" she asked quietly.

The angel looked back at her with eyes filled with the deepest sadness. "Helm fell before Tyr," he said. His voice, usually so rich and confident, sounded weak, like a frightened child's. He could not hold her gaze and returned his own to the floor in front of him.

"What? I don't understand. Tyr defeated him? Isn't that what you wanted? An end to the bickering between them?"

"Not like this," Kael said when Tauran would not answer. "Tyr slew him."

The words crashed against Aliisza like a storm-tossed wave. One god had slain another. "How is that possible?" she breathed. "Your gods don't *do* that."

"Not often," Kael conceded. "Certainly not by choice. Whatever drove him to do it . . . the ravaging of the House was both his fury and his sorrow."

Tauran looked at Aliisza again, and she saw something new in his face, something she had never thought to see in an angel's visage. Shame. "Tyr, and many of us who serve him, will not see it this way," he said quietly. "But he has fallen from grace today. No matter how much power and wisdom he wields, the Maimed God took a misstep in his decision to debate Helm, and the results have weakened the entire House."

"Cyric drove him to it," Kael added. "There can be no other explanation."

Tauran nodded. "Perhaps that is true, but even so, Tyr made the choices he made. I love him like no other"—at that point, the angel's voice cracked—"but today, I look upon his glory and find it tarnished. He has betrayed my trust."

Aliisza found the deva's words stunning. "You can't just turn your back on him," she said, surprised by her own conviction. "He is your life, your whole reason for being. You can't just cast all that away."

"What would you know of such things?" Kael said coldly. "You, who have never served any higher ideal in your long, corrupt life."

Aliisza stared at her son but said nothing. The alu was surprised how much his words stung. He is wounded, she realized, perhaps embarrassed. He blames us for some of this.

"Leave her be, Kael," Tauran said. "She may not have devoted much of herself to greater causes before, but that doesn't mean she isn't learning. Remember, she is still here of her own accord, by choice."

Kael frowned for a moment, then grimaced and nodded in acquiescence. "You are right. Forgive me, Mother."

That was the first time Aliisza could recall her son addressing her as such. She blinked in surprise but still said nothing. Was that deferential or demeaning? she wondered. Then she dismissed it. A question for another time, she decided.

"Tyr is not my whole reason for existing," Tauran said, drawing Aliisza back into the conversation. "The ideals he represents are what I have devoted my life to. I have believed with all my heart what he believes in. I still do, which is why I am so disappointed. He did not live up to those ideals, at least not in my mind. Micus and the others must see things differently, but I cannot abide leaving this tragedy uninvestigated. We must find out what caused this, if Cyric is indeed at the root of it."

"Through Zasian," Aliisza added. "If Zasian acts on Cyric's behalf, as you claim—"

"He does," Kael interjected.

"—then we must find him to find out his—and thus, Cyric's—plans."

Tauran looked pointedly at Aliisza. "Yes. And that's why I still need your help. You and Vhok know more about him than we do. Help me figure out where he's gone, what he's up to."

Aliisza glanced over at Kaanyr. The cambion had risen to his feet and was standing near the edge of the temple, gazing out at the storm-tossed clouds beyond. He had his hands clasped behind his back, looking calm and confident for the first time in a long while.

At least he's not sulking, Aliisza thought. "Kaanyr knows Zasian far better than I," she said. "He conspired with the man to get here. He traveled with him. I only interacted with Zasian peripherally. And mostly I tried to avoid him." She had to fight to keep the bitterness at her lover's trickery from infecting her tone. Then she leaned close and lowered her voice. "Kaanyr will do the minimum necessary to adhere to the rules of your bonds," she warned. "I will try to convince him that it will be more useful, even to him, if he does more—if he really helps. But you should know that he will find a way to repay you for your trickery." She gave Tauran a steady stare. "He does not take well to being manipulated."

"I did nothing of the sort," the angel replied, his tone bristling. "He freely relinquished control without fully investigating the situation."

Aliisza clicked her tongue in disapproval. "You were almost gleeful when you revealed his mistake to him," she said. "Don't deny that you were looking forward to seeing his reaction."

Tauran grimaced and nodded. "Indeed," he said. "There is a certain righteous satisfaction in out-clevering such a cunning adversary. I did let my pride cloud my emotions." He sighed. "But you cannot deny that if I had revealed the lost time to either of you before securing your agreement to aid me, you would have departed at once."

Aliisza smiled. "You don't understand," she said. "It's not that Kaanyr feels the maneuver was unjust. He is just resentful that he fell for it. In his mind, your desperate clinging to such lofty ideals as 'honor,' 'nobility,' and 'law' make you vulnerable to crafty deceptions. He let his guard down because he assumed that you would consider yourself above that sort of underhanded duplicity. If he took a moment to allow himself, he might actually, begrudgingly, admire you for it. But he is too proud to admit it, even to himself most of the time. And"—she glanced the cambion's way once more—"his pride will drive him to pay you back. I should know. I've been watching him do it with other adversaries for many, many years. That's what brought him here in the first place, you know."

Tauran shrugged. "So be it," he said. "So long as it doesn't prevent me from exposing Cyric and Zasian's actions to the rest of the Court." The angel rose to his feet. "Now," he said, stretching to his full height, "what can you two tell me about Zasian to get us started?" He spoke those last words loudly enough for Kaanyr to hear.

"It's about time you stopped sulking," the cambion said, striding over to join the other three. "Your friend Micus is sure to think to search for us here. We should depart, at once."

"I agree," Tauran said. "But to where? Without some sort of clue, some evidence leading us, there is no point. What can you tell me of the priest?"

Kaanyr gave a long sigh and stared off at nothing, thinking. "I don't know nearly as much about him as I should," he said.

"He posed as a servant of Bane—part of a well-organized cabal hidden among the citizens of Sundabar. They had strategic plans for taking over the city when the time was right, but most of them seemed to be all talk and little action. Among them all, Zasian was the only one who seemed to have any brains. I should have known better than to trust a Banite with common sense."

Tauran folded his arms across his chest. "Anything else?" he asked.

The cambion shook his head. "Not really. He was clever. He was logical. He had a way of arguing things that always made sense. If he was truly a servant of the Prince of Lies, as you say, he hid it well."

"What about you?" the angel asked, turning toward Aliisza. "What can you remember?"

"Very little," the alu replied. "As I said, I tried to avoid him in Sundabar, not knowing his true role in Kaanyr's plot"—and she gave the cambion a brief glare before continuing—"but all he said upon arriving within this temple was that our ways must part. He claimed to have things to do, but there was nothing else."

Tauran nodded, frowning. "That doesn't reveal much about his intentions, I'm afraid. Can either of you perform divinations of any significance?"

Both the half-fiends shook their heads.

"Nor can I," the deva muttered, looking wistful. "It was never my strongest talent, even under normal circumstances, but certainly not now."

"Why not now?" Aliisza asked.

Tauran sighed. "My rebellious attitude has clearly put me out of favor with Tyr," he said, and though he seemed to be trying to make light of it, Aliisza could see a shudder pass through the angel. "Much of my spiritual power has vanished. My divine link to the Just One has been severed." He smiled, but there was a profound sadness in his eyes.

"Your god has abandoned you, your kind has named you outlaw, and yet you still wish to pursue this?" Kaanyr asked. His expression was one of incredulity. "What worth is there in pursuing a path blockaded by the very ones you try to save?"

"I want to save them from themselves," Tauran replied. "I want to remind myself that the cause we all served was a worthwhile one." He looked at the cambion. "I don't think it would be so hard for you to understand. There are things for which you are willing to sacrifice yourself."

"Not the way you would do it."

"Truly?" the angel asked. "Did you not urge Aliisza to flee, to escape into the beyond when we were within your quarters, confronting Micus?"

"I said no such thing," Kaanyr snapped, his gaze flickering back and forth between the deva and Aliisza. "You speak lies."

"You did not say it with your words, Vhok, but I heard it in your heart," Tauran said. "I sensed the struggle within you, the conflict between a need for her to stay and fight on your behalf and a desire to make amends to her, to give her the freedom you had a hand in stealing from her."

Kaanyr's face darkened, and he took several rapid, deep breaths as though he meant to tell the angel off, but the words never came. Finally, with a long exhalation, he muttered, "She's endured enough of my desperate schemes," he said. "I thought maybe it was time to cut her loose."

Aliisza flushed. She stared at Kaanyr, watched him struggle to admit that he had considered such a selfless act, and grinned. She couldn't help it, and she knew if he saw her he would likely misinterpret it and grow incensed, but it spread across her face despite her efforts. He's showing all sorts of new facets, she thought, and grinned even more.

"What?" Kaanyr said when he spotted her. "What's so damned funny, you winged tramp?"

"You," she said, beginning to chuckle. "You, who are always scolding me for letting my human side appear, and you're just as bad. Worse!"

"Well, don't let it go to your head," he grumbled. "And you," he said, turning to Tauran, "stay the Hells out of my thoughts!"

The angel smiled, though it was a bit thin and didn't last long. "We understand one another better than you would like to admit," he said.

Kaanyr walked a few paces away and fumed by himself.

Aliisza glanced at Kael. He tried to adopt a look of stoic disinterest when he caught her glance, but she noted that he had been watching the entire proceeding with great curiosity.

"We still aren't any closer to tracking down the priest," the half-drow said. "We have nothing, other than the fact that he stole away in the storm dragon's form."

Tauran snapped his fingers. "Of course!" he said, half to himself. "Not just in the form of the body, but in the body itself. And I know someone who can find him that way."

"Wait," Aliisza said, concerned. "Everyone in the Court believes you are a rogue and outlaw. How can you approach someone you know? How can you even trust him?"

Tauran shook his head. "Not him, her. Her name is Eirwyn. And I don't know the answer to your question," he said, getting a far-away look in his eyes. "I don't know at all."

"It will be easier than you might think," said a woman's voice.

❖ ❖ ❖ ❖ ❖ ❖ ❖ ❖

Micus looked over the collection of soldiers that had gathered in the courtyard. In addition to a half-dozen other astral devas, nearly twenty hound archons milled around, awaiting orders. They were competent warriors, elite troops capable of standing up to the half-fiends running with Tauran.

Micus knew he would need every last one of them.

The angel sighed softly, wishing it were otherwise. He didn't want to be chasing down his friend, certainly not under such circumstances. Not only did it pain him greatly to be forced to apprehend Tauran, but there was so much else that needed to be done in the aftermath of Helm's death.

The demise of the god still stunned Micus whenever he gave himself a moment to think on it. Though he had no doubts that Tyr was justified in his action, he had no understanding of what that justification might be. It was not his place to question. He understood that, unlike Tauran.

And that's why I have to go get him, Micus reminded himself. *Whatever else he may be, he abandoned his calling and his responsibility when he helped them escape.*

Micus dismissed the gloomy thoughts from his mind and refocused on the job at hand. His immediate problem was figuring out where Tauran and the others might have fled. Micus knew that Tauran had not made up his claims of believing Cyric had a hand in the chaos erupting within the House. The angel still believed in duty and responsibility, even if their execution had become twisted.

So where did Tauran think Cyric's minion might have

gone? Micus asked himself. What path will he take to pursue this fabled trickster?

"Micus," a voice, soft and musical, spoke behind him. The angel turned to behold a dancing ball of glowing light. It winked softer and brighter, changing hues like the colors of a soap bubble in the bright sunlight. "I have news," the lantern archon announced. "Very grave news, indeed."

"What is it?" Micus asked, disheartened that more sorrow was being heaped upon him.

"You should come to the High Council's chambers to hear this," the lantern archon replied, its voice a tinkling melody that belied the seriousness of its words. "It may have some bearing on your mission."

"Very well," Micus said, rising into the air upon his white wings. "I will make my way there as quickly as possible."

"I will be waiting," the archon replied, then vanished.

Micus winged his way toward the temporary home of the High Council, a small open tower that rose from the midst of the Court. As the angel climbed higher into the gray, humid sky, he studied the vast marble city below him.

The damage from the reverberations of Tyr and Helm's battle was extensive. Some sections of the city had fared better than others, but there were places that had been knocked flat. Of the High Council's hemispherical gathering place, there was no remnant. The entire floating island upon which it had originally been built had vanished along with the shattered dome.

Micus did not fret over the physical destruction. Eventually, Tyr would conceive of a new dome, and the High Council would return to its majestic meeting place. But the Maimed God was not yet of a mind to address any of the repercussions of his actions, and so the host that dwelt within, the angels and their petitioners, made the best of things until such time as he recovered.

No, Micus thought, it's not the walls and buildings that cannot be healed. How many followers of Helm suffer today? he wondered. How many loyal servants, stunned at their patron's destruction, sit now in stricken solitude or run screaming in the wild, all hope lost? How many despair at the shame they must feel, their own piety called into question merely by the fact that they focused it on a doomed deity? How many have just lain down and died?

There but for the grace and majesty of Tyr go I, the angel thought.

But whatever sympathy he felt for those abandoned, crushed souls, it was not his duty to see to their comforts and grief. They had chosen a path, and in the grandest scheme of things, they had chosen poorly. The righteous ruled in all things; all others must be cast low. And Tyr, above all else, was righteousness incarnate.

Micus arrived at the tower to find the High Council and the lantern archon waiting for him. He stepped into the center of the gathering and executed a graceful bow. "I am yours to command in all things, high beings. May I serve you to the best of my abilities."

"Thank you for returning to us so quickly, Micus," the High Councilor said. "We have learned dire things since last we spoke."

"So I have heard," the angel answered. "I have completed my preparations for finding and returning Tauran, Kael, and the two interlopers. I only need a direction to travel. Perhaps your grave news will offer some insight into where I should begin?"

"Perhaps," the High Councilor said. "Though such insight will be subtle."

There was a long pause, and Micus turned from one face to another to see the entire Council looking uneasy, on guard.

"You all seem troubled," he said, wondering what could cast worry into the hearts of the nine most powerful solars within the Court of Tyr.

Other than the tragic death of Helm, he reminded himself.

"A prisoner has escaped," the High Councilor explained. "One that was very dangerous, very connected, and heavily guarded." Micus held his tongue and waited for the solar to continue. "Her name is Kashada," the High Councilor said.

Micus stifled a small gasp. He and Tauran had assisted in that wretched witch's capture a number of years previous. He knew both her prowess and her value to foes of the Court. "I know this prisoner," he said. Then the unthinkable occurred to him, and that time, he could not suppress his gasp of dismay. "Tauran didn't—"

"We do not believe so, no," the High Councilor answered. "Evidence points to Tekthyrios having been there."

Micus felt the floor grow a little less steady beneath him. Tauran had claimed that the priest of Cyric had taken the form of the storm dragon before fleeing. Micus voiced his thoughts to the Council.

"That had occurred to us as well," one of the female Councilors replied. "If what Tauran claimed is accurate, and this third intruder is a priest of Cyric, there is a certain mad sense to it."

"But for what?" Micus asked. "A bargain? A collaboration?" Could what Tauran have believed be true? "If this priest Tauran spoke of truly is a servant of Cyric, then freeing one of the most powerful and loyal maidens of Shar does not bode well for the entire cosmos. Whatever those two are planning, it means dire trouble."

"Yes," the High Council agreed. "And we must know what that plan is."

"Tauran is trying to accomplish that very thing," Micus said, a surge of hope filling him. "Perhaps I should aid him instead of capture him?"

"No," the High Councilor said. "Although we no longer question Tauran's loyalties nor his intentions, his judgment may still be suspect. His new companions may have more to do with this plot than he realizes—or wishes to realize. They may be manipulating him in ways that none of us can yet see. They may, in fact, be in league with the Cyricist. We must assume the worst."

"Then what would you have me do?" Micus asked.

"Take no chances," the High Councilor ordered. "They must be stopped so that we can determine their role in this scheme. Capture them at all cost."

Micus sighed. "Of course," he said. And he meant it.

"Micus," the High Councilor said.

"Yes?"

"Do not, under any circumstances, allow your personal friendship with Tauran to cloud your judgment. If he stands in your way, you must not hesitate."

Micus felt his heart grow heavier. "I understand," he said. In all his long years of service, he had never been so unhappy to be carrying out his duties as he was just then.

❖ ❖ ❖ ❖ ❖ ❖ ❖ ❖

Aliisza had her blade free and a spell on her lips before the mysterious, disembodied voice finished speaking. To one side of her, Kael held his sword before him, and to the other, Kaanyr had both Burnblood and a wand raised. The three of them spread out, wary, and peered into the distance. Aliisza could see nothing but mist. The alu risked a glance back over her shoulder at Tauran.

The deva stood still, relaxed, and was actually smiling. "Eirwyn!" he said. "You found me again."

"Indeed I did!" replied the voice. "You knew I would." From perhaps twenty paces away, near the water's edge, another angel stepped out from behind one of the eerie, fading columns that filled the chamber. Deep lines filled her mature, grandmotherly face, and her hair flowed like silver over one shoulder and down to her waist in a single, thick braid. Despite her apparent age, Eirwyn looked far from frail. She had a gleaming silver mace at her belt very similar to the one Tauran wore. She strode toward them all with a stately gait.

Kael was the first to sheathe his blade again. Aliisza put hers away a moment later. Only Kaanyr still held his before him.

Eirwyn closed the distance between them and stopped a pace or two from the cambion, staring hard at him. "If you've learned nothing from your time with Tauran and still intend to strike me, then do so. Otherwise, put your weapons away; you insult me when I mean you no harm."

"For the moment," Kaanyr replied, but he sheathed the sword and slipped his wand back within the folds of his tunic. "But like most of your kind, sooner or later you will not abide me."

"Oh, pshaw!" Eirwyn said, cracking a grin. "Bluster all you want, but I have more important things to worry about than one half-fiend with a chip on his shoulder." She stepped past Kaanyr then, as though dismissing him, and went straight to Tauran. She said nothing, just embraced him.

"I am so sorry," Tauran said.

Aliisza cocked her head to one side, not understanding Tauran's comments.

"Thank you, dear one," the angelic woman replied. For a moment, immense grief crossed Eirwyn's face, but then it was gone and the deva was smiling again.

"I wasn't sure you'd even try to return to me, Eirwyn," Tauran replied. He smiled at the other angel, but then his expression sobered again. "Others will be coming after us," he said. "You cannot remain here, or you will be accused of collaborating. Micus already knows of our earlier conversation."

"You let me worry about that," Eirwyn said, waving his concerns away with her hand. "You have more important tasks before you."

"What do you know?" Tauran asked. "What can you tell us?"

"As to the first question," the elder deva replied, "I know much. I have been here long enough to have heard most of your conversation. So there's no need to worry about formal introductions." She winked at the other three.

Tauran grimaced. "Forgive me," he said. "I have lost my manners."

"That's all right," Eirwyn said. "As I observed, you have more important tasks before you."

"Can you help us?" Kael asked. "We need to find someone. A priest of Cy—"

Eirwyn chuckled and took Kael by the shoulders. "Calm yourself, young one. I already told you I heard the entire conversation. I will do my best. And don't worry," she added, dropping her voice to a whisper, "your loyalty and devotion will do you proud. So stop berating yourself for your perceived shortcomings."

Kael blinked and stared at the angel, obviously surprised. He said nothing, though, just nodded once.

"Now then," Eirwyn said, growing serious and officious. "This clever priest of yours has snuck off with our beloved Tekthyrios's body, has he? Let's just see where he has ventured off to, then, shall we? I will need a few moments. And some room to work."

She sat down cross-legged and closed her eyes. Very softly, such that Aliisza could hardly hear her, Eirwyn began to chant. As she did so, she began to rock back and forth in a slow, steady rhythm.

The alu watched the elder deva for a moment, but then Kael tapped her on the shoulder and drew her attention to Tauran, who had walked some distance away. Kaanyr stood next to him. The angel motioned for mother and son to join them.

"Eirwyn is one of my oldest and dearest friends," Tauran explained in a soft voice once Aliisza and Kael had joined the gathering. "She is a mentor of sorts. She's also one of the most powerful diviners in the Court. If anyone can track down Zasian, she can."

"Yes, but can you trust her?" Kaanyr asked. "She is part of the Court, after all. For all you know, Micus sent her here to convince us to let down our guard. All that chanting and head-bobbing over there could just be a stalling tactic."

"Vhok, that's the most intelligent, thoughtful idea you've contributed to this journey yet," Tauran said. "But in this case, there is no doubt I can trust her." His face become somber. "She lost everything today," he said, his voice weary. "She has more cause to want to see us succeed than just about anyone."

"What do you mean?" Aliisza asked. "Lost what?"

"She does not serve Tyr," Tauran replied. "She has devoted her life and her service to Helm."

Aliisza turned to gaze at the woman, who still sat serenely chanting. "How can she be so calm? Her god is dead!" The alu felt sorrow wash over her, but she quelled it. I can't ache for *everyone* who's ever suffered, she thought.

"How can she be praying?" Kael asked. "To whom?"

"I don't think she is," Tauran answered. "I think she somehow sensed before this even happened that she would need certain divine magic. She's always been intuitive that way. She will sacrifice what little spiritual energy she has left to aid us, if she can."

Aliisza looked over Kaanyr. "Good enough for you?" she asked.

The cambion shrugged. "If she's actually doing what she claims and provides us with what we need. Besides," he added, grimacing, "what choice do I really have?"

Tauran nodded. "She will provide us with what we need," he said.

Eirwyn emerged from her meditative chanting. She looked thoughtful. "If this priest still travels within the flesh of Tekthyrios the storm dragon," she said, "then you will find him within Deepbark Hollow."

Tauran looked at the older angel quizzically. "The World Tree?" he asked. "Truly?"

Eirwyn nodded. "Yes," she said. "It appears your quarry is planning to depart the House of the Triad."

CHAPTER EIGHT

Though he longed to leap into the air and strike—he imagined that impulse was a bit of the dragon's instinct bleeding into his own mind—Zasian forced himself to wait. No, his role would come soon enough.

The first sounds of combat grew louder, and soon, a horn rang through the forest. The tone was somber, urgent, and muffled. The clash of steel on steel accompanied it, and the screams of the wounded. Zasian thought he could detect the feral snarls of beasts, too, but he wasn't certain.

Only when he began to feel the first subtle thumps did the priest of Cyric know his time was at hand. He launched himself up into the sky and raced forward, scanning the land below for a sign of what he sought. Between the thick fog and the heavy canopy of trees, it was difficult to see much, but he knew he wouldn't need to pierce that veil in too fine a fashion. His quarry would be more than visible.

He spotted a small group of humans racing through the odd, twisted trees, leaping over the gnarled, angled trunks or ducking and scrambling beneath them. At first he thought they were chasing their foes, but then several dark streaks shot into view, sprinting after them. The streaks were all shadow, and lithe, like some sort of hunting cat. They made no sounds, and they closed the distance with their prey in a few bounds.

As Zasian glided past the point where the two groups became entangled he heard the screams of the humans, but he was already past the gap in the canopy and could not see the results of the conflict. Angling himself slightly to the right, he continued to search for something more suitable.

When the priest at last found what he sought, he banked around for a better look. At first, he didn't see the creature at all, but rather the route the beast was taking. The trees near where it passed shimmied and shook from its bulk. Zasian angled into a shallow dive and zipped just above the treetops where it seemed to be moving, seeking a better glimpse of it. The first time, he did not spot much, but upon circling past again, he got a much better view.

The thing stood nearly as high as the treetops themselves, and it shuffled along in huge strides on all fours. Even looking directly at it, Zasian had a hard time picking it out from the surrounding foliage, for it was made of living greenery and blended in well.

On his third pass, the beast must have sensed him, for it rose up on its hind legs and roared. The sound it made reverberated through the entire forest and shook Zasian where he flew. It lunged at him and snapped its jaws, trying to latch onto his tail, but Zasian rolled completely over to evade the thing and swung back around behind it.

The creature, still on its hind legs, looked every bit like Zasian had imagined. Its thick body supported an ovoid head with small, round ears and a stubby snout. Its forelegs ended in wide, flat paws, which themselves sported long, curved claws. For all intents and purposes, it would have been one of the most massive dire bears Zasian had ever seen, except that it was all brambles and vines and greenery.

Zasian swooped in from the rear and raked his claws at the mammoth beast, slicing through numerous strands of the plant growth along the thing's neck and back. The creature roared in fury and whirled around, but Zasian was already out of reach.

A cluster of long, javelin-like shards sliced through one of the priest's wings. They gouged a series of holes in the thin skin and passed straight through, stinging his snout. One of the barbed projectiles nearly caught him in the eye.

Zasian issued a rumble from deep within his chest at the pain, but he did not otherwise react. The injury was superficial and did not affect his flying at all. He circled around for another go at the creature. The wood elemental dire bear had dropped to all fours again and began charging through the woods after other prey.

As he closed in, Zasian lined his flight path up with the path the bear-thing was taking. He let loose with a powerful blast of lightning from his mouth. The jagged bolt of energy ploughed through the thick, gnarled plant growth all along his opponent's back. Bits of vine and earth flew in every direction, and the massive thing reared up in agony. As Zasian swooped past, another clump of spikes smacked against his flank, but they did little more than sting. The dragon's thick hide protected him from harm.

Zasian circled around for one more attack. He could see that his assault was taking its toll. The creature thrashed on the ground where he had hit it during the previous pass. It bellowed in anguish as it rolled back and forth, and smoke rose up from the deep wound on its back. It was knocking trees aside in its throes, and Zasian could see more of the humans gathering near the beast. He suspected some might even be trying to heal the thing.

He swooped in low, aiming for the newly made clearing, and raked the entire area with a swipe of his massive tail. The satisfying thunk of scale on flesh and the abrupt screams of several of the defenders let him know that his attack had been effective. He circled once more, scanning the area. Numerous unmoving figures lay scattered around. The giant wooden bear still thrashed, but its movements had become feeble and sporadic. It wouldn't survive much longer.

That ought to do it, Zasian decided.

The priest selected a tree from among those still standing at the edge of the clearing. It was larger than most, and it jutted at just the right angle, toward the dying creature. He rolled toward it and flew hard, zipping just to one side of the trunk. As he soared past, he slapped at it with his tail. There was a tremendous booming crack, and the tree splintered in half, leaving a jagged stump. The rest of the tree toppled over to one side.

The jarring impact sent agonizing pain up the storm dragon's spine. Zasian was fairly certain that he had fractured bones. He gritted his teeth and spun away, trying to climb.

Fighting the pain of his injury, the priest gained altitude. He climbed in a spiral, circling above the ruined tree. When he was high enough that he could not even make out the clearing for the fog anymore, he spun over and dived.

No! Tekthyrios screamed from within the confines of his mind prison.

Yes, Zasian replied. *Your usefulness has ended for me.*

As he plummeted down toward the clearing, the priest began to cast one final spell. The jagged spike he had created came into view, and Zasian angled toward it. At the last moment, he finished his spell, releasing the magic. Just as the wyrm's body plunged down atop the sheared-off tree, impaling itself upon it, Zasian felt himself recede from sensation as a dragon. He coalesced into his own form, freshly recovered from the pocket dimension where he had secured it. When the rejoining was complete, the priest found himself trapped inside the belly of the beast.

The impact slammed Zasian hard, jarring him even within the relatively protected environs of the dragon's stomach. The blow left him woozy, but even in his muddled state, he heard the horrific howl of agony reverberate through Tekthyrios's body. The priest felt the creature shudder once, then the dragon wretched, and Zasian was thrown clear.

He landed atop a mound of coarse earth and bounced to the far side of it, sliding into a gully. The cool dampness of the soil felt pleasant against his scorched skin. Still unsteady and in pain, Zasian rose up onto his knees and peered back at his handiwork.

Tekthyrios thrashed feebly, impaled upon the sheared-off tree. The dragon's eyes rolled back in his head and he gave one plaintive cry. As Zasian watched, he struggled to get his clawed legs beneath himself. He tried to lift himself free of the deadly spike. After several unsuccessful attempts, Tekthyrios gave up and sagged back down, his head lolling to one side.

"Priest," the dragon gasped, his eyes closed. "You will . . . pay," he said, his last word little more than a death rattle in his chest.

Zasian watched for a moment to make certain the dragon was truly dead, then wove a quick spell of healing to cleanse away the acid burns he had endured while within the beast's belly. Once renewed, Zasian turned and trotted into the mists, seeking his companions.

Kashada chuckled and initiated the delicate, intricate gestures of a spell.

The elf advanced several more steps and raised her glowing, preternatural sword with both hands. As she closed the distance between them, she kept her milky, iridescent gaze on the mystic.

Kashada found those strange, opalescent eyes unnerving. She nearly lost her concentration and her spell and had to take a step back as she completed the incantation. She wanted to stay well clear of that incandescent blade's reach.

Near the warrior's feet, beneath a thick clump of ferns at the base of a large tree, shadows began to writhe. Tendrils of them thickened and darkened. The tendrils then snaked outward from beneath the ferns and lashed at the elf's ankles, rapidly encircling them.

The elf paused in her advance and stared down at her feet as the tendrils grew to become grasping black tentacles. The tentacles thickened and climbed like unholy vines. In the span of a couple of heartbeats, they had engulfed the woman's legs and hugged her waist, squeezing tightly.

Kashada smiled, though she knew her adversary could not see the expression. "Don't scream," she advised. "You'll lose your air faster that way." She giggled then and started to turn away.

The aura that surrounded the elf blazed brighter, hurting Kashada's eyes. The glow pulsed once, twice. The third time, the mystic felt her magic dissolve as the black appendages disintegrated and vanished.

Kashada gasped.

"What were you saying?" the elf asked, stepping closer and raising her blade high again.

Bitch, Kashada thought and spun away. The glowing sword arced down and sliced very near the mystic. She felt hot, shadow-sapping energy warm her skin where the blade passed. She darted to one side and sought a spot of deeper darkness.

The warrior hoisted her weapon high again and stalked after Kashada, following her step for step. "Don't run, witch. You'll lose your air faster that way."

Kashada spied a small draw where water rushed through during wet weather. A large branch, fallen from some nearby tree, had become wedged there, and debris had piled against it in rainy days past. The resulting natural lean-to protected a dark recess. The mystic dived toward it, engaging her magic.

As she hit the ground beneath the debris, the servant of Shar saw the world change around her, becoming faint and faded. At the same time, the shadows deepened, firmed, became more substantial. Of the elf woman and her wicked sword, there was no sign.

Kashada lay for several moments where she had landed, catching her breath. Then she rose to her knees and peered out. In almost every way, the shadow-forest mirrored its material counterpart, with the exception that everything sat absolutely still. No branches swayed in the breeze, no birds flitted from limb to limb, no rain fell. All was dim, unearthly silence.

The mystic smiled and crawled out from beneath the dead branch. She climbed to her feet and scanned her surroundings, seeking some sign that her adversary had found a way to follow her. Satisfied that she was alone, Kashada turned and followed her original path, making her way toward the cave.

Zasian did not mention there would be ghaeles in the

woods, the shadow-mystic thought. Just as he failed to mention in Sundabar that I would remain imprisoned within that Shar-forsaken sphere for twelve years, she added sourly. Such oversights will come back to haunt him, she vowed. Blessed Shar will make certain he has his day of reckoning. Cyric cannot protect him from that.

As Kashada neared the point where she suspected she was to meet the others, she sought another place of deeper shadow. She spied a felled tree ahead. The massive trunk had snapped from its stump perhaps five feet up from the forest floor and still rested against the rotting base, forming an angular, offset arch. Beneath that span, welcome darkness invited Kashada. She quickened her pace and stepped beneath it. She slipped one of her daggers free and flipped it around to grasp the blade end. She took a slow, calming breath and shifted.

The forest came alive again. Green replaced faded silvery gray. Leaves danced and whispered as breezes ran through them. The smell of earth and decaying wood filled Kashada's nostrils. Somewhere, a bird chirped.

The Sharan held still and peered around. She saw no sign of the ghaele. Somewhere in the distance, a horn wailed, a distressed call for help. Perhaps the ghaele had heard it too and had gone to assist whoever was sounding it.

Confident that she had slipped away from her pursuer, Kashada stepped out from beneath the fallen tree. She checked the surroundings once more. There was no one.

Satisfied, the mystic turned toward where she believed the caves to be and began walking again.

The baleful call of the horn ceased, replaced by a faint roar. Then a rumble of distant thunder reached Kashada's ears. She suspected that Zasian, in the form of Tekthyrios, was wreaking havoc among the folk guarding the cave.

Hopefully he's torn that horrid ghaele into pieces with his claws, she thought.

Kashada noticed that the land had changed around her, and she knew she must be close. The ground had become coarse and dark, more like bark than soil. The trees had thinned out a bit, too, and the air was thick with mist. She could not see more than a handful of paces in any direction.

A blinding flash engulfed Kashada. She threw her arms up protectively, trying to shield her eyes from the blazing glow, but the damage was done. Pain wracked the mystic, searing hot agony that made her crumple over and fall to the ground. Her first instinct was to fall into a shadow, but she couldn't clear her vision of the white afterimage in order to seek one out.

"Very clever, shadowwalking to try to evade me," the ghaele said. Her voice came from somewhere overhead. "But the stench of your evil fills these woods. You are too easy to find."

Kashada's vision began to return. She could make out the basic shapes of tree trunks, but everything was still blurred and too bright to focus on. She fought the pain of keeping her eyes open and scanned the sky, trying to spot her adversary.

As her sight continued to improve, the Sharan finally spied what must be the ghaele. A sphere perhaps five feet wide hovered among the tree tops. A panoply of eldritch colors shimmered across its surface, intensely hurtful to look upon.

Why must it fight with light? she lamented. Anything but light. Where in the Hells are Myshik and Zasian?

"Ah, friends to come to your rescue," the ghaele said. "Thank you for letting me know."

Kashada gritted her teeth. Fool! She can read your mind. Flee!

Before the mystic could rise and get away, another beam of light flashed from the sphere. Kashada pitched herself to one side to evade the attack and slammed into the bole of a tree. She grunted, feeling the blow on her ribs. The searing whiteness struck the ground where she had lain a heartbeat before.

Not waiting to see if another attack was eminent, Kashada gestured and spoke a word of magic. Blackness enveloped her. She scrambled to her feet, using the tree for support, and moved around it, hoping misdirection would throw the ghaele off. She had not taken three steps when the blackness vanished again.

The ghaele stood before Kashada in elf form. Those lustrous, pearlescent eyes fixed on her face, boring into her own. "If you crave the darkness so much, then allow me to send you to your grave." She gestured and uttered a word that rang in Kashada's ears. The mystic fell back as vibrant light surrounded her. The glow clung to her, shredding the shadows in which she cloaked herself. Her carefully crafted illusion of mysterious beauty vanished, leaving her weak and terrified.

"No!" she croaked. She dropped to the ground, one arm raised to ward off the debilitating power of the ghaele's magic. "Shar, help me!"

The ghaele stepped closer, pulling her sword free. "Your deceitful goddess will not aid you, witch," she said, raising her weapon for the killing blow. "You are finished."

The blade reached its apex, but the ghaele did not strike. Instead, those milky, opalescent eyes glanced away, at something behind Kashada, and widened in alarm. "No!" the ghaele screamed, putting a single hand out before herself as if to ward off an attack.

A beam of sickly green energy struck the warrior in the

chest. She threw her head back and screamed in agony, a sound that was cut short as her entire body turned to dust and scattered across the forest floor near Kashada's feet.

The mystic gaped for a moment at the ghaele's disintegrated remains, then she turned to look over her shoulder as footfalls approached.

Zasian strolled up to Kashada and offered her a hand up.

"Sorry I'm late," the priest said. "I was delayed by a rampaging shrub. I take it Myshik hasn't arrived yet?"

❖ ❖ ❖ ❖ ❖ ❖ ❖ ❖

Kaanyr nudged the blackened body at his feet with his toe, flipping it over so that it faced upward. The unseeing eyes were still open, the face smudged with mud and blood. Whatever had hit the fellow, it had killed him quickly, and not that long before. Smoke still rose from the charred remains.

The cambion stepped away and checked another, slumped over the boughlike trunk of one of the twisted trees in the area. That one, too, was dead, though there was no outward sign of injury. When he flipped the corpse over, he saw a look of horror upon the elf's face. The body was still flush and warm to the touch.

"They're all dead," he said, turning and striding back to where Aliisza and the other two stood gathered next to the corpse of the dragon. "Every last one of them."

"As I expected," Tauran said, not looking up. He knelt next to the storm dragon's head, his hand upon its ridged brow, as though comforting it. "The ghaeles do not leave wounded behind, if they can help it. They either carry their brethren away or stand to the last defending them."

Aliisza looked all around. "Zasian did this?" she said,

appearing a bit awed. "Even in dragon form, this is a formidable force to confront."

"Yes, it is," Tauran said, still kneeling. His eyes were closed and he kept his hand upon the dragon's forehead. Finally, he stood up, looking around. "But I don't understand what happened to him."

Kaanyr snorted. "He bit off more than he could chew, and this little army of wood elf fellows and their giant bear-plant did him in."

"I wish it were that simple, if tragic," Tauran replied, "but there is no sign of the priest within the dragon's corpse. Whatever happened here, Zasian did not die in Tekthyrios's form."

"So he's still running loose," Kael said, whacking his blade against a nearby tree in frustration. "We're not done, yet."

"It appears not," Tauran said. "And what's worse, he left the dragon behind, so he's more difficult to find, and I think he's left the House of the Triad, making that difficult job even trickier."

"Why did he come here?" Aliisza asked. "What is this place?"

Tauran sighed and began walking in an ever widening circle around the dragon. As he surveyed the area, he explained. "Some of those who fought here today are eladrin, fey creatures. Those here have dedicated themselves to being champions of good across the cosmos. They are a bit more free-spirited than most of us who dwell here within the House, flaunting our laws when such strictures do not suit them, but Tyr abides them because they are dedicated to defending this place."

The angel stopped and knelt down next to a patch of earth, tracing his finger through something there. "It would seem that whatever happened to Zasian, here is where he got up and walked away."

Kaanyr moved next to the angel and peered down where he indicated. A set of bootprints wandered off through the underbrush. They would be easy to follow.

Tauran stood again. "It doesn't appear that he's injured, so he's moving rapidly. But these kills are very fresh. He can't be far ahead."

"Then we should not tarry," Kaanyr said, sensing that the end of his servitude might be near. He loosened Burnblood in its scabbard and gestured for the angel to lead the way. "Let's go."

❖ ❖ ❖ ❖ ❖ ❖ ❖ ❖

"You!" Myshik snarled as Zasian walked into view. The draconic hobgoblin scrambled to his feet and reached for the war axe strapped to his back. "Where is Tekthyrios?" he demanded, drawing the axe back as if to strike at the priest.

Beside the half-dragon, Kashada shifted her gaze back and forth between the two. Her eyes, peering out from behind that shimmering veil of black cloth and shadow, glittered in amusement.

The shadow-mystic had been genuinely grateful to Zasian for rescuing her, but afterward, he noted something dangerous in her demeanor. She had appeared flustered at first, at least until she managed to redeploy her shadow-illusions. Even afterward, she became aloof, and he caught her staring at him more than once. She would bear watching, he decided.

"The storm dragon is no more," Zasian answered, stopping

a few steps out of Myshik's reach. "And if you don't put that down, the same will hold true for you."

"How then will I cleave you in twain to avenge his death?" Myshik asked, a taunting smile appearing on his lips. He took a single stride forward, and Zasian finished the spell he had begun before he and Kashada had joined the half-dragon.

Myshik's eyes bulged when he realized he could not move.

Zasian watched, smirking, as the hobgoblin strained to break free of the repulsive magic. *You truly are a simpleton, whelp of Morueme. Always two steps behind the rest of us. As bad as the half-fiends and their fool angel.* "Are you done, yet?" he asked, folding his arms across his chest.

"I could heave this blade such that it would lop off your head, Banite," Myshik growled. He continued to struggle and did not notice Kashada step behind him.

"Yes, but you don't know what other little tricks I might have up my sleeve," Zasian replied and nodded to the shadow-cloaked woman. She nodded back and stepped closer, planting what Zasian assumed was a dagger against the small of the hobgoblin's back.

Myshik froze, and his eyes rolled as he tried to peer back over his shoulder at the woman. Her free hand snaked up and took hold of the axe. He resisted for a moment then arched up straighter. Zasian chuckled, imagining how she was pressing her point home. Myshik released the axe and Kashada tossed it to the side. She did not move away from the half-dragon.

"Have you heard the saying, 'The enemy of my enemy is my friend,' Myshik?" Zasian asked. "I believe the nomadic tribesmen who roam the desert near your home use it often, as do the genies in various parts of the cosmos."

Myshik glowered, but he did not say anything.

"Yes, I killed the storm dragon, but you never served him. It was me in control of his flesh and blood, me to whom you swore fealty."

The half-dragon's eyes widened the slightest bit as that realization sunk in.

"I shouldn't think that it would matter too much to you what happened to Tekthyrios," Zasian continued. "I don't believe your father or uncle would be too keen to hear that you were in the service of a storm dragon. The storms and the blues never have gotten along too well, have they? Always squabbling over territory, domains, or some such, right?"

Myshik frowned, but eventually he nodded. "But why?" he asked. "Why the disguise, the trickery?"

"In due time, whelp of Morueme, in due time," Zasian answered. "For now, just know that I am no friend of Vhok's. He was a tool to me, nothing more. In fact, he still serves me in that fashion, though he does not yet realize it. Also know that I do not serve Bane. That lie was a necessary part of my deception with Vhok." Zasian paused and studied the half-dragon, gauging his reaction. Myshik had stopped glowering. So far so good, the priest decided. He continued. "You have two choices to consider now. One is to take a stand, try to fight against me, and die as a result. That is no threat, it is a certainty. It isn't, however, a particularly appealing result to me, because despite your stubbornness and rather simple outlook, I find you useful.

"Which brings me to the other choice. Serve me, as you had been serving me when you believed I was a storm dragon. The terms will be the same. Do as I ask, willingly, eagerly, and I will make certain you receive generous compensation for your efforts. Plus, you get the opportunity to thwart

Vhok, make him one miserable demonspawn. That ought to convince you right there."

"I accept," Myshik said.

"What?" Zasian said, taken aback. "No need to think about it? No deliberations over which choice is the lesser betrayal to your conscience?"

Myshik smiled. "As you said, 'the enemy of my enemy is my friend.' What is there to think about? My uncle gave me very clear instructions."

Zasian's eyes narrowed in suspicion. *Perhaps he is more cunning than I gave him credit for. I will have to watch him,* he decided. He nodded to Kashada, who stepped back from the half-dragon and slipped her dagger back into her belt.

Myshik relaxed and moved to pick up his axe. He stopped before he actually took hold of it and glanced back at Kashada. "You're not going to use me for target practice when I scoop this up, are you?" he asked.

"Does she have a reason to?" Zasian asked.

"No," Myshik replied, "but I wasn't sure if she knew that."

"I don't think we need fear a reprisal from you," the priest said.

Myshik gave him an even stare for just a little longer than Zasian thought appropriate, then he lifted the axe from the ground. He slipped it back into its spot upon his back and turned to face the other two. "So, what is your intention?" he asked.

"Kashada and I have business elsewhere," Zasian answered. "We must take a journey, one that is likely to be a bit treacherous."

"Yes, this cave you have brought us to," Myshik said. "But where does it lead? Where are we going?"

"Follow me," Zasian replied. He turned and began to walk through the mist-filled forest, pushing past the foliage that sprouted up from every direction. The dampness clung to everything, and the sounds of its dripping echoed softly through the woods. The priest could see a faint path winding among the odd, rolling ridges of ground. Zasian picked his way along it, listening for sounds of pursuit or ambush.

"This ground is odd," Myshik commented from behind Zasian. "What is this place?"

Zasian smiled. "It's not really ground at all," he said. "We are passing from the House of the Triad into the World Tree. This is the veil between those two places."

Myshik was silent for a moment, then he exclaimed, "It's bark! This is a branch!"

Zasian grimaced. "Yes, but lower your voice, Morueme. There are a few enemies still around—and new ones on our trail—that will not take kindly to our passing through here."

The priest grinned as he imagined Vhok and the others pursuing him, trying to catch up before he slipped away. Stay close, cambion, he thought. I am not finished with you yet.

They walked on in silence for some time longer, Zasian keeping a watch ahead as he followed the path. It wound between the rounded, rolling ridges of the rich, brown, woody substance and the twisted, angled trees.

Not trees, Zasian reminded himself. Branches. Twigs, perhaps.

The surrounding terrain grew higher and steeper on either side of the path, forming a narrow defile. As the trio descended into the canyon, it began to rain. The patter of drops from the gentle downpour caused little more than a whisper on the spongy ground.

Zasian pulled the hood of his cloak up and around his head, shielding him from the moisture. "Keep an eye out, now," he cautioned the other two in a soft voice. "Other things live on the World Tree, and some of them are not friendly. Sometimes, even the tree itself becomes your enemy."

The defile grew narrower and narrower, until Zasian felt his shoulders brushing against the sides as he walked. Just when it seemed that the walls had closed together too much for them to continue, the canyon ended in the entrance to a cave. The path vanished into the darkness beyond.

"Here we go," Zasian muttered, half to himself. "A bit of light, and . . ." He muttered a quick prayer, waved his hand over the head of his mace, and the weapon glowed with the light of day, illuminating the passage. "Kashada, Myshik, wish this unhappy place a fond farewell. We're beyond its reach, now." And with that, he ducked into the narrow opening and entered the blackness.

CHAPTER NINE

"Where are we going?" Kaanyr asked as he trailed after the angel. "You seem to know what this place is and why Zasian would come here."

"It is a doorway between worlds," Tauran replied, his gaze still turned toward the ground. "This part of the House borders on the World Tree. I think Zasian is going to try to travel along it to reach another plane."

Kaanyr caught sight of a second set of booted prints in the soil, smaller and more delicate than the first. "It doesn't look like he is alone," the cambion said, pointing.

Tauran stopped and knelt down, again running his finger through the depression. "I think you're right."

"Look," Aliisza said, pointing a bit farther down the path. "There's more over here. It appears someone engaged in a scuffle."

The angel rocked back on his heels, gazing into the distance, deep in thought. "This makes things quite a bit more interesting," he said, pulling on his chin. "Where did he get an ally?"

"From the same place as before," Micus said from above them.

Kaanyr flinched and darted to the side, ripping Burnblood free. He peered upward and spotted the angel standing upon a thick branch in one of the odd, sloping trees. The cambion's companions reacted just as quickly, jumping into defensive postures and freeing their weapons.

"From among the conniving fiends he calls friends," Micus continued, "like the ones you're wandering around with, Tauran."

The sound of footsteps behind Kaanyr drew his attention away from the deva in the tree. He spun and saw three hound archons fanning out to surround him. Two more materialized just behind them.

"It's a trap!" the cambion shouted. "They're surrounding us!" He backed away, considering his options. He risked a quick glimpse in other directions. Perhaps a dozen more dog-headed warriors stood on guard; a handful more instantly appeared as Kaanyr watched.

The enemy had position; the group was encircled.

"Time to surrender," Micus said. "You cannot keep running, Tauran."

"Micus, look around you," Tauran said, his frustration evident in his tone. "Look what has happened here! Isn't it obvious now that we have to find this priest? We have to stop him."

Kaanyr took a couple more steps back, away from the archons and toward his companions. The hound-headed warriors followed him, wary. As he retreated, the cambion reached into his tunic and pulled a wand free. He made the decision to speak the command word and fire glowing missiles at the nearest foe, but he couldn't quite muster the will.

Damn it to the Nine Hells! he silently seethed. "Tauran!" he growled softly, hoping the angel would understand without tipping his enemies off that he could not attack them. "What's the word?"

"Micus, this is the proof we needed!" Tauran said, ignoring Kaanyr. "Isn't this enough to go back to the High Council and convince them?"

"The High Council is already convinced," the other angel replied. "They know something is up, just as you said. But they also believe it is very unwise to trust these two. They have given me explicit instructions to bring them back to the Court. With your help or without it." Micus's last words were slow and deliberate.

Wise up, you fool of an angel! Kaanyr thought. They're never going to listen to you! Give the go-ahead!

"I gave them my word, Micus," Tauran said. "I must honor that."

"No, you must not," Micus replied. "Not to them. You have other duties, like obedience and loyalty. Those must come first."

"I'm sorry, Micus. I don't see it that way."

"Then you leave me with no choice," Micus said, his voice sounding weary. "I'm sorry, too. Take them!" he shouted. "You know your orders!"

Kaanyr snarled, and he almost didn't hear Tauran's voice ringing through the din of battle cries as the archons rushed at him.

"Fight, Kaanyr! Fight and flee!"

There we go, the cambion thought, smiling as he raised the wand. That's what I like to hear.

He uttered the magical phrase to trigger the wand and sent four glowing missiles streaking directly at the nearest hound archon. The arcane projectiles whistled through the air and slammed into the creature with staccato popping sounds. The warrior barked in pain and twitched away, stumbling to the ground.

Kaanyr didn't waste time watching to see how badly he had injured that one. He spun to another, swinging Burnblood. His smaller, lighter blade whipped toward the canine head, but the archon knocked it away with his sword. That was just what Kaanyr had hoped the creature would do, and he spun back around, getting inside the sword's reach. He rammed his enchanted blade into the archon's chest.

Before the warrior could even gasp and go wide-eyed, Kaanyr had his boot planted against the archon and yanked his sword free again. He leaped away as three more of the dog-headed warriors tried to close with him. He leveled the wand at them. Just the gesture of aiming the wand made the trio draw up, and Kaanyr used the delay to leap into the air and begin rising, drawing on his innate magic to escape their reach.

The creatures recognized the feint and renewed their efforts to come after him, but Kaanyr sent a volley of shrieking missiles in their direction, and it was enough to get him beyond their blades. He spun in place to scan the rest of the battle. He could see his companions, three isolated pockets of resistance within a swarm of archons. He had faith that Aliisza could extricate herself. Of the other two, he cared not a whit.

Tauran had commanded him to flee, and flee he would.

And I won't stop until I get well away from him. For good.

The cambion reached into his tunic and fumbled free a bit of gauzy fabric wrapped around a tiny glass tube sealed with wax. Kaanyr didn't waste time with the seal. He simply snapped the tube in half, freeing the smoke that had been trapped inside. As the two arcane components merged together, he swirled the whole thing around himself.

Kaanyr transformed, becoming insubstantial. He felt odd, disembodied, but he had experienced such before and ignored the sensations. He could see in every direction at once, all around, above and below. He watched the hound archons struggle in vain to see where he had gone, and he wanted to laugh, but he had no voice.

Vhok continued to rise into the air, sliding through the foliage of the strange, twisted, angled trees. He could not travel very fast, but he did not care. He was virtually invisible, particularly with the swirling mists all around, and every moment that he slipped farther away from the fighting made him feel safer, more at ease.

When he was well above the tree tops, Kaanyr searched for some landmark, a direction by which he could navigate. He wasn't sure where he wanted to go, but he wanted to disappear silently and completely from Tauran's grasp forever.

He initially considered the World Tree. It was nearby and it offered so many possibilities. But that was where Tauran had intended to go, and Kaanyr did not want to risk a reunion with the angel.

No, he decided, I think another direction entirely is in order.

He had just begun drifting toward the nearest edge of the great, forested island—intent on reaching its underside to hide—when he saw two angels rise from the trees and fly in his direction. Like Tauran and Micus, they were astral devas, and it was clear to Kaanyr that they were homing in on him.

Damnation, he thought.

Before the cambion could react, one of the angels gestured at him, and his spell of gaseousness dissipated. In corporeal form once more, Kaanyr plummeted. He got his wits about him in time to invoke his levitating ability before he crashed into the canopy below.

Apparently, that was precisely what the two angels expected him to do, because in the next instant, he heard the second one speak a single word. It echoed in the cambion's mind like a thunderbolt.

Everything went black.

❖ ❖ ❖ ❖ ❖ ❖ ❖ ❖ ❖

Myshik and Kashada followed close behind Zasian as they moved along the passage between planes. The shadow-mystic's footfalls, already faint, became lost amid the clomping of Myshik's boots.

The walls of the passage remained close at hand on either side of the trio, and Zasian imagined he could have forgone the light and felt his way easily enough. The tunnel twisted and turned occasionally, ascending at times and dipping sharply at others. Once, it grew so narrow that Myshik was forced to slip free from his breastplate to squeeze through.

"What catacomb do you lead us to?" he grumbled as he tugged his armor back on. "You said nothing of tight spaces before."

"We will be free of this confined space soon enough, Morueme," Zasian replied.

As soon as Myshik had donned his armor, they resumed their travels. As if to prove the priest a prophet, they rounded a bend and discovered light seeping from the next turn ahead. Zasian quickened his pace and reached the opening of the tunnel. Stepping free of it, he took in the surroundings.

Much like at the other end, the trio stood within a narrow

gorge of rich, dark wood rising up to either side of them. The trail continued out of sight ahead. Also similar to before, gray mist filled the air, casting a pall over the place. Unlike the moist air that hung within the House of the Triad, though, the mist was much more silvery.

Eventually the canyon walls began to drop away from the sides, until at last the priest and his companions stood upon what appeared to be a great ridge of the same woody landscape. Much of the ground was bare, but in spots, the same large, angled trees jutted from it. Lush green tangles of some sort of thick bracken covered other large stretches.

The ridge did not rise from some larger plain, however. Instead, it just fell away to either side, its edges seeming to grow steeper as it faded from view, making the whole thing round, like some gargantuan barrel. The crown of the ridge ran off both ahead of and behind them into the distance, eventually fading from sight into the pervasive silvery light. The narrow gorge from which they had ascended appeared as a crack in the surface behind them.

Zasian halted and took it in for a moment. He scanned the horizon in every direction, as far as he could see. *I'm actually standing here,* he thought, pleased. *I'm actually standing on the World Tree. It is grander than even I could have imagined.*

"What is this place?" Myshik asked, peering around in wonder.

"The World Tree," Zasian answered. "Or rather, a single branch of it."

"Where does it lead?" the half-dragon asked. "Why are we here?"

Zasian glanced at his companion, irked. *Can't you even appreciate the grandeur of this place? Do you not grasp what* a monumental moment this is? He shook his head in disgust. "It leads everywhere," the priest explained with a sigh. "And we are following it to get . . . elsewhere." He stared at the hobgoblin with a steady gaze, as if to say, *Do you really wish to keep testing my patience?*

Myshik returned the stare with displeasure, but he didn't press the issue further. Instead he asked, "Which way do we go?"

Zasian studied each direction before deciding on the path leading back alongside the crack. It seemed to him that the ridge grew larger in that direction, whereas the route in front of them became the slightest bit narrower. Without a word, he set out along that path.

The trio walked for some time, passing numerous thick, angled tree trunks. Zasian recognized them as other, smaller branches jutting from the larger one upon which they strolled. In some places, great fanlike expanses of green material as large as a ship's sails clung to them.

Ah, the priest realized, *leaves. Magnificent, monumental leaves. Extraordinary!*

They skirted large patches of undergrowth, and eventually, he recognized the dense, tangled vines as oversized clumps of moss.

Before long, unease replaced Zasian's elation. For a while, he thought it was simply a wariness of the unfamiliar place, or an expectation of encountering some hostile denizen of the tree, but eventually he knew it was something else entirely.

No wind blew and no sound reached the trio other than their own footsteps. The odd, silvery surroundings were utterly devoid of any noise, any hint of life.

I guess I keep thinking I should hear birds singing and

breezes blowing through the leaves, he decided. On the other hand, he added wryly, I don't really think I want to see the bird that nests in this tree. Stifling the chuckle at his own grim joke, Zasian refocused his attention on the trail, the offshooting branches, and the moss. Many things could hide in those places, waiting to spring out and attack them.

The trio walked on in utter silence. The landscape never changed, although it was very clear to Zasian that the thickness of the branch upon which they hiked had grown considerably since they had set out. That observation convinced him that he had chosen the right way, and that they were, indeed, headed toward the trunk.

"Look," Myshik said, and Zasian glanced back at the half-dragon to see him pointing off into the distance, ahead and to one side.

Zasian peered into the silvery murk and spotted what the hobgoblin had noticed. A second great branch was just beginning to become visible, running at an angle and from a slightly higher plane such that it would most likely join with their own branch within a few more moments of walking.

Zasian nodded. "Yes, we draw ever closer to the nexus of the World Tree, to its trunk. Its branches spread throughout the Astral plane, connecting to every location in the cosmos."

"How will we know which new branch we will need to follow?" Myshik asked.

"Why, we'll have to hire a guide, of course," Zasian replied. "I'm certain we will run across a local inhabitant of the Tree very soon."

In another few moments, the trio neared the point where the two branches intersected, and Zasian smiled to himself. Ahead, right at the junction, he spotted clear evidence of habitation. A whole series of elevated structures, like children's tree houses, filled the branches rising up from the larger one. Ladders and bridges of rope hung between the different levels, making the whole place a tiny interconnected community.

As they grew closer to the small tree village, Zasian could make out the distinct forms of creatures. A small group of them were emerging from the mist and approaching the trio.

"Perfect," the priest said softly, still smiling in anticipation. "A welcoming committee."

❖ ❖ ❖ ❖ ❖ ❖ ❖ ❖ ❖

Aliisza parried a strike from one of the hound archons trying to surround her and took another step back. The celestial warrior closed the gap and swung his sword at her again. Her foe wasn't trying to injure her. His attacks were slow, methodical, not designed to slip past her defenses so much as wear them down.

"Surrender," the archon said, raising his sword for another two-handed strike. "It's only a matter of time before you must. Save us all some aggravation."

Aliisza smiled and whipped her more delicate sword up and out to block his. The blow rang in the mists of the forest, and it sent a tingling up her arm, but she didn't let that show. Instead, she took another step back until she pressed against a tree. Out of the corner of her eye she saw two more archons closing in. They held a net between them.

Aliisza followed up her parry with a feint to the archon's knees, then used the space she had created to duck around the tree. She heard the creature's blade strike hard against the trunk, but she was already sprinting toward a fallen log with another clump of bushes, nearly as thick as she was tall, nestled against it.

The archons had relentlessly pursued her since she had become separated from Tauran and Kael. Kaanyr had gone off in his own direction, but the other three of them tried to remain together, closing ranks to defend themselves from the swarming onslaught of archons. They could not maintain their positions, though. The creatures utilized a clever tactic to divide them through rapid and repeated teleportation. They used their attacks to drive her to one side or another, then they popped into the area she had just vacated, becoming wedges, separating her from her allies. They were herding her away from her compatriots.

Once Aliisza had realized their intentions, she abandoned her efforts at staying near the other two and sprinted through the forest, ducking and weaving in haphazard directions to evade their attacks and confound their strategy. The new tactic prevented them from closing in on her initially, but they had the numbers necessary to surround her.

The alu nearly took to the air then, thinking to outrun the archons by winging her way into the canopy and beyond. She had gotten only a few feet off the ground when that innate sense of danger she sometimes experienced washed over her. She peered up into the trees and spotted devas awaiting her there.

Giving up on fleeing by wing, Aliisza returned to the branch, where the archons continued to close in. Over and over, she managed to evade the creatures, but each desperate maneuver took her farther and farther away from her companions.

She no longer even heard the sounds of distant battle ringing through the misty forest to indicate where they might be.

She was alone in her fight.

Nothing you can do about it now, she chided herself. *Find them later. If they're still standing.*

"Surrender," the one chasing her demanded.

Aliisza did not turn around. She leaped and spread her wings. She glided over the low scrub brush and came to rest atop the fallen log. She turned to survey her pursuit.

The archon closest to her took one faltering step before drawing up at the edge of the scrub. He eyed the greenery as if considering how best to get past it, then he shrugged and blinked out of existence.

Aliisza had anticipated his tactic, and when he appeared next to her atop the log, she muttered a quick arcane phrase and looked away. A flare of magical light flashed right upon the tip of the archon's nose. He yipped in surprise and flinched, falling backward. He swatted at the afterimages dazzling him, but Aliisza was already moving away.

She sprinted the length of the log and leaped, spreading her wings to soar over the other archons closing in. The pair with the net tried to unfurl their rope trap in time to throw it up and over the alu, but she lunged past them and glided to the ground on the far side.

Her newfound freedom didn't last long. Once again, the archons materialized ahead of her, cutting her off . No matter which way she turned, they appeared there. It was maddening.

Can't outrun them, she decided. Got to outsmart them. Got to hide, slip away.

Aliisza turned to sprint in yet another direction, aiming for a small draw between two large and rather prominent trees. Her sense of foreboding warned her that something menaced her from above the hollow, but she ignored the sensation. If she executed her plan well enough, she might be able to slip away undetected.

The alu darted into the shallow depression and flourished one hand in the air as she uttered a magical phrase. A cloud of mist arose, thickening into an impenetrable veil that obscured Aliisza from everything around her.

In the next breath, she reached within her tunic and pulled out two different bits of material needed for another pair of spells. The first one, a small lump of a sticky substance, she squeezed between her thumb and forefinger as she verbalized the magic needed to render herself completely invisible.

Once she had vanished, she took the second one, a small fragment of fleece, and tossed it to the ground near one of the two trees. Instantly, an image of herself appeared. The illusory version of the alu crouched down next to the bole of the tree as though hiding.

Satisfied, Aliisza turned and pushed herself up from the ground as quietly as she could and spread her wings wide. Just as she was rising from the thick, cloaking mists in which she had hidden, the first of the archons drew near. With one last mental command, the alu sent her illusory image aloft, causing it to wing its way in the opposite direction from her own path. The mirage version of the half-fiend appeared from within the mists and shot forward.

The closest archon gave a shout and pointed, and other celestial warriors took up the pursuit. Giving a small, silent sigh of relief, Aliisza flew away.

She hadn't made it twenty feet before she became visible again.

Above and slightly behind her, a commanding voice yelled, "Here! She's trying to sneak away!"

Cursing, Aliisza glanced up and spotted one of the angels swooping toward her. He was pointing at her and motioning for the archons to pick up their pursuit again. A heartbeat later, several of the archons appeared nearby, teleporting into positions to surround her once more.

Aliisza cursed again and drew up into a hover. She spun and flew straight at the deva, hoping to catch him off guard.

You're not taking me back there, she swore. Not so you can play mind games with me.

The deva, who wore his golden hair trimmed short, started at the sight of the alu rushing at him. Aliisza thought she might have stunned him enough to feign an attack and zip away, but the angel recovered and opened his mouth to speak.

The next thing Aliisza remembered was spinning dizzily as she fell to the ground. Her ears rang and she could not orient herself so that up was up. She struck the soft forest floor with a jarring exhalation and bounced across it until she finally came to a stop. She lay there, gasping for air.

A pair of archons appeared near her and began to unfurl their net. "Surrender," one of them said dispassionately as he worked to envelop her within the confines of his snare. "It's pointless to keep fleeing. You cannot get away."

To the Hells with you, Aliisza thought, but she had no strength to resist.

Two more archons gathered around her and the deva joined them. As a group, they stretched the net out over Aliisza and pinned her to the ground.

"This doesn't have to be painful," the deva said, and he smiled at her. "We're not trying to kill you. But there are laws here, and you must obey them."

"Rot in the lowest levels of the Abyss," she snarled. "I came willingly before and had the word of one of your own that I was free to go whenever I chose. So don't lecture *me* about breaking laws!"

"Tauran was not in a position to—"

The deva's sentence died in his throat as Kael dropped to the ground next to him. The flat of the half-drow's blade crashed hard against the back of the angel's head and sent him staggering forward, where he collided with one of the archons holding the net down.

"Get out of here!" Kael shouted, spinning to smack another of the celestial warriors with his weapon. "Now!"

Aliisza stared at the sight of her son waging furious combat with the three archons still surrounding her. He flowed from one stance to another like a dancer, all grace and balance, shifting with the weight of his sword. Even attacking to stun rather than kill, he wielded the sword with exacting precision. The archons were no match for him, but as soon as one was put down, two more appeared.

"Go!" Kael shouted. "I can't do this all day!"

Recollecting her wits, Aliisza tried to wriggle herself free from the netting, but the archons devoted at least a small part of their attention to standing on the snare, keeping her pinned down.

Fine, she decided. *There are other ways to depart.*

She summoned one of her magical doors beneath herself and slipped through it. Acting as much on instinct as reason, the alu positioned the other end of the magical portal near the corpse of Tekthyrios. Aliisza tumbled through the opening and sprawled upon the loamy earth, hoping none of her pursuers were nearby. When she heard no immediate shouts of discovery close to her, the half-fiend gingerly crawled to the storm dragon's body, seeking a place to hide.

One of the dragon's wings was cocked at such an angle that Aliisza could squeeze under it and nestle up against the impaled beast's body. She slunk into the hiding place and collapsed, still suffering the residual effects of the deva's divine attack. She closed her eyes and sat still for a few moments to allow the last vestiges of dizziness to leave her.

The forest was quiet, though she could discern the sounds of battle continuing in the distance. Aliisza wondered if it was Kael in the midst of that, or Tauran.

It's certainly not Kaanyr, she decided with a grimace. He took off like a roc when Tauran gave the word. He's halfway to Sundabar by now.

The alu sighed and settled back, wondering how long she would be safe where she hid.

What difference does it make? she thought ruefully. Without Tauran here, I have no idea how to get out or where to go. I'll find no friends, either.

Feeling a little bit sorry for herself, Aliisza tried to relax and wait. Tired, aching muscles reminded her of the harsh fight she had endured against the archons. She wanted more than anything to sleep for a short while, but her worries about being caught kept her on edge, unable to give in to her weariness.

Despite her angst, Aliisza must have drifted off for a least a few moments, for the next thing she knew she was startled awake by a noise. She jerked forward, then remembered her situation and froze, listening for the sounds of discovery. Whatever had roused her did not come for her in her hiding place, but she could clearly hear something rummaging around near her concealment.

She peered from deep within the shadow of her secret lair but saw nothing. Worried about capture but hating not knowing what was out there even more, Aliisza moved to get a better look. Very slowly, she inched her way forward to the edge of the hollow until she could widen her view.

A pair of hound archons worked nearby, gathering the bodies of the humanoids that had been slain alongside Tekthyrios. The two creatures seemed to be stacking them, perhaps for some form of funeral pyre or similar last rites.

As she studied them, several more arrived in the clearing, appearing magically. The creatures spoke to one another as they worked, but their words were too soft to be understood.

How long before they decide to do something about this dragon? Aliisza wondered. I can't stay here.

But there was nowhere for the alu to flee, at least not yet. A far greater number of the archons were unaccounted for, most likely still roaming the forest around the clearing. And regardless, she had no clue where any of her companions might be.

Careful to remain quiet, Aliisza crept back into the depths of her hiding place and waited. She continued to watch the work being done beyond her shadowy enclave as the celestial warriors passed in front of her field of vision.

Eventually, it grew dark. The warriors never bothered to light lamps or torches, and as Aliisza watched, it became clear that they could see perfectly well without the need for such illumination.

So much for sneaking out under cover of darkness, the alu thought. What a wretched mess this has become.

Aliisza remained huddled in her secret sanctuary. She hoped the angels and their soldiers would eventually move on or settle in for the night and she could find the means to slip away undetected. She dozed from time to time, but always some noise, some shout or shuffling near her spot, jerked her awake again, heart thumping rapidly. Each time she would curse her circumstances, but the celestial warriors were still hard at work, moving around the clearing.

Aliisza, came Tauran's voice. *Aliisza, can you hear me?*

The alu was hesitant at first, leery that it might be a trick. But she knew the sort of magic being employed, and she doubted it could be used to determine her location.

Yes, she answered. *I hear you.*

Where are you? the angel asked.

How do I know it's really you?

Well spoken, Tauran replied.

There was a long moment's silence, and Aliisza began to grow worried that she had miscalculated, that it was a trick, that soldiers with nets were closing in on her position right at that moment.

Just when the alu was on the verge of bolting from her hiding place in panic, Tauran said, *How can I prove it to you?*

Answer me this, Aliisza said. *Tell me the name of the boy I saved, in the dream world where you kept me imprisoned. The one who worked for the tailor. Who was he?*

It was no boy, Tauran replied without hesitation. *Lizel was a girl.*

Aliisza's relief cascaded through her. She sank back into the cool earth and sighed. *Yes,* she said. *It's you. How did you find me—reach me?*

A little trinket Eirwyn gave me before we parted ways. I had forgotten about it until just now. Where are you? Can you come to us?

I don't know where you are. I am hiding within the clearing. There are devas and archons everywhere. What's happened?

Kael and I are safe, the angel replied. *We are watching Micus. He and some of his warriors are concealed near the passage to the World Tree. Probably expecting us to make a break for it.* There was a pause, and then, *Where are you hiding?*

Under Tekthyrios's wing, she answered. Then, biting her lip, she asked, *What about Kaanyr?*

There was another, longer pause. *Micus's troops captured him. He's there, in the camp, very near you. I'm sorry.*

Sorry? You didn't help them, did you?

No, Tauran answered. *But I'm sorry they turned against you. I'm sorry it all fell apart like this.* The angel sounded tired and defeated. *Kael and I are considering offering a trade: me for Vhok.*

No, Aliisza replied. *They won't agree, and you know it. They are sworn to uphold your many and sometimes ridiculous laws.*

I know, Tauran replied. His voice was without hope. *But we have no other choice. There are too many of them. We can't free him by force, and I will honor my word to him to let him go back to Sundabar.*

Aliisza thought for a moment, then inspiration struck. *I have a better idea*, she said.

CHAPTER TEN

"How do you know they aren't hostile?" Myshik asked. Kashada saw the half-dragon reach for his war axe out of the corner of her eye. "They don't look like they're very happy to see us."

The figures approaching them did seem wary. As they drew closer, Kashada saw that they resembled elves in appearance, though they had eschewed clothing and their deep brown skin mimicked the bark of a tree.

Dryads, the Sharan thought with a mixture of distaste and surprise. A whole colony of them. Annoying little fey.

On her other side, Zasian chuckled. "You leave that to me, young Morueme. In a moment, they will be falling all over themselves to please us." The priest pulled a pendant from his shirt and rubbed it between his thumb and forefinger, chanting softly.

When Kashada saw that it was the silver skull of Cyric, she grimaced. Though she was grateful to Zasian for his timely rescue of her at the hands of the ghaele, it only made her further resent the necessity of associating with one of his ilk. *He is merely a tool,* she reminded herself. *As Cyric is Shar's.*

Use him to achieve the ends you desire. Such thoughts were of little comfort when she felt so dependent upon him for seeing the plot through.

Zasian completed whatever divine invocation he had engaged in and paused expectantly. The half-dozen dryads, who had slowed and stopped once they were within a few paces of the trio, broke into shy grins and closed the remainder of the gap, arms outstretched. They fawned all over the strangers in their midst, gently pawing at buckles, jewelry, and other shiny bits of outfit. They chattered and giggled like young girls, but Kashada could understand none of it.

Zasian began another spell, murmuring softly as he caressed his pendant. When he finished that one, he let the thing slip back inside the folds of his shirt. He began speaking words that Kashada did not understand, but whatever the priest was saying, it made the dryads beam all the more. One of them replied, and Zasian nodded.

"They are more than happy to lead us where we need to go," he explained to his companions. "But they would welcome us to their village as guests first. They have invited us to rest and partake of whatever meager fare they can provide."

As if it somehow understood, Myshik's stomach let out a pronounced rumble.

Zasian and the dryads chuckled. "I think they're taking that as a yes," the priest said.

"Is that truly necessary?" Kashada grumbled. She did not relish the idea of spending any more time than needed among the pesky creatures. She was already fighting the urge to fling their infuriating little hands away from herself. "We will lose precious time."

Zasian turned toward her. "It is, in fact," he said, "for reasons you will come to understand soon enough."

Kashada sighed, thankful that her veil hid the frown she knew she wore. His smugness and condescension were wearing thin. "I suppose a bit of rest would do me good," she said, hoping she sounded agreeable. "My body's just not used to all this activity after so long confined within my prison." She batted her eyes at the priest, hoping he got her little dig.

Zasian's level stare told her he had, but otherwise, he did not react. "Very well, then," he said, turning to the dryads. He said something with a warm smile, and the dryads eagerly led the three of them into the village.

❖ ❖ ❖ ❖ ❖ ❖ ❖ ❖ ❖

The entire population of the little woodland community could not have numbered more than two dozen or so, but they were more than enough to make the tiny hut feel crammed beyond reason after a couple more of Zasian's charming spells brought them all merrily under his sway. The dryads prepared a simple meal for their guests that consisted of some type of greenish paste served on sections of thick leaves and garnished with giant ant abdomens.

Kashada watched as Myshik looked at his for a few moments, then shrugged and grabbed up an ant abdomen. He split the carapace with his teeth, sucked out the soft flesh within, then used half of it as a scoop to shovel mouthfuls of the green stuff as fast as he could past his lips and tongue. He hardly seemed to taste the fare at all.

Kashada tried not to make a face as she turned to Zasian. "The fact that he seems to think it delicious gives me pause," she said. "What exactly is this?"

The priest looked thoughtful as he finished a bite, then he said, "I think it's some sort of fermented moss." Kashada nodded and had a bite halfway to her mouth when he added, "But it also might be caterpillar flesh."

Kashada did make a face, then, and she set the food back down uneaten. "I am no longer hungry," she said as gently as she could. "Perhaps one of you two would like to finish mine? I think I'd like to rest for a bit, now."

Myshik had his face pressed against his leaf, licking the last dregs of the paste from it. "I'll take yours," he said. He leaned over and snatched the leaf from her lap and began devouring it.

Zasian laughed. "Suit yourself," he said. "There will be plenty to eat that's more to your liking when we get where we are going next."

Kashada rose to her feet and glared down at the priest. "Just let me know when it's time to go," she said, hoping her sour tone conveyed her overall displeasure. "The sooner, the better."

At a word from Zasian, two of the dryads took Kashada by the hands. The mystic allowed them to lead her out of the overcrowded hut. She was forced to tread carefully so as to avoid stepping on anyone's feet. She followed her escort along a curving, swaying rope bridge to another shelter.

Not rope, Kashada realized as she ran her hand along one of the flexible rails of the bridge. What is this? Woven silk? Webbing? How odd!

The dryads showed her into the hut, where a soft mat made of more of the thick, soft leafy material lay in the middle of it. They gestured and said several things, but Kashada just tried to smile and nod, then shooed them out of her way.

She lay down on the mat, and weariness washed over her at once. She had not realized how exhausted she was until that moment. She knew she would not be able to sleep so long as the constant, silvery glow of the environment intruded on her. The chattering dryad dinner party a stone's throw away only made it worse.

Kashada gestured and muttered a phrase of arcane power. The illusory shadows surrounding her grew and thickened. She gestured again, and the shadows wrapped themselves around her like a cocoon. Once safely inside their embrace, Kashada smiled and drifted off.

❖ ❖ ❖ ❖ ❖ ❖ ❖ ❖

Kashada did not know how long she had slept when she came awake to gentle shaking. Disorientation made her start, but she gathered her wits quickly and unfurled her shadows to see who was disturbing her rest.

Zasian loomed over her. "It's time," he said softly. "There is work to do."

Kashada sat up, rubbing her eyes. "Very well," she said. "Give me a moment to collect myself."

Zasian rocked back and stood up. "Take a few moments," he said. "Myshik and I are journeying on ahead, but I want you to remain behind for a bit longer."

Kashada gave the priest a sharp glare. "What scheme are you concocting? This was not part of our plan."

Zasian gestured in the air, trying to reassure her. "I only want to get a little bit ahead, so that our guides cannot see what you are doing."

Kashada did not stop glaring. "And what would that be?"

Zasian smiled. "I want you to leave behind a little surprise for our pursuers," he said. "Something to make sure they don't catch up too fast, but also to make it clear that they are on the right path."

Kashada thought for a moment, then she returned the priest's smile. "I think I know just what to do."

Zasian and Myshik departed with a pair of dryads to guide them along their way. Before leaving, the priest had explained to the remaining dryads that Kashada wished to remain for a while longer in order to learn how to prepare the fermented moss.

You will pay for that, Kashada fumed. She watched as her companions departed, then she turned to her hosts. They had gathered together, cooking supplies in hand, and awaited her with eager, expectant expressions. She resisted rolling her eyes and motioned for them to begin.

The dryads swarmed around, chattering and laughing incessantly. Kashada pretended to watch. She began a spell, keeping her movements subtle and whispering the arcane words. The shadows draped across her body darkened and spread out. They grew thicker, more rigid, more substantial. They cocooned her body, but unlike before, when she had manipulated them merely to aid in her rest, the new ones hardened and formed a shell of darkness. She breathed another phrase, and the gloom deepened. It began to glow very faintly in the silvery light of the plane, a purple hue that was nearly black.

One of the dryads stopped her work and stared at Kashada, mouth agape. When she noticed the mystic returning her gaze, her eyes grew wide and she cowered, shouting something in a shrill voice. The other fey creatures halted their tasks. Some watched their guest, dumbfounded, while others began to scramble to escape her presence.

Kashada smiled, then she laughed. "It's much too late for that," she said. Then she uttered the final phrase of her spell.

The purple-black shadows expanded from her body in

a great sphere. The dryads shrieked and tried to flee. One attempted to meld into the great branch upon which the tree-house had been constructed. Another dived toward an open window to escape. Most of the rest flailed and clamored to slip through the doorways.

None were fast enough.

The blackness engulfed all of the dryads. Its boundary soared outward, catching each and every one of the elflike women in its embrace. They wailed and babbled in their odd, woodland language and staggered around, blind. Kashada laughed, for she could still see. The world had turned a beautiful, shadowy plum to her eyes.

One dryad shuffled toward Kashada, a small dagger in her hand. The dryad felt for the woman, and Kashada did nothing to evade her. When her hand brushed against Kashada's arm, the dryad stabbed at her, trying to ram the dagger deep into the mystic's flesh.

The blade struck shadowstuff and snapped.

The dryad wailed in dismay and fell away again.

The dryads thrashed and flailed as the arcane gloom did its work. Tendrils of the stuff wrapped around limbs, encircled waists, coiled around necks. It grappled with those trapped inside it, enveloping them with darker, firmer umbra.

Kashada laughed as the fey fought against the snaking tendrils. She smiled as the one who had tried to stab her clutched at her own throat, gasping for breath. Kashada walked among them, watching in delight as one by one the dryads' struggles grew weaker, then stopped altogether. The shadowstuff continued to wind itself around them like black, gauzy funeral wrappings. Tighter and tighter it wove, until each dryad was nothing more than an oblong lump of black within the purple nightworld Kashada had created with her magic.

Finally, the spell finished its work and vanished, returning the surroundings to their original silvery hue and brightness. Kashada sighed. She had so enjoyed watching the transformation. It had been particularly satisfying to see the wretched fey succumb to her magic. She was only sorry there hadn't been more of them to ensnare. All in all, though, she was content.

She spoke, then, in a language few would understand in the normal world. Her voice carried, ringing loudly and clearly to pierce the veils of shimmering shadow that still surrounded the dryads. "My pets," she said, "I have a task for you. Others come along the path that I followed to arrive here. You will wait and watch for them, and when they appear, you will destroy them."

Before she left, Kashada took up flint and steel and ignited a bit of tinder. She then lit an oil-soaked rag wrapped around one of her long-bladed daggers and walked among the tree houses, setting them ablaze. She fired the strange, silky ropes that made up the bridges and ladders. She looked back once and watched as the little dryad community became charred ruins.

❖ ❖ ❖ ❖ ❖ ❖ ❖ ❖

Kaanyr sat cross-legged and stared at the ground. The sullen glare he had leveled at his two guards had done nothing to make him feel any better, so he gave it up. That and the fact that holding his head up while it was encased in so much iron exhausted him. The strange harness held a thick metal brank in place in his mouth, keeping his tongue flattened so that he had no way of speaking. Kaanyr's jailors had locked the thing behind his head, where he could not see.

Even if he could study the security, it wouldn't make a difference. Thick leather bags wrapped tightly around his hands kept them secure, as well. He sensed that he was clenching some sort of round object, like a ball, in each hand, which forced them into fists. He could barely move his fingers within the confines of the bags. To further restrain him, they had fastened metal manacles to his wrists, and those were locked to a metal belt that encircled his waist.

There was no way he was going to work the brank harness free, even if he could see the fastener.

Nor could he unlock the thick chain that held him fast, one end around his neck, the other around a large tree. His jailors were taking no chances.

The hound archons who had captured Kaanyr had said nothing to him. He came to from his blackout feeling woozy and disoriented. It took a few moments for him to remember where he was. By that time, the warriors had subdued him with rope and threats of worse if he even tried to resist them. Other than that, they simply escorted him back to the clearing where the ambush had begun.

No one's even asked me any questions, Vhok thought. Wasn't that why they wanted to capture us so badly? To see what we know about Zasian?

Recalling the traitorous priest made Kaanyr scowl. The cambion still couldn't decide at whom he was angrier. Though most of his woes could be traced back to Zasian's underhanded manipulation, Kaanyr knew he was still responsible for setting the events in motion in the first place.

Aliisza was right, he thought glumly. I became so caught up in seizing Sundabar from Helm Dwarf-friend that I grew careless. But they're still bastards. All of them. Zasian and Helm can rot in the Abyss. And Tauran and Kael. And Micus and Tyr. All of them! And you can toss that no-good alu in with them, too.

Kaanyr had spent the first part of his captivity anticipating a rescue from Aliisza, but as the time dragged by and it grew dark, he began to doubt that she would return for him. The logical part of him realized there was no way his lover could overwhelm an entire camp of astral devas and their hound archon minions. That would just get them both caught.

But damn it, I want her to try! I'm still supposed to matter to her, despite what happened here. It's still her, isn't it?

Kaanyr snorted then, an expression of resignation. *Of course it's still her. And she's long gone by now. She and her two holier-than-thou fops have left me here to rot. Hells, I would have done the same thing to her.*

"Good evening, Vhok," an angel said as he approached the cambion. "I imagine you are hungry." He was one of the two who had captured him earlier.

An archon stood behind the deva holding a tray of something that smelled delicious. He set it on the ground near Kaanyr as the angel squatted down next to the cambion.

"I want to take this brank harness off you, Vhok, but if I do, I have to have your vow that you will not speak, only eat. We can't have you attempting to cast any spells. Do you understand?"

Kaanyr eyed the food, which consisted of a thick slice of roasted meat, a slab of cheese, a hunk of bread, and some berries still on a snip of vine. The aroma of the meat and bread made his mouth water, but he hated giving in so easily to the wretched celestials. He looked away from the tray and back at the angel and made no gesture at all.

"If I don't get your promise, I can't let you eat," the deva said. "I know you must be very angry right now, but there's no point in refusing our food. I have nothing personal against you, half-fiend—beside the obvious issue of your base nature, of course—but you have broken the laws of the Court, and I have a job to complete. Now, do you want to eat or not?"

Nothing personal indeed, Kaanyr thought. *If I wasn't wearing all this iron, I'd wipe that self-important grin off your face.* He still made no effort to convey an answer.

"Very well," the angel said, rising. "I'll leave the food right over here and you can think about it." He walked off then, followed by the archon who had brought the tray. Kaanyr watched the two of them go and sniffed loudly to express his disdain. His two guards paid no attention to him, so Kaanyr went back to studying the ground in front of him.

Though he tried to ignore it, the smell of the roasted meat haunted him, and when the angel returned a little while later, Kaanyr began to have second thoughts about his stoic resistance.

What difference does it make if I eat? he asked himself. *It doesn't change anything.*

The angel paused. "Having a change of heart?" he asked.

Kaanyr nodded, albeit reluctantly.

"Very well," the angel said, smiling. "I have your promise that you won't say anything if I remove the harness?"

Again Kaanyr nodded.

"Good, good. Now, if you decide to break your vow, I'll be forced to speak the divine word of power we used before to subdue you, and I really don't want to have to do that. So please be agreeable."

Kaanyr sighed in resignation and nodded a third time.

"Now," the angel said as he reached around behind the cambion, "I'm going to have to feed this to you, because we just can't risk freeing your hands." Kaanyr could feel and hear a click as the harness loosened. The deva pulled the vile metal from Kaanyr's mouth. As he did so, the two guards went a little stiffer, warier, watching him.

The cambion ignored them as the angel held out the meat. Kaanyr eyed the beef, juicy and lean, but he hated having to be fed like a helpless child. He grimaced and hesitated.

"I know this must be demeaning, I really do," the angel said in a sincere tone. "But this is the price you pay for your choices in life. Now, go ahead."

There will be a price for you to pay, too, Kaanyr thought.

He leaned forward and grudgingly took a bite from the meat. It practically melted in his mouth, it was so lean and tender. The cambion began to tear huge bites from the well-seasoned beef, gulping it down. Bits of gravy and juice ran down his chin, but he didn't care. In no time at all, he had finished the meat.

The angel grabbed up the cheese and the bread, holding one in each hand. Kaanyr no longer cared how shameful he looked. He tore into the food with a ravenous hunger.

How long has it been since I've had such a good meal? he asked himself. *The spreads we had within the magical mansion,* he realized. *Too long.*

The thought crossed his mind that the food might be poisoned in some way, but he dismissed that notion quickly.

If they wanted to slay me, they wouldn't have gone to all the trouble to bind me in this manner. Besides, angels don't do that sort of thing. Then the idea occurred to Kaanyr that they might not try to kill him but make him more compliant. *A truth serum or suggestive magic,* he realized. He stopped chewing as the cold thought washed over him. *You're a fool, Kaanyr Vhok.*

"What is it?" the angel asked, puzzled. "Full already? Head movements only, please."

Kaanyr wanted to spit the tainted food out, spit it right at the angel. Instead, he just grimaced.

"Don't want to answer? Very well, if you're done . . ." The angel replaced the remnants of the bread and cheese on the tray. "I guess we'll save the rest of this for later, then." He set the food aside and picked up the brank harness. "This has to go on, though, my friend. No arguments."

Kaanyr glowered at the angel, but the threat of divine magic was real enough, so with an exasperated sigh, the cambion opened his mouth and allowed the hated thing to gag him once more. When the angel had secured it behind Kaanyr's head, he stood.

"You cooperated very nicely, Vhok," the deva said. "I'm sorry it has to be this way, I truly am. I will mention this to Micus when he returns. Maybe it will reflect favorably upon you when it comes time to bring you before the High Council. But that is not for me to promise."

The angel turned to stride away, but at that moment, a commotion erupted from just behind Kaanyr.

The angel turned back that way and his eyes widened the slightest bit. "Micus," he said, standing a bit straighter. "What news?"

"We have all three of them in custody," Micus said, flying into view and settling to the ground. He looked down at Kaanyr. "They're being taken back to the Court now. I want to take him there as soon as possible."

The other angel looked confused. "But you said that we—"

"I know what I said before! Things have changed! They tried to ambush us near the entrance to the World Tree.

They didn't realize we knew they were there, so we were ready for them. I want to get them all back to the High Council, get this distasteful job finished as quickly as possible. Now, get him unchained so I can take him with me! Don't bother with that gag, just get him free of the post."

"Of course, Micus," the other angel said. He reached down and began to fidget with the lock keeping the chain on Kaanyr's neck. "Shall I send an escort with you?" he asked Micus as he unlocked the restraint. "Or do you have some other means of transporting him?"

"Is he still wearing the dimensional shackles?"

"He is," the angel answered.

"Remove them," Micus said.

The other angel paused. "You said we should not remove those shackles under any circumstances," he said, suspicion plain on his face. "What is going on, Micus?"

"By Tyr, do I have to do everything myself?" Micus said in exasperation. He stalked toward Kaanyr and grabbed at the cambion's wrists. "I said I wanted to move fast. Don't you listen?"

"Don't let him do that!" the other angel ordered. "That's not Micus!"

Kaanyr gave the other deva an incredulous look, and then peered at Micus. The deva's eyes were wide, looking right at him. They had a familiar shape to them.

Aliisza!

Kaanyr thrust his shackled hands toward the disguised alu. Over her shoulder, he could see the two archons hesitating, unsure what to do.

Aliisza reached down and took hold of the clasps of the shackles and snapped them open. At the same time, the other angel lunged toward them, trying to grab hold of the false

Micus. When the shackles came free, the alu wrenched them from Kaanyr's waist and let them drop to the ground. Then she kicked backward with one leg, catching the deva squarely in the chest. The force of the blow sent her forward, right into Kaanyr, and knocked him backward.

The cambion expected to crack his head upon the bole of the tree he had been chained to, but instead, he found himself falling through a magical portal. Both he and Aliisza tumbled through the doorway, but the two hound archons were a step too slow.

The portal winked out, leaving his guards and the angel behind.

"Hurry!" Aliisza hissed softly, scrambling to her feet. She shifted from the image of Micus back into her natural form as other hands struggled with the bonds that still held Kaanyr.

The cambion looked up to see Tauran and Kael crouching over him, working frantically to free him. He saw that the four of them were in a small hollow surrounded by short but steep ridges. The moonlight made the still-heavy mist glow, creating a veiled backdrop to their hiding place.

When Tauran managed to slip the brank harness from Kaanyr's mouth, the cambion let out a soft groan. "Thanks," he said, and he meant it. "Throw that thing far, far away."

"Keep your voice down," Kael said, working to slip one of the leather bags free of Kaanyr's hand. "Micus and his coterie are not far off."

The cambion nodded. "I'm surprised you came back for me," he whispered. "That was a big risk, by all of you." He shifted his gaze from one face to the next. "Why?"

Tauran cocked his head to one side. "I gave you my word," he whispered back. "It was the only thing *to* do."

Kaanyr thought on that for a moment. It was hard to wrap

his mind around. He shrugged and nodded. "Well then, I thank you for keeping your word. I'm not so used to people doing that."

Tauran gave him a quick nod in return.

When the other three finally had him unbound, he sat up and stretched aching muscles. "What's the plan?" he asked, rising to his knees. "Where now?"

Tauran pointed to something out of sight beyond the nearest ridge. "Micus and a patrol are guarding the passage through to the World Tree just over there," he said. "They are hiding, setting up an ambush. Of course, the camp will get word to them very quickly that we've managed to free you, so we have to get through there now, before they're alerted."

"How do you propose we slip past them?" the cambion asked as the four of them crept to the crest of the ridge and peered over. Kaanyr could see nothing but trees and mist.

"The same way we got you out of there," Aliisza whispered.

"We don't have much time," Tauran said. "Once that doorway opens on their end, they're going to know what we're trying to do. They will do everything they can to block us from escaping. You and Aliisza are more vulnerable to Micus's divine magic, so you're first. Don't look back, just run."

Kaanyr opened his mouth to query the angel on a few more points, but a light appeared in the misty gloom a stone's throw away.

"Lantern archon," Tauran said, "coming to inform them. Time to go."

Nodding, Kaanyr saw Aliisza turn and summon one of the red-tinged doorways directly in front of them. A shout arose from the direction of the enemy before Kaanyr even had a chance to step through it.

"They see the other end!" Tauran said. "Go!"

Kaanyr reached for Burnblood and the Scepter Malevolous as he stepped through. He only realized once he was on the other side that he no longer had his enchanted weapons. Lamenting their loss, he took a couple of paces forward and spotted a narrow tunnel directly ahead of him. He cast a quick glance over his shoulder and saw Aliisza come through the doorway right behind him. Beyond her doorway, past the mouth of the tight canyon in which they stood, he could see the glow of lights and could hear more shouting.

"Go!" Aliisza urged him, pushing him forward. "Into the tunnel!"

Kaanyr hated leaving his treasures behind, but he knew it was a fool's errand to try to retrieve them at that point.

I'll be back for them, he vowed, then he ducked into the cramped tunnel and fled.

CHAPTER ELEVEN

Micus stood in the middle of the clearing, surveying the area. The archons had performed suitable funeral rites upon the bodies of the elves and ghaeles and were almost finished freeing Tekthyrios's corpse from the jagged tree. The angel watched it all, his heart heavy.

"Explain what happened, Garin," he said.

The other angel standing beside him exhaled. "She came in disguise, appearing as you," he said. "She acted a bit peculiar, but not so much that I was suspicious, at least not at first. When she insisted that you had caught the other three and were ready to take them all back to the Court, I freed him enough to allow her to escape with him. By the time I realized what was going on, it was too late to stop them. I'm sorry, Micus."

"No, my friend," Micus said. "Do not apologize. The fault is mine. I should have expected some trickery from them." Then he added, half to himself, "Even from Tauran." The angel scuffed his foot in the dirt. "He has fallen so far in such a short time. I should never assume that any part of our doctrine is still sacred to him. I was the fool."

"What are you going to do now?"

"That is not for me to decide. I must report my failure to the High Council."

"Your heart is heavy, Micus," Garin said. "You have experienced setbacks before in your quest to bring goodness to the cosmos, and I've never seen you so grim. What is troubling you?"

Micus sighed and weighed his next words carefully. "There is a part of me that regrets all of this, Garin," he said. "There is a part of me that thinks Tauran might be right, and that he's the only one who can see the truth of the matter."

"Truly?" the other angel asked, surprise clear in his voice. "You honestly believe that?"

"It doesn't change a thing," Micus said. "I still have my duties. But yes, I suspect we're all in for much more grief."

"And that's why you're sad?" Garin asked. "Because you dread what is to come?"

"Partially," Micus answered. "But also because, even if he's proven right, Tauran is lost to us. He has betrayed everything we stand for. And I grieve for him when he realizes it."

❖ ❖ ❖ ❖ ❖ ❖ ❖ ❖

"How are you certain Zasian came this way?" Kaanyr asked. The cambion trudged along behind Tauran, who was leading the group. Aliisza followed Kaanyr, and Kael brought up the rear.

As they hiked, the alu surveyed the surrounding terrain. To her, it seemed like they followed the crest of a great ridge that stretched on indefinitely in each direction, swallowed up in the odd, silvery haze that surrounded them. To either side, the ridge became a gentle slope dropping away. The path they followed passed through largely open ground, spotted in places with the occasional copse of trees or scrub. No sky showed through, nor any sense of the direction of the sun. Everything seemed isolated, enclosed in the mist.

"There are really only two ways they could have gone," the angel said over his shoulder. "And this path leads to other places. If we had followed the other direction, we would eventually find ourselves on the tip of this great branch, at a dead end."

"How can you even be sure he walked?" the cambion retorted. "For all we know, Zasian magically transported himself in an instant. I've seen the kind of divine power he wields. I know his methods."

"For the same reason we can't just fly to where we want to go," Tauran replied. "It's too easy to get lost in the Astral plane if you leave the branches. The World Tree has bizarre properties; geography doesn't work on it the way you think it should. He didn't whisk himself away magically."

"We never even determined who else was with Zasian when he passed from the House," Kael said as he trudged along behind Aliisza. "Those other sets of bootprints continued right into the passageway we took to escape. I checked."

"You could see prints on the ground, in the dark, while running," Aliisza said. It was more of an incredulous statement than a question.

She could hear the half-drow chuckle softly behind her. "I inherited my father's eyes, too, you know," he said. "But the ground was very soft there, and it was easy to make out."

"So who is it?" Aliisza asked.

"That is a question that will have to wait a while," Tauran said. "Until we catch up to Zasian."

"The important thing to remember is that he has allies," Kaanyr said. "Wherever Zasian is going, he could accumulate even more. We must be on watch."

"A fine point," Tauran said. "And one that we should . . ." The angel's voice trailed off and he slowed to a stop, a look of unease on his face.

The rest of the group caught up to him and peered where he stared into the gloom ahead. Aliisza could not make out much, but the air was filled with a cloud of gray, something slightly darker than the surrounding silver.

"What is that?" she asked.

"I don't know," Tauran replied, still staring. "But I fear it does not bode well for us."

"We should not all approach it," Kael said. "It could be dangerous, or even a trap laid for us."

"I'll scout it out," Kaanyr said.

The offer caught Aliisza by surprise. She stole a look at her companion and noted that his expression seemed genuine. He was frowning as he stared at the smudge of blackness in the distance, but he sensed her stare and turned to look at her.

"What?" he asked. "I can avoid being seen when I wish it. You know that."

"Yes, of course. But since when have you volunteered to do anything around here?"

Kaanyr's smirk was fleeting. "Since the three of you came back for me," he said. At Aliisza's widening eyes, he added, "I've come to figure that perhaps the best way to survive this escapade is to make sure it succeeds. Don't go thinking I'm getting all soft and caring, fool girl. I just don't want to spend the rest of my days trapped here."

Tauran studied the cambion for a moment. "Very well," he said. "Sneak up a little way and see what you can find out. But at the first sign of something dangerous, you slip away again and return. No exceptions."

Kaanyr's smirk returned. "Well, since you put it that

way, I guess I have no choice, do I?" he said. "I'll be back in a moment. Make yourselves comfortable." With that, the cambion slipped away, quickly disappearing among the lush growth.

Kael led the three of them down into a partially concealed hollow surrounded by scrub brush and trees. He sat and pulled a bundle free of one of his satchels. He unpacked some dried meat from it and popped a chunk into his mouth. He held the bundle out to Tauran, but the angel just shook his head. Kael next proffered some of the meat to Aliisza. She took a couple of thick strips and nodded in thanks.

Tauran turned away and found an outcropping of rock. He plopped down on it and hunched over, placing his face in his hands. The weariness in his body made him wilt in the alu's eyes. He sat there unmoving for several moments.

"Rest, my friend," Kael said, rising to his feet again. "You've pushed yourself hard and need the respite."

"I'll be fine," Tauran mumbled. "Everyone else is tired too."

"Tauran, I mean it," Kael said. "The grief wears you down. I know. I've been there."

Aliisza started when she heard that. She looked up at her son's face. What have you grieved for? she wondered. Me, perhaps? That thought strangely comforted her.

"Please," Kael said. "You're no good to us exhausted. I'll keep watch for a while."

Tauran sighed. "Very well, but only for a few moments. Wake me when Vhok returns."

With that, the angel slid down from his rocky seat and stretched himself on the ground, using the stone for a pillow.

"I won't be far," Kael said to Aliisza softly. "I'll stay in sight. You can rest too, if you want." He turned and climbed out of the little depression and walked a few paces out from it, where he proceeded to begin circumnavigating in a casual stroll.

Aliisza watched her son for a few moments, but his gaze seemed always outward, away from their hidden haven. He was an enigma to her, and one that piqued her curiosity in new ways every day. *For what do you truly grieve?* she pondered again.

Aliisza turned her attention to Tauran. The angel lay still, and the alu wondered for a moment if he actually slept, but just when she decided that he must be dozing, he sighed and shifted around. In his new position, Aliisza had a better look at his face, and what she saw wounded her. Lines furrowed his expression, and his eyes seemed clouded and watery. He stared at nothing, sadness radiating from him.

Aliisza got up and moved close to the deva. She knelt down next to him and took hold of his face. He raised it up to look at her, and she leaned forward to kiss him on the forehead.

"Aliisza, I can't—"

The alu placed her finger upon her lips. "Shh," she said softly. She guided his head toward her and urged him to place it upon her lap. "Just rest," she whispered. "Close your eyes."

She began to stroke the angel's head, then, twining her fingers in his golden locks. Occasionally she would run her hand down the back of his neck, squeezing gently in a reassuring way.

At first, Tauran lay rigid, his body stiff and his muscles corded. He couldn't seem to get comfortable. After a time, and with Aliisza's gentle caresses, he began to relax. He let out a series of small sighs, and his body seemed to melt into hers and into the ground. In another few moments, his breathing had become the slow and even exhalations of one asleep.

I can't begin to imagine what you've sacrificed for this,

Aliisza thought. Or even why you would do it. Nothing can be worth that, can it?

Thoughts of the lessons he had tried to teach her, when she had been his prisoner, crossed Aliisza's mind. *The only way to truly know love is to give in to it,* she recalled. *You have to be willing to expose yourself, make yourself vulnerable, to reap the rewards.*

Whom do you love so much? Tyr? Is a god worth loving like that?

A pang of jealousy hit Aliisza. She wasn't sure why she would be jealous of Tauran's love for Tyr, but slowly, as she dug deeper into the emotion, she realized that she wanted the angel's love for herself.

Why not me? she thought. *Am I any less deserving of that kind of devotion and dedication? At least I'm not some lofty, mysterious, obscure being no one understands,* she sniffed.

And I would love you back, she silently told the angel. *I would give you everything you ever wanted. Let's just leave this place, find a home somewhere, and love each other.*

"What are you doing?" Kaanyr asked, quietly entering the hollow. Kael stood right behind him, peering over the cambion's shoulder.

Aliisza started at Vhok's sudden appearance. "Nothing," she said as Tauran stirred and sat up. The angel looked first at Aliisza, then he followed her gaze to Kaanyr.

The cambion's stare was emotionless, and at the same time, his eyes glittered dangerously. He looked at Aliisza for a long time.

The alu swallowed, wondering why she felt guilty. *What have I done?*

Kaanyr turned his attention to Tauran. "It's smoke," he said, his voice a bit colder than usual. "There's some sort of village up there, and it's been burning. I see no signs of life."

"Oh, no," Tauran muttered, rising to his feet. "We must go there, see if anyone survives."

Kaanyr shrugged, then turned to look at Aliisza once more.

The alu shuddered beneath his pointed stare. At the same time, she felt herself growing cross with Tauran. He seemed oblivious to Kaanyr's displeasure. Why? Why does that bother me?

Because he wasn't thinking of you enough even to feel guilty, she realized. Damned angel. Damn both of you! she fumed.

The cambion turned and walked past Kael back out of the hollow.

The half-drow shifted his stare back and forth between the angel and the alu. His expression was grim, and he shook his head in disapproval. Aliisza climbed to her feet as Tauran pushed past Kael, his focus turned entirely on whatever was burning.

The alu returned her son's stare for a moment. "What?" she said. "You, too? What is your problem?"

"Leave him be," Kael said. "He doesn't need your wicked, twisted games playing with his head right now. He has enough to deal with."

Aliisza barely restrained herself from slapping his face. "You have no idea what you're talking about," she said. "Stay out of it." I'm your mother, she silently added. How dare you speak to me that way. But the words rang false, even in her own mind.

"I won't," Kael said. "I watch his back for him, and I'm not going to let you hurt him." With that, the half-drow turned away and left the hollow.

Aliisza bit back the insult she wanted to hurl after him

and instead took a deep, calming breath. Then she understood something, and she almost laughed. *That's not it at all, my son*, she thought. *What you really mean is, you won't let me hurt* you. *I've become a threat. You don't want to share.* The thought almost made her laugh again, but there was a deeper emotion, too. Hurt. *You can't see room in your life for two parents.*

That realization made her clench her teeth till they hurt. She climbed up and out through the scrub into the open.

Tauran was already at the head of the group, walking briskly in the direction of the black smudge, which had dissipated somewhat since they had first spotted it. Kaanyr was right behind him, and Kael's rapid strides were catching him up to the other two.

All three of them, leaving me behind, Aliisza thought wryly, trying to make herself feel better. *Isn't that always the way with men?*

The alu hurried after them.

❖ ❖ ❖ ❖ ❖ ❖ ❖ ❖

Tauran led them to the outskirts of a tree-house village. He didn't hesitate to enter it, walking along the ground beneath the dwellings high overhead. Much of the place was in ruins, and Aliisza noted that many of the means to get up into the bowers of the trees had been destroyed or removed. The singed remains of rope ladders and bridges hung uselessly down from the structures, out of reach of those on the ground.

"Damn him," Tauran murmured, gazing around helplessly. "He didn't have to do this."

"Where is everyone?" Aliisza wondered. "There aren't even any bodies."

"Oh, by Torm," Kael muttered softly. He reached for his sword.

The other three followed his stare upward into the trees.

There, scrambling down the thick trunks like strange, smoky spiders, were shadowy beings. They looked human in shape, though they crawled on hands and feet. They had no real faces, only red, glowing eyes. Aliisza could hear a strange sound emanating from them, a kind of hissing.

When they dropped to the ground, they charged the four visitors and those hisses became unnatural howls of misery, rage, and death.

❖ ❖ ❖ ❖ ❖ ❖ ❖ ❖

Kael took a single step back and rotated away from the nearest of the shadowy assailants. Its red eyes glared, but Kael could tell the creature had once been a dryad, a fey being native to the World Tree. Whatever magic had been used to slay her had transformed her into a force of dark and evil hatred, bent only on his destruction.

The half-drow's maneuver brought him just far enough back to evade her lunging attack, and as she leaped through the point in space where he had stood a moment before, Kael completed the pivot, bringing his sword up and around to slash at her from behind. The blade glided easily through her shadowy, insubstantial form, its divine enchantment crackling against her malevolence.

The shrieking wail of the shadow-dryad rose in pitch, changing from a scream of fury to one of agony. She arched her back as she tumbled through the apex of her leap, landed awkwardly, and went sprawling. She stumbled as she tried to right herself.

Kael was still angry, but he didn't want to be. Seeing his mother within that glade, entwined around Tauran, had infuriated him, but he shouldn't have allowed it to creep into his thoughts and disrupt his concentration. Yet that's just what was happening. He could not get the image out of his head. He felt . . . something. Something he could not name.

Two more of the disfigured dryads rushed at him. They began their charge shoulder to shoulder, but as they drew closer, the twin phantoms diverged so as to come at him from either side. Kael adopted a defensive stance, blade out and to his left side. As the left-hand creature leaped at him, he shifted forward, dragging the blade up and under his foe. The sword raked her from knee to shoulder without any resistance at all as she passed him. He fought to control the momentum of the heavy blade, unused to dealing with incorporeal opponents.

As he fought to regain his balance, the other shadow-dryad struck his shoulder and raked her claws against his armor. Though the holy protection of his plate mail repelled most of the blow, he felt a numbing cold pour into his flesh. Kael grunted and swung his blade the rest of the way around as he shrugged her off. The sword came down hard upon her back, passing completely through her torso as she tumbled in a heap.

Learning from the fight as he went, Kael let the momentum of his strike carry the blade down hard to the ground. He used it as a brace to spin himself back the other way, then hefted the weapon into a defensive position and surveyed his foes.

The two abominations that had just assailed him writhed upon the ground, shrieking in pain. The first creature that had rushed at him circled, wary of the magic of his blade.

He shifted to keep her in front of him and checked on his companions.

Aliisza and Vhok had taken positions back to back, each with a weapon in hand. The cambion wielded a pair of enchanted daggers the alu had given him after the loss of his own blade. Three shadowy dryads circled them. On the far side, Tauran stood before two more of the transformed fey, his shining mace gripped in both hands. One lunged at him and he batted it away with a well-placed blow to the head.

A dozen more bounded down from the trees above, rushing to join the battle.

"Let us just fly away and be done with this!" Vhok snarled as he sliced at one of the creatures opposing him. "This isn't getting us any closer to Zasian!"

"We cannot leave these poor, cursed creatures as they are," Tauran replied, panting as he swung his mace back and forth in large arcs. "They must be put out of their misery."

Vhok snorted and slashed with both his daggers at the nearest of the shadowy beings. He struck her squarely in the chest and head. Her wail of rage split the air as she fell back, clawing at the wounds. "Get your priorities straight, fool angel," he grumbled as he turned to slash at another of the things attacking him. "We're no good to you butchered by these wretches."

So much for the new and improved helpful cambion, Kael thought. *Though I can't imagine he's very happy to see Aliisza and Tauran cuddling, either.*

"Nonetheless," the angel replied with a hint of disdain, "I will not suffer such twisted abominations to live. They deserve death rather than a cruel existence such as this."

And you don't even see what's going on, Kael thought of Tauran. *You don't even see the way she looks at you!*

The one circling Kael chose that moment to attack him, and the half-drow was forced to shift his attention back to the work at hand. He swung his sword at her as she darted in, only to discover too late that her attack had been a feint. The momentum of his swing carried him around and past her, and she leaped high toward his head.

Kael staggered as he tried to slide out of the way. His movement carried him out of reach of her black, gleaming talons, but the other two he had wounded rejoined the fight, and both of them took advantage of his unbalanced state to slip inside his weapon's reach.

Idiot! Concentrate!

The three of them became a blurred whirl of inky howls and slashing pain as they swarmed Kael. He tried to swipe at them with his sword, but the weapon was simply too bulky to use in such close quarters. He cast the sword aside and swung his mailed fists instead.

As he punched at the three horrific creatures battling him, Kael felt a more righteous anger swell within him.

Kael murmured a prayer to Torm, calling on the Loyal Fury's blessings to aid him in his fight.

Torm heeded Kael's call.

A bit of the deity's divine essence coursed through the half-drow. Kael felt glorious strength and holy wrath overtake him. With renewed vigor, he slammed his armored fists left and right, landing preternaturally powerful blows upon the shadow-dryads. Each strike burst with spiritual light and energy and sent the battle-crazed creatures scattering and yowling in anguish.

Kael strode to his sword and picked it up. Brandishing it, he roared, "I am punishment incarnate!" His voice, magically amplified, reverberated across the battlefield.

The three grotesque fey flinched and fell back from the divine knight.

Kael swung the blade once. He turned to the nearest of the three sprawled horrors. "Feel my wrath!" he bellowed.

The thing screeched and scrambled to escape.

Kael lunged.

The blade whistled through the air, crackling with holy power. As it struck the shadow-dryad, a thunderous boom emanated from the point of impact, and blinding white light flashed. The shadow-thing let out a single ear-splitting scream and vanished in a burst of purplish smoke.

Kael roared in triumph and turned to the next of the three.

The two creatures jabbered in fright and turned to flee.

Before either of the creatures had covered five steps, Kael was on them, carving them apart with shattering, thundering blows. When he drew up and paused, neither one of the shadow-dryads remained.

Around Kael, the battle raged. Tauran and the two half-fiends worked furiously, staving off a multitude of the things as they continued to swarm. Several of the creatures came at him.

Kael advanced to meet them, the thrill of divine power urging him forward. Gone was his petulance. Gone was the sense of betrayal, the jealousy—yes, that's what he had felt, he knew—at seeing his mentor and his mother comforting one another. In their places, there was only the fulfilling glory of Torm's divine might.

Kael stepped among the horde of twisted, cursed dryads, cutting and lunging with his blade. He moved through sword form after sword form, his motions swift, compact, and precise. Everywhere he turned, his blade parted the shadows, cleaving them into nothingness.

Conducting the battle required no more thinking on Kael's part. Each move was logical, the correct response to the previous step, the shifting of the opponents. Everything he did was a continuous flow of motion. He was a river maneuvering among the stones.

Each slice of Kael's blade connected with his enemies. The spiritual energy of Torm coursing through the sword blasted those enemies, ripping them apart and annihilating their shadowy flesh. Puffs of purplish smoke erupted around the divine champion as he carved his way through his foes.

The fight led the half-drow into the midst of his companions. As he conducted the battle, he worked in concert with the other three, attacking in unison with them to flank an opponent or catch it off balance.

Tauran drove one back within reach of Kael's blade, and Kael sent it to oblivion.

Vhok faced two at once, and Kael stepped between them, dispatching both in a fluid series of swings.

Aliisza became trapped within a gathering of three, and Kael ran to her side, going back to back with her until none remained to threaten her.

It was over. Kael drew his blade back for another devastating strike, and he had no more enemies to battle. All their foes had fallen. The twisted, cursed things were no more.

Yes! Thank you, blessed Torm. That's what it's all about.

With the danger past, his god's divine wrath left Kael and weariness crashed into the knight. He felt light-headed, barely able to stand, and numbing cold pulsed in half a dozen spots on his body—wounds taken during the fight. He sank to one knee, laying his sword at his side, and panted.

Aliisza also settled to the ground, sitting cross-legged. She stared wide-eyed at Kael. Vhok remained standing, though he breathed heavily and had to lean down with his hands on his knees. Tauran came down to one knee as well, though he immediately entered into a silent prayer, presumably for the immortal remains of the dispatched dryads.

"I hope we don't have to do *that* again," Vhok said between ragged breaths. He eyed the surroundings as though looking for more enemies. "It seemed like they would *never* stop coming!"

"Funny you should say that," Kael replied between hard breaths. "I was just starting to get into the moment, myself."

Tauran looked up from his completed prayer and frowned at Kael. "They rest now," he said quietly. "They are at peace. I pray we don't encounter any more warped souls like that." The comment seemed directed at the half-drow.

Vhok smirked and shrugged. "Well, good for them. I still say that was a fool's errand, angel. Clearly Zasian did that to slow us down. We played right into his hands by staying here and fighting. I thought you wanted to catch him."

"I'm not so sure that was his only purpose," Aliisza said. She shifted herself so that her legs stuck out as she leaned back on her hands.

"What do you mean?" Kael asked, finally beginning to catch his breath. "What other reason could he have for torturing those dryads, other than mere capriciousness? That seems counterproductive to his task." He felt calmer, serene. The battle had been good for him, he decided. A cleansing of the mind to remind him of his purpose.

"Aliisza's right," Tauran said with grim purpose. "Zasian is leaving a trail for us."

"A trail?" the half-drow asked. "Why?"

"Two reasons," the angel replied. "First, he wants to

make sure we know where he's going, make sure we can track him."

Aliisza nodded. "The slaying of the storm dragon right at the portal between the House and here," she said. "At first, I thought it was just a means of throwing us off the path, but it seemed odd to me that he would do that right there, where we would know which way he departed. Now it seems like a marker, a beacon left for us. Especially because he never bothered to hide his tracks."

"Left for us?" Vhok asked. His voice was full of doubt. "Why?"

"I don't know," Tauran said. "But clearly he wants us to follow him. Whatever his plans are, we are a part of them."

"And what is the other reason?" Kael asked.

Tauran's face grew grimmer still. "To reveal his power," the angel said. "To taunt me with the alliance he has formed."

"What are you talking about?" Vhok asked, impatient. "What alliance? And how do you know this?"

"The shadow creatures," the deva answered. "They are Shar's doing. Or rather, the doing of one of her most talented minions."

"Zasian didn't do that to them?" Aliisza asked.

Tauran shook his head. "No. I'm sure it was his idea, and part of his greater plan, but the magic was another's."

"Who?" Kael asked. "And why does the priest wish us to know it?"

"As I said, to taunt us, I'm sure," Tauran replied. "To show us his strength. As for who, I know of only one person who is capable of such. Kashada the Nightwraith."

Kael flinched at the mention of that name. "But she is imprisoned!" the half-drow protested. "Back within the House!"

"Apparently not any longer," Tauran said.

"By holy Torm," he murmured. The warrior knew well the story of Kashada the Nightwraith, sometimes called Kashada the Veiled. Renowned as one of Shar's most deadly assassins and mystics, capturing Kashada had been Tauran and Micus's biggest triumph—and had come very close to being their downfall. Kael had still been in the early stages of his tutelage among servants of Torm when the two angels managed to ensnare her.

In Sundabar! the knight realized. Kael better understood the angel's grim expression then. "She was planted," he surmised. "Just like Aliisza."

Tauran nodded. "Zasian has been three steps ahead of us for twelve years. And he wants us to know it." The angel sounded morose.

"Who is this Kashada you speak of?" Vhok asked.

Tauran explained the tale to him. "She was posing as a young girl in the employ of Helm Dwarf-friend. She was also spreading deceit and strife throughout the city and establishing a dark temple dedicated to Shar. At the time, I thought she just got sloppy, but now I see she was supposed to get caught."

"Wait a moment," Aliisza said, sitting forward with an incredulous look on her face. "She was pretending to be Ansa?"

Tauran looked at her oddly. "Yes," he said. "How did you know?"

"That was *my* cover story! She stole it from me after you, you . . ."

"Zasian!" Vhok growled. "He knew it, planned it from the start. That bastard set me up so many different ways. But why? Why that?"

Tauran shook his head. "The night I claimed you—claimed Kael, to be precise—you were in Helm's chambers, but I had no idea you had been posing as Ansa. You were in your own form."

"After Zasian and his lackeys intruded, it no longer seemed worthwhile to pretend," Aliisza said. "And as for why," she added, turning to Vhok, "what better way to minimize the uproar than to have nothing seem amiss? Replace one false Ansa with another, and Zasian's got his finger in another pie. Regardless of his intentions for this Kashada to get caught, it was *his* agent holding Helm's trust, not yours."

Kael stared at his three companions, shifting from face to face. He saw his own dismay reflected in each of their expressions. "So what does this mean?" he asked.

The cambion grimaced. "It means they are a formidable team," he said. "Whatever they intend to do, it won't be easy to stop them."

Tauran drew himself up straight and stood. "Yet we must try."

Kael shook his head. Noble statements aside, they had to break the cycle of duplicity. "That's fine, but you said he's been three steps ahead of us this whole time. Twelve years! So what can we do? How can we get a step ahead of him?"

"You're right," Tauran said. "It is time to change our strategy. Too long have we been reacting, following, like his lackeys, each moment doing exactly what he expected. Instead, we must circle around, come at him from ahead."

"Very well," Kael said, warming to the idea. "How?"

"Divination," Tauran answered.

"You said you were no good at it," Vhok rebutted. "And none of the rest of us are, either. And I don't see Eirwyn around to do her little trance-thing again, so how do you propose we make that work?"

"Savras," the angel said. "We must travel to Dweomerheart and consult with Savras."

Aliisza grimaced. "Taking that path risks losing Zasian altogether," she said. "It may cost us more than it gains us."

"If the priest of Cyric truly wishes for us to follow him, we will be able to pick up the trail again," Tauran said. "And if we are successful, then it won't matter. We will be ahead of him, waiting for him."

Vhok shrugged. "Sounds like a plan to me. Anything is better than wandering about, fighting shadow-fey."

Kael grinned. For the first time, he truly sensed that they were working as a team. Maybe Tauran's faith in the two half-fiends was not so misplaced, after all.

CHAPTER TWELVE

"You would defy this Court?" Micus asked, incredulous. "You would stand before this High Council and refuse to answer the questions put before you? I find that irresponsible, short sighted, and unwise."

Eirwyn shrugged her shoulders and smiled. "Nonetheless," she said, "I do not wish to discuss this."

Micus pursed his lips to contain his anger. He stared hard at Eirwyn, trying to fathom why she would choose to betray herself in the face of almost certain punishments. It made no sense. He could not understand how the elderly deva could hold her loyalty to Tauran above her duty to the law.

The solars sitting on the High Council murmured among themselves. Micus could sense their growing restlessness, perhaps to the point of irritation, with the entire proceedings. He had asked much of them of late, and he suspected their patience with both him and his lack of progress was growing thin. Not only was Eirwyn exacerbating the situation, but she was also putting him in an uncomfortable spot.

He felt betrayed.

"Micus," Eirwyn said in a tone that conveyed her nurturing

instincts, "I know you want to do what's right, but sometimes, you let your devotion to the balance veil your sight from what's sensible. Tauran is one of your oldest and closest friends. Why do you not trust him to do what's right?"

Micus drew a deep breath. "It pains me, Eirwyn, to watch him fling himself into the proverbial Abyss, and I have given him every chance to correct his path, but he has refused. And it is not I who have decreed him outlaw, but this Council." He gave her a pointed stare to drive home his next point. "The very same Council that holds your own future in its hands."

Eirwyn drew herself up into a regal pose. Her next words were a bit colder than usual. "I do not answer to this Council. I came here today merely out of a sense of obligation to you, Micus. And to Tauran. Not because I fall under this body's jurisdiction. I do not serve Tyr. My loyalty always has been and always will be to noble Helm."

Micus bowed his head. He did not want to witness what was coming next, but he had no choice. She had to understand.

"The moment the Watcher fell before Tyr's blade," the High Councilor said from his position at the middle of the raised dais, "it was decreed that all who had been loyal to Helm would be offered a place under the Maimed God's protection and guidance. Those who refused would be found guilty of abetting Helm's own crimes and punished accordingly."

Micus watched as the other deva's eyes widened, first in disbelief, then in dismay. He felt a great weight upon his heart. "Tyr has spoken, Eirwyn," he said. "You cannot hide behind the protection of your abolished faith any longer. Your loyalty to Tauran is not only misplaced, but criminal."

"I weep for us all," she said. "Whatever drove the two of them to battle, the outcome has harmed everyone, on both sides. There is no glory in this victory for you." She bowed her head.

Micus paused, giving her a moment to collect herself. When she looked up again, her eyes were cold and defiant. He could sense that she knew her options were limited, and despite her earlier refusal to adhere to the Council's demands, Eirwyn still served the law before all else.

"Do what's right, Eirwyn," Micus said gently, coming to stand before her. He took her hands in his to show that, despite the harsh circumstances, he still cared deeply for her. "Tell us what you know of his destination."

Eirwyn smiled then, and her eyes returned to that warm, comforting look. But her words belied her expression. "I told you, Micus, what's right and what's lawful aren't always in accord. The fact that you have yet to learn that very important lesson tells me you didn't spend enough time with Tauran. Perhaps you are not the friend of his I thought." With that, she pulled her hands free.

"Nonetheless," she said, "I hear and obey the ruling of this body. If a law has been established that I am beholden to this Council, then however unjust I perceive it to be, I accept its jurisdiction. You may punish me for my crimes." She laid her mace down upon the floor at her feet. "May Tyr in his wisdom see fit to overturn your decision." She bowed her head once more.

"Eirwyn!" Micus said, pleading with her. "This is madness!"

The elderly angel did not answer him, but Micus could see her eyes glisten with the beginnings of tears as an escort of archons led her away.

After Eirwyn departed, Micus turned to face the Court. "I did not expect that," he said, feeling helpless. "I fear that with Helm's death the foundations of our society, the very tenets of our existence, have been shaken far more than I believed."

"Indeed," the High Councilor said. "This is not a unique case. The entire Court struggles to make sense of the tragedy of the Watcher's passing."

"Without Eirwyn's knowledge, my hunt is all the more difficult," Micus said. "How shall I proceed?"

"Eirwyn is not the only citizen of the House with great skill in divination," the High Councilor answered. "Others have revealed that Tauran and his entourage have crossed—or will very soon—into the realm of Mystra. Therefore, you must travel to Dweomerheart and find them."

"As you wish and command," Micus said, bowing his head.

"You will be there as an official emissary, Micus," the solar said. "You must secure permission from Mystra's agents to continue your hunt. You may not pursue this agenda independently. Is that understood?"

"Clearly, High Councilor."

"We have been assured that you will be given full cooperation."

Micus bowed again then took his leave from the High Council.

He had many things to plan, and he would need help.

❖ ❖ ❖ ❖ ❖ ❖ ❖ ❖

"Are you certain there isn't an easier way?" Kaanyr asked from beside Aliisza. "This is absurd!" Panting, he struggled to free himself from a bundle of grasses that had wrapped around one leg.

"Certain," Tauran grunted from the other side of the alu. He pounded the ground with his mace, making the soil jump in rhythm with his blows. "I cannot whisk us there, however much I would like to. My power to do so is a manifestation of Tyr's benevolence. Since he and I aren't seeing eye to eye at the moment, he has withdrawn his favor from me. This is the best—and only—path!" He finished with a particularly powerful down-stroke.

Aliisza slashed at another clump of writhing, entwining vines and roots with her sword. Hearing the angel's explanation in such a casual tone saddened her. *He tries to make light of it,* she thought, *to keep the rest of us focused and moving forward. But he must hurt at such abandonment. Like a parent turning his back on a loving child,* she added.

Or her back, the alu reminded herself with a sudden stab of guilt. She turned to look at Kael. Her son was busy cleaving some thrashing bushes that were trying to entangle him. *Seems we're all struggling with the same battles.*

Something caught Aliisza's eye, some movement just beyond where Kaanyr fought alongside her. Behind him, a massive tree leaned forward, limbs splayed out as if to swat at him. Kaanyr, unaware of the danger, continued to cut at the tendrils of growth that entangled him.

"Kaanyr, watch out!" Aliisza shouted. She leaped into the air and flew across the open space between her lover and the animated tree. As she reached the tree, she flipped herself around so that she traveled feet first. She rammed both heels against the trunk in an effort to slow it down.

The blow caused the tree to shiver, but it continued to swing its limbs at her. Aliisza darted and wove around, narrowly soaring clear of its reach before the thing could envelop her with its flailing branches. But she bought Kaanyr time, and he scurried out of its reach.

"Two more!" Kael shouted.

Aliisza hovered in place and looked to where the half-drow pointed. Two more swaying trees waddled toward the group, shuffling their roots through the soil.

What madness is this? she wondered as she settled to the ground near Tauran to help free him from the grasping plant life that ensnared him. Walking trees?

"What in the heavens is going on?" she asked the angel as she helped cut him free.

"The World Tree is angry," the angel answered as he broke loose from the last of the clinging tendrils. "It doesn't always like being used as a conveyance, and though it seldom turns on angels, Zasian's cruel attacks on its denizens must have raised its ire." He stepped away from the reaching, grasping plants and up onto an outcropping of rock, evading them. "It might even believe we are the cause of its distress. It may sense the fiendish heritage of you, Vhok, and Kael."

"Well, we need to get out of here," Aliisza said. "Now the trees are walking! Every moment we remain here, more things start wriggling and trying to catch us."

Even as she spoke those prophetic words, several thick vines snagged her around the waist and began to pull her down toward a clump of bushes. Growling in exasperation, the alu whipped her sword around and sliced through the creepers. She heaved herself skyward as she tugged on the severed portions, unwrapping them from her body and tossing them to the ground.

Kael, too, had gone airborne. The knight zipped and

dashed before the towering, mobile trees, trying to distract them and slow their advance. Tauran, seeing the dire turn the fight was taking, took to the air and began to circle. "Let's go! Follow me!"

Kaanyr, however, had become snagged in more shrubs, and it seemed that for every clump he cut free with one of his daggers, three more snaked forward to grasp him. Aliisza could see the frustration growing in his every move to escape.

"We have to help him!" she shouted and swooped in to assist.

Tauran followed her, and together they managed to slash enough grass and weeds away from the cambion to free him. Kaanyr immediately rose into the air, levitating to get out of reach. Once hovering, though, he gazed around wistfully, just as trapped as he had been before.

"We'll have to carry you," Aliisza said. "Get his other hand, Tauran."

The cambion frowned, indignant at how he was to be transported, but he reluctantly reached out to grasp their proffered arms, and soon they were wending their way through the forest, leaving the shambling trees and clutching bushes behind. Kael caught up to them a moment later and they settled to the ground.

"Fortunately for us, the trees cannot move very fast," the knight said. "But who knows how many more of them there are?" He gestured around them. The woods through which they had been traveling remained thick and overgrown, with no end in sight.

"Let's not stick around to find out," Kaanyr said, straightening the sleeves of his tunic like a preening bird. "I'd rather not suffer that indignity again."

Noting that her lover did not actually protest the indignity itself, Aliisza hid her smile. *At least he's learning*, she thought. *That's something.*

"Come," Tauran said, heading off in the direction they had been traveling before the attack. "We're not far, I think."

"How will we find the path in all this mess?" Kaanyr asked after a time, peering down at the ground as they hiked. "If the crack in the ground leading to Dweomerheart is as narrow as it was before, we'll miss it for certain."

"I don't think it will be a problem," Tauran said, coming to a stop at the edge of a clearing. "I believe we're here."

Aliisza peered over the angel's shoulder into the clearing and saw a ring of stones standing upright, perhaps thirty paces across. In the center of the ring stood a stone archway, and within the arch a shimmering, yellow curtain of light rippled. The alu could feel the magic radiating from the doorway, even at such a distance. Just for a moment, she let the magic of Pharaun's ring reveal the emanations to her. The glows that appeared dazzled her and made her blink.

"Powerful magic," the alu said. "Can you feel it?"

"It spills over from Dweomerheart," Tauran explained. "This is definitely the way."

"Let's go, then," Kaanyr said, and he took a step forward.

"Wait!" Tauran shouted, reaching for the cambion, but he wasn't quite fast enough.

The trees along the edge of the clearing writhed and shuffled, shifting around to block Kaanyr's progress.

"It's well guarded," Tauran explained as more of the trees closed in around them, sealing them off from escape in any direction.

"*Now* you tell me." Kaanyr sighed as he stepped back toward his companions to avoid getting separated. "What now? Fly over them?"

"I don't think that will work," Kael said, looking skyward. The boughs of the trees had folded in around them, closing off every space.

"I could become insubstantial," Kaanyr said, "turn to smoke, but that won't help the rest of you."

"Why don't I just create a doorway?" Aliisza asked. She started to conjure one, but Tauran gestured for her to hold.

"No," the angel said, frowning. "I think this is one time we're going to have to wait it out."

Kaanyr glared. "Wait for what?" he asked. "To be crushed to death by these abominations?"

Before Tauran could reply, the ground shook beneath their feet. It was gentle at first, but rhythmic, like massive footfalls somewhere out of sight. The steps grew stronger until the four companions gently bounced with each one.

"What comes?" Kael asked, fingering the hilt of his sword nervously. "It must be huge!"

Tauran nodded. "Yes, undoubtedly, but I think a gentle giant," he said. His eyes shown brightly in anticipation. "I have heard stories . . .," he began, but he did not finish his thought.

Aliisza tried to peer through the boles of the trees crowding around them, hoping to spot what kind of thing could shake the ground so. She spied something big and dark, but the gaps were too narrow to give a clearer picture.

"Let's just go," she urged. "Let me make a doorway, Tauran."

"No," the angel said. "I am honor-bound to seek its consent before passing through the gate."

"That didn't stop Zasian," Kaanyr grumbled. "We're losing precious time."

Aliisza had to agree with the cambion. She saw no sense

in tempting fate. But Tauran was adamant, so she continued to try to steal a glimpse of whatever it was.

The thundering, jarring steps grew even stronger, then suddenly stopped.

The tops of the trees parted.

Aliisza, her heart hammering, caught a glimpse of silvery sky for just a moment. Then a massive face moved into view and peered down at them. It was dark and rough, etched into the bark of a tree that rose twice as high as any that imprisoned the companions. The face was oldness incarnate, deeply lined and furrowed into a perpetual frown. Only the eyes seemed to be made of something other than weathered wood.

"Intruders!" the thing spoke, and its voice was low and rumbling. It drew the word out over several of Aliisza's rapid, gasping breaths.

She could do nothing but watch, all thoughts of fleeing through her magical doorway forgotten for the moment.

"You defile," it said, its voice rumbling so low that Aliisza felt it in her feet, "the World Tree."

"Actually, noble treant," Tauran said, bowing, "we do not tarnish the majesty of your glorious home. We do, however, pursue the ones responsible for the recent blights upon the great branches of the World Tree."

The titanic tree-creature blinked several times as it pondered the deva's words. "Long since angels . . .," it said.

Aliisza and the others waited expectantly. A dozen thoughts went through her head as the gargantuan treant took a breath.

". . . have traveled," it continued.

"Yes," Tauran answered, "It has been a long—"

". . . this way," the creature finished.

"Indeed," Tauran said, smiling at his own impatience.

"My brethren do not often have cause to travel the World Tree. Yet I ask you now to grant us safe passage."

"The World Tree . . .," the treant said.

Aliisza knew Tauran had learned from his brashness and was waiting it out.

". . . is angry."

"Yes, precisely," Tauran said. "Our enemies have awakened it and hurt it. We merely wish to catch those villains who are doing such unspeakable things. Will you help us?"

"Creatures," the giant tree-creature said, "not angels, are hurting it."

"I know," Tauran said. He seemed at a loss. "We are trying to stop them."

"Creatures," the treant said, and then one massive arm appeared. It pointed down into the companions' midst and said, "Like those!"

"No!" Kaanyr said, puffing his chest out. "We're not all guilty. Did you see how many of those cursed shadow-things I put out of their misery?"

Tauran placed a quieting hand on the cambion's shoulder. "These are different from the others, noble treant. They are are helping me. Can you see your way to assisting us? We wish to pass through the gateway to the world beyond the stone ring."

The tree-creature stood very still and said nothing. The four of them waited and watched, until Kaanyr sighed and sat down.

"We're never getting out of here," he muttered.

Aliisza began to think it had gone to sleep. "Maybe we should just fly past it," she suggested softly. "Try to slip through the arch before it notices."

Tauran shook his head and continued to wait.

Aliisza and Kael had both found seats on the ground before the treant finally began to move again. It vanished from view. A short time later, the regular trees began to part, allowing space between them for the quartet to pass through.

Tauran led the way out into the clearing, toward the ring of stones. The tree-creature stood there, to one side, watching them.

Aliisza paused and gaped at it for several moments, stunned anew by both its height and its mere existence.

"Catch them," the treant said. "Stop them . . ."

"W-we will," Aliisza said, nodding and smiling. The idea of making such a behemoth angry frightened her more than she would care to admit. "We promise," she added.

". . . from hurting the World Tree," it finished.

Aliisza snapped her mouth shut, feeling foolish.

Tauran led the way to the shimmering curtain of yellow light. He paused right before it and turned back toward the tree-creature.

The gargantuan treant raised two of its mighty arms, which looked in their own right like the trunks of ancient trees. It brought them together in front of itself and clasped them like two hands. Then, ever so ponderously, it bowed.

Tauran returned the gesture with a formal bow of his own, as did Kaanyr and Kael. Aliisza caught herself bending a knee, too.

Something that old just deserves a bit of respect, she would tell herself later. *It just does.*

Tauran was the first to turn and step through the arch. The other three followed.

Once on the other side of the portal, Aliisza could feel the change immediately. Magic radiated all around her, coursed through everything she beheld. The night sky blazed with a multitude of glamours and enchantments. Architecture that should not have remained upright dazzled her with its beauty and uniqueness. Inhabitants rode upon conveyances both fantastical and mundane, but in nearly every case, they bore the mark of magic.

The alu knew, without even testing it, that magic poured through her being. She sensed how it enhanced her, made her more powerful. Any spell she could recall would burst forth from her in a heightened, more robust state. Everything she might conjure would appear bigger, faster, more potent. More impressive.

They stood in the middle of an urban park. A pleasant stone archway, very similar in appearance to the arch within the clearing they had just left, made up the portal. However, instead of a ring of standing stones guarded by sentient trees and unfathomable tree-creatures, here gravel paths meandering among manicured grasses and shrubs surrounded the focal point of the arch.

Numerous trees, their limbs trimmed and sculpted into interesting shapes, also lined the walks, and at various points beneath their spreading branches, stone benches invited strollers to sit for a bit and rest. Indeed, a handful of casual walkers followed some of the paths, as did a few more who did not walk at all, but instead drifted along upon the air itself, or upon rippling, undulating carpets.

Few of the park visitors paid any attention to the newest arrivals.

"It's amazing!" Kaanyr breathed, turning his gaze back and forth as he tried to take in all the sights. "So much magic."

"Indeed," Tauran said, though the angel seemed far less delighted. "You cannot walk a city block in this mystical place without crossing paths with a potent practitioner, one of their preternatural works, or both. It is, truly, a city of magic."

"You're not impressed," Aliisza said, looking at Tauran with a smile of accusation. "You disapprove of magic?"

Tauran shrugged. "It's not that," he said. He seemed to search for the right words. "Let's just say that I have little use for such a conspicuous display of secular power. It seems pompous and . . . misguided."

"To you, perhaps," Kaanyr said. "But this is not your home. Here, the goddess is magic. Everyone sees her as the embodiment of what they know best."

"Yes, precisely," Tauran said, disdain creeping into his tone. "An uncaring, unconscious force, relied upon far too much as a measure of one's worth. It pales in comparison to the power of faith. That comes from within. That's what makes you who you are. Magic is just a tool, and often a crutch."

Aliisza sniffed, a bit put off by the angel's proselytizing. "Not very open-minded of you," she said. "All tools have their uses. Magic happens to be a very valuable one."

"Agreed," Tauran said with a faint smile. "But it should never define who you are." Then he waved his hand to dismiss the discussion. "It's irrelevant at the moment. We need to find our way to the Eye."

"That may be difficult," Kael said. He had been watching the group's surroundings more intensely as the other three conversed, and when he spoke, he pointed.

Aliisza could see a contingent of hound archons approaching. Seven blue-white stars arranged in a circle adorned their fancy red livery, marking them as servants of Mystra.

Not again, she thought, and on instinct turned in a different direction.

More of the celestial warriors approached from that way, too. As the alu turned in place, she noted that teams of the archons came at them from every direction, covering all the different paths leading from the arch.

"A welcoming party," Kaanyr said. "Doesn't look like there's much welcome to them, though." He pulled his borrowed daggers free of his belt.

"Easy," Kael said, though Aliisza noted that he fingered the hilt of his own blade restlessly. She had her hand upon the hilt of her sword, too. "We're not in trouble here," the knight added. "I hope."

"Put away your weapons, Vhok," Tauran ordered. "All of you. They are understandably cautious when visitors arrive through a portal from elsewhere. There's no need to lend credence to their suspicions. I've been met by this sort of greeting before, and it has worked out without trouble. Just let me speak with them."

Kaanyr scowled, but he slipped the daggers back into their sheaths and folded his arms across his chest. "Very well, angel," he said.

As the archons drew closer and formed a circle around the four, Tauran raised his hand in a peaceful gesture. "Well met, noble soldiers. Who speaks for you?"

"I do," one of the dog-headed warriors said, stepping forward from the circle. "State your name and where you came from."

"I am Tauran of the House of the Triad, and these are my companions," he said, gesturing to the other three. "That's Kael, loyal knight of Torm and my trusted pupil, Vhok of the Scourged Legion, based near Sundabar on Faerûn, and his lieutenant and consort, Aliisza. We come seeking only information. We wish to visit the Eye."

The archon nodded. "The House of the Triad, you say. I'm afraid that's going to be a problem. We have orders to detain anyone hailing from Tyr's domain for questioning before we let them into the city."

Aliisza felt her blood run cold. *They know,* she thought. *Micus is here. It's a trap.*

❖ ❖ ❖ ❖ ❖ ❖ ❖ ❖ ❖

Myshik crouched and waited at the railing of a pagoda that hovered in midair. Across an expanse of shimmering fountains that glowed like sparkling gems in every hue of the rainbow, he could see the stone arch through which Zasian, Kashada, and he had come. He was supposed to be watching for Vhok's arrival, but Myshik was distracted by the myriad sights and sounds surrounding him.

Dweomerheart truly was a wondrous place.

So much treasure, the half-dragon mused. *I could gather up an armload of precious magic at any street corner and return home a hero.* Yet again he asked himself why he didn't do that very thing. *Zasian will cross me,* he thought. *Sooner or later, he will turn on me. When he thinks my usefulness to him has ended. It is the way of his god. I should leave now.*

But he didn't.

Myshik had been troubled by comments he had heard exchanged between Zasian and Kashada. The two of them had been cryptic, but based on what he had gleaned, the shadow-witch was angry with Zasian for not revealing a time differential to her. He wasn't entirely sure what that meant, but he feared that it could affect him, too, should he try to return home by himself. He was certain he was going to need Zasian's help to return safely to the mountain of his father and uncle.

So the draconic hobgoblin bided his time and watched.

A sled came into Myshik's view, crossing in front of his line of sight to the arch. Two great golden lions pulled the device, and it glided along on glittering silver runners. Where they passed, the runners left a trail of what Myshik could only assume was ice. Even more peculiar were the pennants that rippled from twin poles at the rear of the sled. The flags were identical, each depicting a dancing hobgoblin dressed as a court jester. Instead of cloth, though, the pennants had been constructed of something more akin to light.

The hobgoblins looked real.

As the sled passed, Myshik ducked a tiny bit lower. He told himself that they were simple hobgoblins, beneath him. He was a scion of Clan Morueme and no one would dare imprison him within a flag.

A flag!

But he shrank back out of sight all the same.

A commotion in the park caught the half-dragon's attention. He peered carefully and saw several archons moving toward the hill and the arch. Squinting, he could barely make out four figures standing before the magical doorway.

He lifted a small crystal lens to his eye. Zasian had given it to him. The priest had told him it was on loan and not to lose it. Myshik had savored the thought of tucking it away and keeping it. He wondered how far Zasian would chase him to get it back.

Through the lens, Myshik could see the figures up close. It was Vhok and his alu whore, as well as two others—an angel and a dark figure with a large sword.

Interesting, Myshik thought. Do they work in concert? How could the cambion manage that? And who leads? So many puzzles.

The half-dragon continued to watch as the archons drew closer to the quartet and surrounded them. The angel began to speak and gesture. The others appeared nervous, fingering weapons and glaring.

Myshik half-hoped to see a fight break out. Though he suspected that Vhok and his friends would be the victors, it would amuse him nonetheless.

But they came to no blows.

Disappointed, Myshik rose from his observation point and turned to go. He reached the top of a series of floating, disconnected slabs of stone arranged like a staircase leading down from the pagoda. They wended their way through the sparkling fountains to the pathways beyond. Rather than bother descending them, Myshik spread his wings and glided to the ground. When he landed, he trotted away to inform Zasian that their pursuers had arrived in Dweomerheart.

CHAPTER THIRTEEN

"Detain us? That's highly unusual, isn't it?" Tauran asked the archons. His voice carried a gracious tone, but there was a concerned edge to it. "I have come to your fascinating city on other occasions, and you never had cause to detain me then."

The archon nodded again and waved Tauran's concerns away. "I know, and I apologize. It's really just a formality. The upheaval there and all, you know. We've been given orders to make certain any conflicts originating there don't spill over to here."

Aliisza saw Tauran's shoulders relax a bit. She did not share the deva's confidence in what they were being told. *This doesn't feel right,* she thought. *Don't be so quick to trust them!*

"Certainly," the angel said. "I understand. We are happy to cooperate in whatever way necessary. Yes?" He looked to his companions.

Aliisza nodded and tried to smile, but both Kaanyr and Kael glared for long moments before each of them gave a single, curt nod.

They don't like this, either. Why is Tauran not more suspicious?

"Lead on, good soldier," Tauran said, motioning with his hand. "We shall follow."

The lead archon smiled and turned. He gave some instructions for a small detail to escort the quartet of visitors to some place called the Palace of Myriad Amazements, while the rest of the force were to return to their duties.

As the four were led out of the park and down a wide street, Aliisza took in the sights. As much as the park and its magical displays amazed her, the street they turned on outdid it considerably. Every establishment they passed, from the meanest vendor to the most elaborate shop, incorporated extravagant arcane contrivances to draw attention to themselves. It was if each attempted to outdo the next.

The first building on their left was made up of a series of long towers constructed of translucent crystal. It reminded Aliisza of a set of musical pipes, and indeed, the whole place resonated with sweet tones, as though the building itself performed some song.

The entire front wall of a more conventional building on the right glowed from multiple dweomers displaying moving images of sailing ships and splashing dolphins, all in garish pinks and purples. From the noise emanating from within that place, it was a thriving taproom.

A third establishment farther down took up the entire block and resembled the dryad tree-community—or at least how Aliisza imagined it before Zasian had burned it to cinders. Unlike that locale, though, the great tree that filled the lot was entirely magical, constructed of nothing more than millions of twinkling lights. The buildings resting within those arcane branches took the form of gilded bird cages. The whole place had a fey quality to it.

A vendor selling meat pies passed the group heading the other way. He attracted business by means of an illusory life-size phantasm of a three-headed lizardman dressed in a jester's outfit that cavorted around the merchant's cart. The pies he hawked smelled delicious to Aliisza, but her escort seemed intent on getting them to their destination as quickly and efficiently as possible. She gave one last, longing look back at the cart and hurried on.

A trio of ogre magi moved casually down the opposite side of one street they followed, dressed in rich silks adorned with magically enhanced baubles. Aliisza stared at them for a moment, expecting trouble, but when no one else in their retinue paid any heed to the powerful wizards, she shrugged and kept going. In her distraction, the alu almost stepped in front of a floating carriage that was missing both its draft animals and its wheels. Inside, a human with long white hair, an equally long white moustache, and even longer fingernails gave her a disdainful stare as she scooted out of the way.

Through all the sights and sounds, hundreds of lantern archons bobbed and weaved, hurrying elsewhere on some errand or another.

Once over her initial shock and awe, Aliisza found the ostentatious nature of the city amusing. She remembered Tauran's quip about conspicuous displays of power.

He wasn't exaggerating, she thought. Whoever has the time and energy to go around creating all of this must be imposing. And wasteful. The alu could still feel the height-ened sense of arcane potency coursing through her own body. But with this kind of power . . . she shivered in anticipation. Anything might be possible.

They reached an open plaza with several buildings facing

the common square, which was dominated by a great basin filled with what looked like liquid silver. A tall stone fountain depicting three incredibly lifelike dragons hovered over the center of the pool. From the mouths of the dragons spewed a continuous stream of tiny points of light, each one bursting into a myriad of colors, much like the tiny missiles that Kaanyr had been so fond of conjuring with his lost wand.

The patrol of hound archons led the four of them across the plaza to a broad-fronted building. It was one of the most mundane structures Aliisza had spotted since entering the city. Instead of steps, a ramp rose up to a colonnaded porch with three sets of immense double doors. The folk coming and going from those doors did not walk upon the ramp, however. Instead, they merely stepped onto an invisible point directly over the ramp and seemed to glide up or down without moving.

The group entered the austere building, where simple stone walls and fluted columns rose to tall, vaulted ceilings. As the visitors strode across the tiled floor, the soaring chambers echoed their footsteps. Large tapestries hung in some of the alcoves, and hallways led to other parts of the building in others.

Aliisza felt a vague sense of unease. It looks like a cathedral, she decided. And not so many amazements. Someone has a sense of humor, I guess.

The archons led the quartet through several halls and down a broad set of stairs until they came to a polished wooden door. The leader of the patrol opened the door and ushered them inside.

"Someone should be here to speak with you shortly," he said, stepping aside.

Tauran nodded and passed through.

Kaanyr hesitated at the entrance. "How long?" he asked, more gruffly than Aliisza thought necessary.

Don't make them more wary, you dolt! she wanted to yell at him.

The archon bristled slightly. "As soon as is reasonably possible. You *will* wait here until they can get to you. As you can imagine, there is a bit of a backlog. We have many visitors to the city every day."

"Quit being a boor and go in," Kael growled from behind the cambion.

Aliisza was glad she wasn't the only one who had been thinking that.

Kaanyr grimaced and rolled his eyes, but he turned and entered the room. Kael and Aliisza followed him, and the archon pulled the door shut after her, leaving them alone.

The chamber was pleasant and comfortable, with several couches arrayed around the perimeter and a side table filled with numerous foods and beverages. Beautiful magically animated landscapes adorned the walls, like moving paintings made of light and sound. Aliisza stared at one, astonished at the way the populace spared no use of arcane power for the most mundane things. She noted that there were no other windows or exits from the room.

Kaanyr headed straight for the spread of food and grabbed up a thick slab of bread. Breaking it in half, he layered some roasted meat simmering in rich, dark mushroom gravy, along with some slices of cheese, onto the crust. He was on the verge of biting into the meal when he froze in place.

"You don't think they've laced this with something, do you?" he asked no one in particular. "Should we eat it?"

Aliisza's stomach was rumbling, and the odors wafting from the spread made her mouth water. She and Kael both had followed the cambion to the food when Kaanyr posed his question. She halted on the verge of pouring a flagon of chilled wine.

"Why? What would that accomplish?" Tauran asked, motioning for them to continue. "They have no reason to be suspicious of us, nor we of them. This is all just a precaution, I tell you."

"How can you be so certain?" Kaanyr asked, eyeing his food. "You can be too trusting."

"I agree," Aliisza said, still holding the wine and empty goblet. "What if this brief detention is nothing but an excuse to keep us here until Micus can come and subdue us? We're trapped in this room."

Tauran shrugged and moved to one of the couches. He sank down and reclined, closing his eyes. "Though Mystra holds sway here, many outsiders travel to Dweomerheart to conduct trade. Whatever else motivates her, Mystra benefits when that trade, particularly in all things magical, is lucrative. It's hard to entice travelers to stop over when you make a habit of seizing them off the streets and incarcerating them for questioning."

"That proves my point all the more," Kaanyr argued. "This is too unusual. They have brought us here specifically because of who we are. For all we know, Micus is behind it and will come through that door in a matter of moments."

"Exactly," Aliisza said. "It feels like a set up." She sniffed the wine in the pitcher but could detect no taint upon it. That doesn't mean anything, she thought.

Tauran didn't open his eyes. "Suit yourselves," he said, "but I know the angels here. They are aware of the disaster within the House and they are just being cautious. They don't want a faction war spilling over into Dweomerheart. Micus is not part of this."

"What about Zasian?" Kael asked. "Perhaps he has put something in place to stall us, trap us. This could be his doing."

Tauran did sit up then. "Perhaps," he admitted, though he sounded doubtful. "But we stopped chasing him to come here. Besides, why would he do that if he *did* know? He went to all that trouble to lay a trail for us. Why would he do that just to get rid of us here? That makes little sense."

Kael frowned then finally nodded. "I suppose you're right," he said, and he began to prepare a platter with some of the meat and mushrooms.

Kaanyr examined his impromptu selection a moment more, then he, too, shrugged and took a healthy bite. "I guess we'll see," he said, his words barely intelligible around the wad of food in his mouth.

Aliisza watched the two men eat, but still she hesitated. If something was going to happen to them, she wanted to be able to react and not succumb to any reagents in the food. Neither Kael nor Kaanyr paid any attention to the alu as they wolfed down the first hearty meal either of them had enjoyed in quite some time.

After waiting several moments and seeing no adverse effects in either of her companions, Aliisza could not stand it any longer. She poured herself some of the chilled wine and sampled it. It was delicious. She grabbed a plate and started in on a piece of poached fish. The stuff practically dissolved in her mouth, it was so tender and moist. She grabbed a clump of fresh, pinkish berries she had never seen before and spied a platter of some sort of glazed pastries. Her stomach rumbling loudly, Aliisza took her meal over to one of the sedans, sank into it, and began eating.

The food tasted every bit as good as it had smelled. The

berries were slightly tart and had a hint of honey to them, and the pastries were decadent. The alu gorged herself on all of it. Kael and Kaanyr both went back and piled their plates high a second time, and Tauran even overcame his apparent exhaustion long enough to sample the spread. No one said anything for quite some time as they all preoccupied themselves with bite after bite.

Eventually, feeling sated, Aliisza set her own plate aside and stretched out on the sedan she had chosen. She grew worried once more that they had walked into a trap of some sort. "It is taking them a long time to come speak with us," she said, resting her head against the armrest. "I still think this could be an ambush."

"I think they must be dealing with a lot of visitors," Tauran replied, his voice sounding vacant.

Aliisza glanced over to the angel and saw that he reclined again on the couch where he had been eating, his eyes closed. "Someone ought to stay awake, keep watch," she suggested, but her eyelids were drooping. "We don't want to get caught off guard." She thought briefly how it odd it was that none of her companions answered her, but it didn't really matter. All she wanted to do was sleep.

◇ ◇ ◇ ◇ ◇ ◇ ◇ ◇ ◇

Kaanyr jerked awake. The lighting was dim, and for a moment, he lost track of where he was. Then he took in his companions, all sleeping soundly on various couches, and it came back to him.

The cambion sat up and peered around. Had something startled him? Had someone come to visit them while they had been out? Or had he simply been dreaming? He couldn't shake the feeling that something had happened, but there was no one else in the room.

How long have we been sleeping? Kaanyr wondered. He remembered seeing an ornate and elaborate candelabra resting on the side table where the food was. He turned toward it and stopped dead in his tracks.

All of the food had been cleared.

Kaanyr reached for his sword, only to remember that he had been forced to leave it behind when Aliisza had rescued him. He slipped his daggers free of their scabbards and scanned the room again. When he was certain there was no one in the chamber, he relaxed slightly and moved to the table. The candelabra was still there, and the candles had burned low. A good amount of time had passed since they had arrived.

That could be a lie, he thought. Whoever came in here and cleared the dishes might have swapped the candles.

Suspicious of why none of them had awakened at the intrusion, Kaanyr decided to investigate beyond the door. He slipped silently across the floor and pressed his ear against the portal, listening.

When he heard no sounds from the other side, he slipped the heavy wooden door open a tiny bit and peered out through the crack. A pair of bobbing, weaving globes of light flitted around just outside. Kaanyr knew they were lantern archons, the spiritual essences of those who had come to Dweomerheart after death and who served in various capacities. They did not seem to react to his presence, so he watched them long enough to confirm that they were deliberately positioned at that particular door.

Guarding us, he realized. The cambion pressed the door closed again and frowned in thought. They aren't powerful enough to stop me from leaving, but it would only take them a moment to summon others. Very clever.

Kaanyr scanned the room again, checking on his companions. Each of them was still in a calm, deep sleep. His gaze fell upon Tauran.

He didn't specifically tell me I couldn't go, Kaanyr thought, trying to justify the act of leaving and avoid the trap of the magical coercion. And sneaking out in order to gather information might be crucial to our plan to stop Zasian, he added, smiling to himself in the dimness of the room. Yes, he decided, a perfect justification. We can all play the game, angel.

Satisfied that he had mentally created a loophole that would allow him to slip away, Kaanyr considered how best to execute his plan. He disliked the thought of leaving the others behind, particularly Aliisza. His gaze swept over her. She seemed so at peace where she slept, he almost wanted to go to her, wake her, and get her to come with him. But the feeling of betrayal still lingered, and when he recalled its source, he started to get angry all over again.

He may be one of the four you love, the cambion silently fumed, but don't expect me to like it. He's a thrice-damned angel, for Hells' sake! You should know better. No, better to be alone right now, he decided. I'll have a better chance if I go by myself, anyway.

He wondered how sensitive the lantern archons would be to his presence if he chose to turn immaterial. Passing through the crack in the door in gaseous form would be a simple matter, but if the glowing spherical creatures had the ability to detect such magical tricks, he would be in trouble.

Noticing me and stopping me are two different things, the cambion decided.

Reaching into the folds of his tunic, Kaanyr produced

one of the tiny glass vials wrapped in gauzy fabric that he used for his chosen spell and snapped it with his fingers. He murmured the arcane words to complete the incantation and felt himself transform, becoming an insubstantial cloud. He took a moment to adjust his senses then proceeded.

Settling to the floor, Kaanyr glided to the door. He inched his way forward until he was partially past the barrier, then he watched the archons. They never changed their random flitting or reacted to him in any way. Satisfied that he went unnoticed, the cambion curled his form around the edge of the doorframe and sneaked away, keeping his shape long and thin and following the corner made by the floor and the wall.

Kaanyr traveled to the end of the hall and then around several corners until he reached the stairs. At one point, he passed a pair of hound archons walking the other way. He held still as they strode by, still compacting himself into the horizontal corner between floor and wall. They didn't seem to notice him, though, and once they were gone he continued on his way.

Ascending the stairs, Kaanyr followed the path he and his companions had taken upon arriving at the Palace of Myriad Amazements and finally reached the great front doors. He was on the verge of sliding beneath the nearest pair when an inner voice warned him to halt. He froze next to the portal and waited, trying to discern the cause of his apprehension. It took the cambion a moment to zero in on the danger, but with the heightened magical senses he had been experiencing since arriving in Dweomerheart, he finally located it.

A magical field surrounded the door, a trigger that he could only faintly detect. No, that's not right, he realized. It surrounds the entire building.

Kaanyr probed it with his mind, sending out magical

feelers to see if he could learn more. After a few moments testing the field, he determined that it was no barrier against him, nor was it going to discharge some magical attack against him. It would, however, sound an alarm throughout the palace if he tried to cross it.

Vhok decided to wait and see if he could determine how others bypassed the signal without setting it off. He remained in the corner next to one of the doors, hoping someone would pass through before his magic was consumed and he reverted to his corporeal self.

The cambion did not have to wait long. A pair of humans, one male and one female, exited one of the many hallways and headed to a set of the doors. Careful to remain unobtrusive, Kaanyr glided near them and waited while they approached the portal. As they drew near the ward, a lantern archon materialized. The archon flitted and danced around the two, seeming to examine them. It appeared satisfied and moved toward the ward. Kaanyr heard the creature speak a single word, and he could tell that a portion of the trigger was suppressed. The two humans passed through without incident.

Kaanyr didn't waste any time. The moment he understood that there was a gap in the alarm, he drifted past it, sliding along the floor just behind the pair of humans. They quickly outpaced him, and he feared that with his slow rate of motion, he would be caught within range when the barrier reactivated.

But the cambion's fears were not realized, and he found himself free of the palace.

Kaanyr drifted along for a few moments more, seeking a concealed location where he could return to his normal physical form. After entering a small alley between the palace and another nearby building, he shifted back into his solid body.

First things first, he thought, peering out into the street. I need weapons.

Initially, Kaanyr remained out of sight as much as possible, using the shadows to best advantage while moving from point to point. But the farther away he got from the Palace of Myriad Amazements, the less concerned he became about being apprehended. In addition, the folk strolling the streets were of so many varied species that he realized he would blend in far better acting casual, as if he belonged.

After a few discreet inquiries, Kaanyr found his way to an open bazaar brimming with merchants. From a variety of stalls, tents, and wagons the vendors offered every sort of magical trinket, spell component, and artifact imaginable. Dealers held their wares in front of him, cajoling him to sample them or buy, but the cambion had a specific destination in mind. He pushed past the merchants without even acknowledging them and headed for a large and colorful tent near the center of the bazaar.

Guards stationed at regular intervals around the perimeter of the pavilion watched the goings-on impassively. The cambion saw mostly humans, though he noted a couple of lion-headed leonals serving, too. The other merchants left plenty of space around the tent, giving it and the sentinels a wide berth.

Kaanyr walked to the entrance of the pavilion and was on the verge of ducking inside when one of the two guards blocked his way. "No one goes inside without an invitation," said the warrior, a big burly human in black-tinged plate armor.

The cambion stared at the man through narrowed eyes then held up his hand for a moment to signal that the fellow should wait. He pulled off his left boot, reached down inside it, and pulled out a small bundle. Slipping his boot back on, Kaanyr opened the pouch and spilled a quantity of uncut diamonds into the palm of his other hand.

"Does this count?" he asked, showing the gemstones to the guard.

The warrior stared at the stones for several heartbeats then said, "Wait here." He ducked inside the tent.

As Kaanyr waited, he slipped the diamonds back into the pouch and hid it in an inner pocket of his clothing. Then he studied the crowds in the rest of the bazaar.

When the warrior returned, a creature followed him. The being stood twice as tall as the cambion, with skin of a deep azure color. His body was long and lithe, with high, pointed ears and a prominent if slender chin. Two small fangs jutted from the fellow's mouth, but his voluminous black and orange robes, cut from the finest fabrics and embroidered with an elaborate pattern of precious metals and stones, belied any feral nature. Kaanyr had only heard of the mercane by reputation, but if they were half as good at buying and selling as most people believed, the cambion could get what he sought.

"I understand you wish to conduct business," the creature said in a high, reedy voice. He spoke in quite refined Abyssal. "You have some commodities you wish to show me?"

Kaanyr nodded and produced the pouch again. He dumped the diamonds out into his palm once more.

The mercane reached out with one spidery hand and took hold of the largest stone between his thumb and forefinger. Kaanyr noted with the slightest revulsion that the mercane's fingers bent with an extra joint. "Ah, decent quality," the mercane said, producing a strange ocular and peering through it at the stone he had selected. "Quite fine, actually. Few flaws, good color. Yes, I think we can do business." He placed the stone back in Kaanyr's palm. "Follow me." He turned and glided gracefully inside, his robes hardly swaying around his legs.

Kaanyr put the stones back into their pouch and followed the creature into the tent. A number of hanging tapestries partitioned the interior of the pavilion, so Kaanyr could not see the entirety of the place all at once, but everywhere the mercane walked, Kaanyr spotted trunks, barrels, boxes, and crates. Oil lamps illuminated each area individually, and in some of the alcoves, buyers and sellers haggled over wares. A few of the dealers were mercane as well, each dressed in finery to rival Kaanyr's host, but each one's tastes in colors and cut varied significantly.

The mercane led Kaanyr to an unoccupied spot near the center of the tent and glided toward a plush chair with numerous cushions that had been pulled up to a low table. As he sat, the mercane offered Kaanyr a similar seat on the opposite side of the table.

"Wine?" the mercane asked, gesturing to a crystal service set on the table. "Perhaps a sweetmeat?"

Still sated from the meal back at the palace, Kaanyr declined. He knew that the mercane considered it customary to engage in pleasantries for a few moments before getting down to business, but he had no time.

"I thank you for your hospitality, and your willingness to do business," Kaanyr said, "but time is of the essence. I need weapons. Can you accommodate me?"

The mercane sniffed, obviously put off by the cambion's brusque manner, but he nodded. "Indeed," he answered. "What sort of weapons?"

"I need an enchanted blade," Kaanyr said. "Something with a bit of bite to it. A good sword."

The mercane sat back and steepled his long fingers together in front of his mouth. "I see," he said. "And your funds? You wish to spend all of what you showed me?"

Kaanyr hesitated. He had other pouches hidden on his person, but those diamonds were a significant part of his fortune. And he wanted more than just a sword. "Perhaps," he said, refusing to commit. "Depending."

"On . . . ?" the mercane asked. "I have the finest quality enchanted swords of every style imaginable in the entire city. I'm sure you can find something you like."

"I'm sure I can, too," Kaanyr said, "but I'm also looking for something a bit more arcane to round out my purchase. I dabble a bit in the dweomers myself, so I have some specific ideas in mind."

"Oh? And what would those be?"

"Well, I prefer wands," Kaanyr said. "Though potions will do in a pinch."

"And what kind of wands would you like?" the mercane asked.

"Something with some power," Kaanyr answered. "Flashy, potent. That's what I like. Oh, and I need a reliable means of flying. It's become an issue of late."

"I think I can accommodate you," the mercane said, smiling.

Kaanyr found the grin a bit predatory, and he fought the urge to shudder.

❖ ❖ ❖ ❖ ❖ ❖ ❖ ❖

Later, after concluding his business—and after cursing himself for spending so much—Kaanyr worked his way back to the Palace of Myriad Amazements. He was still thinking how best to sneak back inside when he spotted Micus.

The angel walked on the far side of the street with another angel alongside, one that Kaanyr recognized as his jailor. Garin, he thought. I think that was his name. The sight of those two made him draw up short and want to vanish into the crowd.

They strode with purpose between a pair of utterly strange creatures. The creatures reminded the cambion of centaurs, though they were certainly not of flesh and blood. In some places, he could see alabaster skin, but in between, gears, pistons, and tubes of brass and steel shone through. The creatures wore golden armor, and they walked with the same sense of urgency that Micus and the other angel displayed.

Kaanyr followed them from a distance, but he already knew where they were headed. When they reached the steps of the Palace of Myriad Amazements, the cambion knew it was time to clear out. He turned to flee, to leave Dweomerheart by whatever means he could find, and then his mind betrayed him.

If you don't do something to warn Tauran and the others, you're putting the entire mission at risk.

That was all it took to force Kaanyr to try to help.

CHAPTER FOURTEEN

Aliisza sat bolt upright and reached for her blade. That innate sense of danger pounded, warning the alu to get out. She had her sword drawn and was on her feet before she even remembered where she was.

A quick check around the room told her that Kaanyr was gone and that Tauran and Kael still slept. The absence of her lover troubled Aliisza, but not nearly so much as the impending sense of a threat. She fingered Pharaun's ring and activated its arcane powers, seeking some evidence that her internal warning was justified.

The entire room erupted in a blaze of magical resonance, as if the whole chamber, including the air she was breathing, was highly magical. It made her worse than blind; it dazzled her with its intensity.

Fool, she told herself. You're at the very home of magic. What did you expect?

Dismissing the power of the ring, she concentrated on her other, more natural senses. There was nothing amiss as far as she could tell, other than the cambion's absence.

Then she noticed the food was gone.

She padded softly to the couch where Tauran slept, his breathing slow and deep. Getting one hand near his mouth, Aliisza reached down with the other and nudged him with a finger against his shoulder.

"Mmm? What?" the angel mumbled.

Aliisza clamped her hand over his mouth and put her other finger to her lip. "Shhh," she whispered. "Something's wrong."

Tauran's eyes widened for a moment, then he recognized her and grew still. Finally, he nodded, and Aliisza took her hand away. "What is it?" he asked.

"I don't know," the alu replied. "I just get a sense sometimes, and it's telling me that we need to leave."

Tauran sat up and looked around. "Where's Vhok?" he asked in a soft but urgent tone.

Aliisza shrugged. "Nothing to deal with right now," she said. "First, we need to get out of this room."

"Don't wake Kael," Tauran said as the alu stepped toward the knight. "Let me do it."

She glanced back at the angel, then shrugged and nodded.

Tauran moved to one side and leaned over the sleeping half-drow. He whispered something in Kael's ear then shifted back, out of the way. In a single smooth motion, Kael bolted upright. The knight had his sword up in both hands and was staring hard at the door. Aliisza gaped at her son. She had no idea where he had been holding it beforehand.

Kael got his bearings and caught her staring. "I inherited more than just your good looks," he said softly with a grim smile on his face.

I'll say, she thought. Remind me never to wake you up.

She moved to the door and placed her ear against it. She heard footfalls growing louder from the opposite side of the portal, and her sense of threat grew more intense as she stood there. Whatever was spooking her, it was coming through that door, and soon.

She wove a simple spell upon the door, sealing it.

"What do you sense?" Tauran asked, freeing his own mace from the loop on his belt. "What's coming?"

Aliisza shook her head. "I don't know, but I don't really want to wait around to find out."

"Can you whisk us away through one of your magical doors?" Kael asked.

Aliisza shook her head. "I can sense that something would prevent it from working," she replied. "We can't escape, but maybe we can hide."

"Hide? How?" Kael asked, his tone filled with doubt.

Aliisza thought for a moment. "Like this," she said, and she grabbed one end of the couch where she had rested. "Help me," she urged the knight, and when he'd grabbed the other end, they pulled it a little less than a pace away from the edge of the room. "Get against the wall," she ordered, even as she moved there herself. The other two joined her, and she pulled a small block of granite free of a pocket inside her bodice. Chanting, she gestured with the tiny block where she wished to spring her spell.

A wall formed there.

Aliisza had conjured the wall so that it ran parallel to the one against which the three of them pressed themselves, giving it the coloring and texture to match. She left a hole in it near the middle and at the floor, large enough that they could crawl through it but hidden from the other side by the couch.

Aliisza put her fingers to her lips to motion for the other two to remain quiet, then she squatted down next to the hole and cocked her head to one side, listening. Tauran and Kael joined her.

For several agonizing moments, the alu heard nothing. Then, though she wasn't sure, she thought she detected the creak of the door opening. She held her breath.

"They're not here!" The voice was muffled, but the voice uttering those words was unmistakable.

Micus.

"You told me you had detained them!" the angel said.

"We did," came an unfamiliar voice. "They must have slipped out magically. I expected that they would still be asleep, after what we dosed them with. I don't understand."

Aliisza heard footsteps enter the room and begin to pace.

"Do you see them in here?" Micus asked. "Are they hiding from us magically?"

There was a pause, then a third voice spoke up. "No. They are not employing magic to hide within this chamber." The sound of that third voice was odd, mechanical.

"But you can still sense them?" Micus pressed.

"Yes," the mechanical voice replied. "They are somewhere in that direction."

"You know how they did it, Micus," came yet another voice, one that was vaguely familiar to Aliisza, though she could not quite place it. "The alu and her magic doorways. That's how she managed to escape with Vhok right out from under my nose."

Of course! Aliisza realized. That's the angel that had been guarding Kaanyr!

"That's impossible," the second voice insisted. "We have the room warded against that."

"Then they probably used another method to get past your sentries," Micus said. "They must have slipped out of here just before we arrived."

"They must still be inside the building," the second voice

said. "I can have my sentries begin searching."

"Yes," Micus said. "Please do so. What a shame. So close . . ."

The sound of footsteps retreating was followed by the slamming of the door.

Aliisza listened for a moment longer, fearful that it had all been a trick and that Micus knew where they were hiding. Tauran and Kael remained still as well, as if sharing her thoughts.

"I think they're gone," the knight whispered. "Push the couch away."

The three of them very carefully and quietly shifted the couch forward, until there was enough room for them to exit. The alu sighed in relief when she saw that the room was empty.

"We can't stay here," Tauran said, rising to his feet. "They'll be back soon enough."

"How do you know?" Aliisza asked, walking around the couch into the center of the room.

"Because I think they're using zelekhuts," he said, and his expression was grim.

"Using what?" Aliisza asked. Fear was addling her brain. Focus!

"I was afraid of that," Kael said, nodding to Tauran. He turned to Aliisza. "Zelekhuts are inevitables—constructs built to enforce laws. They are very good at hunting down anyone who has broken an agreement or has tried to escape justice. We sometimes use them to track and capture criminals."

"That strange voice you heard," Tauran said, "and what it said about not seeing us hiding by some magical means. That is the mark of a zelekhut."

"Your idea to make a wall was brilliant, Aliisza," Kael

added. "It wasn't magical. No illusion, no invisibility or other means of masking us. Just a second wall. It made the room look normal to the zelekhut."

Aliisza shrugged. "It was a snap decision," she said. "I had no idea." She had to fight not to grin at the compliment.

"Regardless, Micus and his zelekhut will be back," Tauran said. "It can track one of us. Probably me. Micus knows me better than either of you two, and he can help the construct get a better sense of what it's hunting."

"Ah," Aliisza said. "It can sense which direction you are, but not how near or far."

"Yes," Tauran said, "but once it starts moving through the building, sensing me from different angles, it won't take long to pinpoint where I am. We must leave."

"How?" Kael asked. "Whoever was trying to curry favor with Micus said he was going to have his sentries looking for us."

"Time for a disguise," Tauran answered, and he shimmered before their eyes, changing form. His wings disappeared, and his clothing transformed from his brilliant white tunic and leggings to a simple brown robe with a deep hood. "Tyr may have denied me many of my powers, but I can still do this." Even his voice sounded different.

Aliisza followed suit, changing herself into a plump, matronly woman in robes similar to Tauran's.

Kael looked back and forth between the two, frowning. "That's all fine for the two of you, but I lack the power to hide myself in that fashion."

"Not to worry," Aliisza said. She reached down and tore a bit of cloth from the corner of her robes, then wove a spell over it. The shred of fabric became another full robe. "There you go," she said, handing it to Kael.

The knight slipped it on over his armor and pulled the hood up. "Much better," he said, "but my sword is a bit too noticeable."

"We'll have to risk it," Tauran said. "Use it like a walking stick, and stay right behind the two of us. All we need is enough time to get out the front entrance, then it won't matter."

The trio moved to the door. Tauran took the lead, cracking it a tiny bit to peer through to the hallway beyond. Aliisza gripped her sword, ready to free it from her robes should they be attacked. Tauran pulled the door a little wider and peeked his head out.

"Come," he said, motioning for the other two to follow him. "Before someone comes and sees which room this is."

The three companions hurried out into the empty hall and Kael pulled the door shut behind him. They moved down the passage in the direction they had come when they arrived.

Aliisza kept fighting the urge to look down, to conceal her face. Despite her disguise, she feared that she would be recognized. She could not explain the irrational fear that coursed through her. *You feel out of control,* she told herself. *You knew the food was tainted and you fell for it anyway. Now you don't trust yourself.*

Kael walked slightly behind the other two, trying to press in behind them as much as possible. The soft, rhythmic ringing of his sword as it struck the stone floor was jarring, and Aliisza expected a crowd of hound archons to come zipping around some corner at any moment, running in search of the offending sound.

"Can you muffle that a bit?" she whispered fiercely as they neared the steps. "*Pretend* you're using it as a walking stick."

Kael said nothing, but the sound diminished.

The trio made their way to the front entrance of the

building and Aliisza thought they might actually manage to sneak out undetected. As they drew close to the doors, though, a lantern archon flitted down and swarmed around them.

Aliisza held her breath and pretended to ignore the creature.

"I don't recognize you," the glowing orb said, hovering in front of the three. "When did you arrive? Do you have clearance to depart?"

Tauran said nothing, just kept walking, so Aliisza followed his lead. They got close to the door and she reached out to push it open. Beyond it, freedom called to her.

"Please stop," the archon said. "I need to know who you are."

"Keep going!" Tauran said, and he pressed his hands against the matching door.

As the two of them touched the portal together, an alarm went off, loud enough to make Aliisza cringe.

"Don't stop!" Tauran said, shoving his way through the door. Aliisza and Kael kept pace with him.

Beyond the doors, the porch was relatively empty, and the steps leading down into the plaza beyond beckoned. Folk there had stopped to peer toward the building, trying to see what was causing the ruckus.

"There they are!" Micus shouted from above.

Aliisza turned to look and spotted the angel perched upon the roof directly over the doors, pointing at them.

By the Abyss! she silently swore, yanking her sword free. Will he never leave us alone?

"Zelekhut!" Tauran shouted, pointing.

The alu redirected her gaze where her companion pointed and spotted a strange being rushing toward them.

It looked to Aliisza for all the world like a centaur, but it had been made, not born. Its skin was incomplete, and she could see mechanical things peeking from beneath, where she would have expected muscles and blood to exist. It wore a suit of gold plate barding.

The construct rushed toward them from one side of the building, its hooves striking sparks on the stone as it charged. Aliisza heard the same clattering sound of steel on stone from the opposite direction. She turned that way and spied a second construct galloping to confront them. It spun a pair of spiked chains overhead that extended from its forearms, just above its hands.

Another deva settled to the ground at the base of the broad steps. Aliisza remembered him as the one who had held Kaanyr prisoner back in the House of the Triad. He stood there with his mace ready, blocking their way.

They were surrounded.

◆ ◆ ◆ ◆ ◆ ◆ ◆ ◆ ◆

The scene confused Kaanyr.

Micus and Garin, the angel who had been his jailor, exited the Palace of Myriad Amazements along with the two strange mechanical centaurs. *Why are they coming back out?* he wondered. *Where are Aliisza and the others?*

Although he had managed to coerce himself into aiding his companions merely by thinking of the ramifications of abandoning them, he had hesitated at the steps of the palace. He had no means of sneaking back into the building without being noticed. Knowing he could do little that way, he hid himself among some vendor carts on the near side of the plaza. Waiting and watching was a better use of his skills than madly throwing himself in harm's way.

The cambion was still hiding and contemplating alternatives when Micus and his cohorts reemerged. Although he had anticipated that they might come out with prisoners in tow, he had not expected them to reappear empty-handed.

At least for the moment, Kaanyr thought as he watched the pursuers spread out around the entrance. Micus flew to the roof of the porch, while the two strange mechanical creatures moved to either flank. Garin took up a position at the base of the ramp.

An ambush.

Well, two can play at that game, Kaanyr decided.

He did not wait long. Some sort of horn began to blare from within the building, and three robed and hooded figures appeared and hurried toward the steps.

It was only when Micus reacted that Kaanyr realized the figures were his companions.

Everything happened at once. Micus swooped toward them, shouting. The two constructs rushed forward, closing in from either side. Only Garin remained in place, standing guard at the bottom of the ramp, keeping the fugitives bottled up.

And that was whom Kaanyr struck first.

Stepping out of the shadows between the nearest carts, the cambion slipped behind the angel with his sword in hand. The blade crackled with a bluish black energy, pulsing in anticipation. Kaanyr drew it back and was on the verge of driving it between the deva's wings when a woman nearby screamed.

The angel spun around just as Kaanyr thrust the sword at him. The blade ripped into Garin's wing, slicing a huge hole in it. The crackling energy dancing along the sword burst out from the wound, spreading like a sickly disease.

Garin's eyes went wide with the pain. "You!" he growled, staggering back from Kaanyr. "Damn you, you son of a rutter!"

"Such unbecoming language for one so enlightened as yourself," Kaanyr said with a mocking smile. He stepped forward, taking the fight to the deva. He brought his sword up for another strike. Garin whipped his mace into place and parried the blow. Blood streamed from the angel's wing as they circled.

"You don't like my language?" Garin asked. "Well how about something a little more holy?"

He opened his mouth to speak again, but Kaanyr had been expecting the tactic. Before Garin could utter the holy word, the cambion flipped a wand into view and commanded it to discharge its magic.

A blazing white bolt of lightning sprang from the tip of the wand and connected with the angel. The electrical energy crackled and swarmed over its target. Kaanyr knew the deva shrugged off some of the power of the wand, but the attack was enough to wound him. Garin went rigid for an instant, then fell to the paving stones with a raw scream.

"I'm sorry," Kaanyr said to Garin in a mocking tone as he raised his sword, "but I didn't quite hear what you were trying to say!" Kaanyr thrust the sword at the angel. He drove it deep into the deva's gut and jerked it free again.

Garin gasped and lurched from the blow. Bluish black energy swarmed across his body in a spiderweb effect. His eyes went wide and rolled up in his head. He shuddered once and lay still.

Kaanyr gave the angel a mocking salute with his blade and sprinted past, heading to his companions to aid them in their own fight.

As Kaanyr closed with Aliisza and the others, he saw Kael battling one of the constructs, while Aliisza faced off with the second one. Tauran and Micus stood toe to toe, appearing to argue more than actually battle. Micus's back was to Kaanyr, so he took the opportunity to close in unseen.

The cambion brought his new sword up, ready to plunge it into Micus's back, as he crossed the distance to his target. As he neared striking range, though, Tauran shook his head.

"No, Vhok!" the angel ordered. "Do not kill him!"

Upon hearing the command, Kaanyr snarled, but he lowered his weapon. His momentum carried him forward nonetheless. Micus, aware by then that the cambion was there, turned to confront the new threat. Kaanyr lowered his shoulder and plowed into the angel, driving him across the porch and into a column. Though Micus wasn't caught completely by surprise, the force of the cambion's attack slammed him hard. Micus's head impacted with the stone and stunned him.

It wasn't quite what he had in mind, but Kaanyr felt a sense of satisfaction watching the angel go down. He drew his foot back to kick the angel, but Tauran grabbed him.

"Go help Aliisza!" Tauran said. "Hurry!"

Grumbling at being forced to acquiesce to every order the angel gave him, Kaanyr spun away from his intended target and sought the alu out.

Aliisza still battled the strange mechanical centaur. The construct had the upper hand in the fight. Twin chains extending from its forearms were wrapped around the half-fiend, pinning her wings and arms to her sides. The thing reeled her in, drawing her closer. She frantically tried to shrug off the restraints.

Kaanyr sprang to the alu's side and leveled his wand at

the construct. He spoke the command and fired a bolt of lightning at the thing. The blinding flash popped between the wand and the creature, leaving afterimages in the cambion's field of vision. When his sight returned a moment later, Kaanyr could see the construct sprawled upon the ground and Aliisza free of the entwining chains.

"Go!" the cambion shouted, gesturing to the night sky overhead. "Get out of here!"

Aliisza shook her head. "Kael and Tauran still need help!"

"I'll stay. Just fly!"

But the alu wouldn't heed him, and his attention was drawn back to the construct, which had regained its feet. Kaanyr knew the dweomer on his blade would have little impact on the creature, but he hoped its preternatural sharpness would still cut through the thing's armor.

"Together," Aliisza said, swishing her own blade through the air. "Flank him." She moved away from the cambion, trying to swing around to the far side of the mechanical centaur. The creature saw the alu's intentions and tried to back away, but Kaanyr grinned in anticipation and leaped into the fray.

Working together, the two half-fiends pressed the attack, wearing the thing down with well-timed feints and parries. Eventually, they scored some serious wounds. It remained in the fight, though, refusing to yield or flee.

Kaanyr drove in with a series of cuts at the construct's upper torso. The rapid attack served to distract the thing enough for Aliisza to slip inside its defenses and run her blade deep into its chest. With a single, gurgling sigh, it sank down to the ground and went still. Strange fluids and wisps of smoke poured from the various openings in its skin.

Kaanyr turned to see Kael dispatch the other construct with his sword. The monumental strike cleaved the creature's head from its body. It crumpled to the ground seeping liquids and smoke.

The cambion turned, seeking another enemy. He spotted Tauran and Micus sparring again. The two had abandoned their weapons and were punching and wrestling bare-handed. As Kaanyr rushed toward the two, Micus grabbed Tauran's arm and tried to spin him around, but Tauran slipped free. When Micus went after him again, Tauran snapped off a punch with his other fist, catching his foe squarely on the jaw.

The blow staggered Micus, and Tauran stepped toward him and jabbed again. Micus managed to evade the second punch, but by then, Tauran's companions had surrounded him. Micus tried to defend himself from all of them, but when his back was to Kael, the knight swung his blade low and caught the angel with the flat of it against the back of his knees.

Micus dropped to the ground and Tauran pounced. He put Micus in a headlock as the other angel twisted and kicked, trying to prevent it.

"Enough!" Tauran growled, tightening his grip. "This is insanity! Let it go!"

"No," Micus croaked, futilely trying to slip a hand underneath Tauran's arms and work himself free. "I have a duty!"

"Of course you do, Micus," Tauran said, "but I am not your enemy! There are worse forces at work here, and you've lost sight of that!"

"The law is the law," Micus said, his voice growing more constricted by the moment. "I swore to uphold it!"

"As did I," Tauran said gently, though he held the choke-hold tight. "But somewhere along the way, I realized that some laws, even good ones, can result in bad things happening. And then we must be ruled by common sense first and fix those laws."

"Blasphemy! You are not the friend I knew!"

"I am. But I have to stop Zasian. Now, please! Quit fighting me and help us. Please!"

"No!" Micus cried. "Surrender! Redeem yourself!"

"I can't do that," Tauran said. "Not until I've stopped Zasian. When that's done, I will gladly surrender to you." The angel took a deep breath. "Now. Garin is gravely injured. When you awaken, heal him. And tell him I'm sorry. It should never have come to this."

Micus tried to say something else, but he was rapidly losing consciousness. He struggled feebly for a few heartbeats more then began to sag. When he went limp, Tauran held the headlock a moment longer, then released the other angel.

A crowd had gathered around the scene of the fight, and a trio of archons emerged from the palace. Kael stepped between them and the rest of the group, his blade barring their way.

Tauran stood and glared at Kaanyr. "Where did you get that blade? Garin might die from that foul thing!"

Kaanyr sneered. "Oh, you're quite welcome. Glad to come to your rescue, noble angel."

Tauran took a step toward Kaanyr, but Aliisza was between them in a flash. "Stop!" she shouted. "What's done is done!"

Tauran hesitated, still glaring.

Kaanyr tightened his grip on his blade, but he didn't strike the angel. He wondered which of them Aliisza thought she was protecting. *Him or me?* He stared at her, feeling jealousy boil up again. *It's time she sees the truth,* he decided.

He gave the deva a surly smirk and waved his hand in

dismissal. "You're so weak. I should have killed Garin. It would have been the smart thing to do. You should slay this fool right now"—he pointed at Micus—"and be rid of his pestering. But I abided by your wishes and spared them both."

Tauran's eyes narrowed, and he clenched both hands into fists. "I should slay you right now and be done with your foul, corrupt influence."

Kaanyr turned to Aliisza then. "Do you see?" he said, pointing at Tauran. "Do you see what you're getting tangled up with? He will never love you. Not like I do. He can't; he's too bound by honor, too caught up in doing what's right. And you've got the blood of a demon flowing through you. What can possibly come of that but ruin?"

Aliisza stared at the cambion, wide-eyed. She worked her mouth to retort, but nothing came out.

Kaanyr waved his hand, dismissing her, too. "Fool alu," he grumbled.

"Enough," Kael said quietly, placing a hand on Tauran's shoulder. "We've worn out our welcome here. Those archons didn't want any part of us by themselves, and they retreated inside again. But they will be back with reinforcements. We must go. We have to find Zasian."

Tauran's jaw flexed, then the anger seemed to go out of him. "Yes, of course," he said. "Thank you for reminding me, Kael."

Kaanyr shook his head in disgust. "I guarantee you, they will be trouble again. Your foolish benevolence will come back to haunt you. Mark my words."

Tauran ignored him. "We must be gone before Micus awakens," he said. "Vhok, can you fly?"

"As a matter of fact," the half-fiend answered smugly, "I can." He took hold of the new cape he had donned and spread it out behind himself. "Lead on, O wise Captain!"

Tauran gave Kaanyr a sidelong glance, but he did not rise to the bait. "Let's go, then." He took to the air.

Beside him, Aliisza still stared. He met her gaze and saw searing anger.

"Bastard," she spat. "You'll never change. You'll never get those self-righteous, condescending blinders off your eyes and see the wider world around you. I should have known better than to start believing you could." She took to the air without a glance back.

Damn straight I won't change, Kaanyr thought, staring after her. *I know who* I *am.*

Tauran led them. As they flew, they passed countless wondrous sights, but Kaanyr did not notice them. He struggled to come to grips with the fact that he was losing the alu. He did not want it to matter so much, but it did.

Maybe it's because of whom I'm losing her to, he thought. *I just don't get what she sees in him. What can he possibly offer her that I cannot?*

The four travelers drew near the edge of the city, and Kaanyr realized the entire community sat beneath a massive, shimmering dome of some transparent substance. Beyond it, a sea of blackness filled with countless stars stretched forever. Where it met the ground, numerous gates punctured it, and Tauran led them to one such portal—a massive pair of valves. As they neared the gate, the angel dropped low and landed.

"We can reach the Eye this way," the deva said as he walked to the towering doors, which stood open. There were surprisingly few people passing either in or out of the gate. "It exists in a set of caverns, below the city."

"Will they let us through?" Aliisza asked. "Do you think they've heard about what happened yet?"

"I don't know. We'll find out. Be ready, but don't get jumpy. Any of you." He looked directly at Kaanyr.

The cambion gave a mocking, ingratiating smile and nodded. "As you command, O Captain."

The hound archons guarding the great gate wore different clothing from those that had been at the Palace of Myriad Amazements. Instead of livery and weapons, they dressed in simple robes, like the monks of numerous orders on Toril. They eyed the four visitors as Kaanyr and the others approached and one of them moved to greet them.

"Welcome, strangers. Have you come to pay homage to Savras the All-Seeing?"

Kaanyr noted that a symbol of a scrying globe filled with eyes adorned the breast of the creature's robes.

"Yes, and also to seek his wisdom," Tauran answered. "May we enter?"

The archon studied them all for a long moment. "You do not seem likely followers of He of the Third Eye."

"Our need is great," Tauran said, "and our generosity greater," he added, holding out his mace. "An offering for the honor of entering."

The archon's eyes widened. "Your need must be great, if you are willing to surrender this," he said. He took the holy weapon and studied it for a moment. "It is useless to us, angel. You know that. None but your kind may wield it. It holds no value for any but you."

"Perhaps, but it is all I have to offer, and isn't the point to give more than you can afford?"

The archon smiled. "Indeed. It is a symbol of all that. Very well. You may enter the Eye. Do you know the way from here?"

"I think we can find it."

The archon nodded and stepped aside, motioning for them to pass through the gates.

Once they were beyond the portal, they found themselves on the edge of a plateau. The path before them wound toward the bottom, a switchback that disappeared from sight because of the steepness.

Kaanyr noticed Kael was smiling. "What are you grinning at, fool knight?" he asked.

Kael didn't answer, but Aliisza grabbed Tauran's arm and turned him toward her.

"How could you do that?" she demanded. "You gave up your sacred mace! An angel never does that!"

"Never by choice," he said. "But our need is great." Then he produced a similar weapon, which he had kept hidden in his tunic. "But that wasn't my mace." He smiled. "It was Micus's."

Aliisza giggled.

Kaanyr grimaced. "Very deceptive, deva," he said. "My bad influence must be rubbing off on you."

Tauran gave the cambion a haughty stare. "Much more than I would like, cambion."

CHAPTER FIFTEEN

The four of them took to the air then, flying down the side of the great plateau upon which Dweomerheart rested. No land stretched beyond its base. Instead, the whole thing floated in the great field of stars. The night sky stretched out both above and below.

At the bottom of the trail, they came to a wide ledge jutting out from the side of the plateau. A large cave mouth led into the depths from there. A second pair of guards stood on either side of the darkened entrance. As the group landed, one of them bowed.

"Welcome to the Eye," he said. "Search for the truth in all things great and small, my friends. Enter and fill your minds with knowledge."

Tauran led the way through the passage from the cave entrance. As they walked, Aliisza noted the width of the path down the center of the tunnel. Compared to the rougher area of the floor on either side, it was smooth as glass and slightly concave, like a trough.

Many, many pairs of feet have passed this way.

The tunnel ran straight and descended slightly. At regular

intervals, torches illuminated the way. Ahead, Aliisza could see the passage level off and the torches end. When they reached the flat area, Aliisza slowed a step or two, awed.

The path ended at a large wooden dock. A hound archon stood at its near edge, watching them approach. Numerous small boats had been tied off to the dock. Each boat bore a boatman, another hound archon dressed in the robes of Savras and who stood in the rear of the craft, waiting. Beyond the dock, water stretched out into an immense cavern, easily as large as some of the great chambers and halls of the Underdark. Scattered throughout the vast emptiness, dozens—no, hundreds—of torches twinkled faintly. They filled the cavern like stars, both near the water's surface and high overhead.

Aliisza felt very small.

"What is this place?" Kaanyr asked in a near-whisper. "Where does it all go?"

"It is the Third Eye," Tauran answered. "The embodiment of Savras's knowledge. The whole place is a honeycomb of tunnels, chambers, and sinkholes. It goes deeper, too. Beneath the water."

"Where do we start?" Aliisza asked. She was overwhelmed with the enormity of the task. "How will we know what to look for?"

Tauran advanced to the dock. "I don't know," he said. He stepped up to the greeter. "We have come seeking knowledge," he said.

The hound archon, his muzzle gray with age, nodded. "May you find it, then," he said. "Do you understand the patterns? The dangers?"

Tauran shook his head. "We have never visited before."

"Few come twice. Trust your insight. Do not rely solely

on your vision. Let the inner force of your desire for understanding be your guide. More, I cannot say."

Tauran cocked his head to one side, pondering. "It's up to us, our instinct, to know where to go," he said. "In every choice, something is revealed. About ourselves, about others. Is that it?"

The hound archon smiled, but said nothing. He merely bowed again.

The angel turned back to his companions. "We have to go on our gut feelings," he said. "If we envision what we need to learn and open ourselves to the subtleties of our subconscious, the veil may be lifted, and we may find what we seek."

"Sounds like a game that's hard to win," Kaanyr said, frowning. "Lots of opportunities to get lost."

"Some that pass through here do not return," the archon said. "Perhaps they never find what they seek, or perhaps they find . . . something else. Something unintended. Whatever the outcome, you are the guide, you must steer the course."

"Are you certain this is what we want to do?" Kaanyr asked. "Is it worth the risk of vanishing in this maze?"

As Aliisza stared out over the water at the distant twinkling lights, she found herself agreeing with Kaanyr's caution. I've never been afraid of the dark before, she thought. What's different about this place?

Tauran gazed levelly at the cambion. "I have surrendered everything I hold dear to right this wrong. What do you think?"

"Well, good for you, angel," Kaanyr said. "I've given up quite a bit, too, and may yet give up more. I still want to think about this before we just plunge into the darkness forever."

"I know of no other way to get ahead of Zasian," Tauran said. "So long as we keep following his breadcrumb trail, we play his game. If we succeed at this, we may have the means to stop him. I'm committed to that possibility. And you are, too."

Kaanyr glared at Tauran, but he said nothing more.

Aliisza watched the cambion and imagined his mind working, trying to figure out a way to bypass the angel's control over him. She was still furious with him for his boorish attack earlier, but at that moment, when she so feared passing deeper into those caverns, she actually felt a bit sorry for him. *I have a choice; he has to go in there whether he likes it or not. Still, he might actually learn something about himself . . .*

But that's what you're afraid of, isn't it? she asked herself. *Seeing too deeply into your own heart.*

"Quit fighting it," she said softly to Kaanyr, so no one else could hear. "Trust me; I know of what I speak."

"How could you stand it?" Kaanyr whispered. "How could you put up with his sneering, condescending arrogance?"

So, he begins to understand at last, she thought, trying not to smirk. *He finally sees how much he betrayed me.* "You'd be surprised," she said, staring pointedly at her lover. "I've had lots of practice."

Kaanyr caught her look and snorted, but she saw his faint smile nonetheless. He inclined his head at her, acknowledging her point. "Let's go," he said, following Tauran.

The angel walked along the dock, studying the different boats. He paused a couple of times, examining a particular craft more closely, but he would move on again after a short time. When he'd traversed the entire row of boats, he shrugged.

"I'm no closer to picking than I was before," he said. "This may take a while."

Aliisza thought for a moment. Then inspiration struck. "What are you thinking about?" she asked.

Tauran frowned. "Which boat feels right."

The alu shook her head. "No," she said, "not like that. Look at me. Now, what do you want to do more than anything?"

Tauran bit his lip. "To catch Zasian."

"How?"

"By knowing what he's planning."

"Exactly," Aliisza said. "Feel that. What is Zasian planning?" She looked at her other two companions. "Fix that in your mind."

The alu followed her own advice. She closed her eyes and imagined the priest, pictured his face. She watched him, studied him, waited for him to act. Then, she imagined which boat would carry her to Zasian, to his next step.

The choice came to her suddenly and clearly.

Aliisza opened her eyes just as Kael said, "It's that one." He was pointing to her own choice.

"Yes," Kaanyr agreed, and Tauran nodded beside him.

"Let's go," the angel said, and they boarded the boat together.

The boatman untied the moorings and pushed the craft away from the dock. The boat moved into the open water and began to pick up speed on its own. The archon stood silently at the stern, occasionally dipping a single paddle into the water to adjust the heading slightly, but he did not row or pole the craft forward.

"Where are we going?" Kaanyr asked. "Or must we choose that, too?"

"I think we do," Kael said.

Aliisza filled her mind with images of Zasian again. She pictured him planning, plotting, scheming. As she did so, subtle hints came to her about the way to follow. The course the boat set seemed to acknowledge her thoughts.

Or maybe Tauran's, or all of us, she thought.

Whatever the circumstances, whenever she glanced at her companions, they all were just as keenly observant of where the craft was taking them, and they all seemed equally as content.

The boat glided along the black water, leaving the docks far behind, until Aliisza could not remember which set of torch lights indicated its location. She peered all around, studying the various points of light. Most seemed to lie along the shores of the subterranean lake, but many more sat up high, perhaps on shelves of cave wall or hanging from the ceiling. She was never certain, for they didn't illuminate much. They simply hovered, distant pinpricks of light against a tapestry of night.

The alu stared down into the water. It was as black as the very depths of the earth, and she could see nothing there—until without warning, they passed over a point where faint light shone up from far, far, below. At first she thought it was just a trick of her mind, a reflection from overhead, but when she looked up and saw dozens of other pinpoints of light there, she knew the water somehow did not mirror them.

Whatever was down there was real, and deep.

"That way," Tauran blurted after they had been traveling for some time. "We need to go over there." He pointed to a set of lights slightly up from the water level.

Aliisza frowned. It did not feel right to her. "Are you sure?" she asked, sensing that they should keep going straight.

"No," Kael said, "I don't think that's right."

Tauran looked at them. "Concentrate," he said. "I know that's where we ought to go."

Aliisza focused her attention once more on Zasian and his impending actions, but the sense that they should continue straight grew stronger. Before she could express her disagreement, though, Kaanyr spoke up.

"No, you're leading us astray, angel," he said. "We need to visit those lights over there."

Aliisza opened her eyes to look where the cambion pointed and felt just as confused. "Both of you are wrong," she said. "We need to keep going forward."

"I agree with Aliisza," Kael said. "It's somewhere ahead, not to either side."

"No," Tauran argued, adamant. "I can feel this. It's right."

"And I say you're all wrong," Kaanyr countered. "I am certain we must go this way over here."

Aliisza frowned. "Boatman," she said, "what are we doing wrong?"

The archon bowed his head slightly at being addressed. "It is said that sometimes, different beings seeking the same knowledge must visit different points of the same path. Perhaps each of you is right, in his or her own way."

The four companions looked at one another.

"I know that what I seek is over there," Tauran said, pointing in the direction he had desired before. "I don't know what each of you is imagining, but if we want to stop Zasian, we *will* find the answers there."

Aliisza knew she felt just as strongly that she would only find what she was looking for if she headed the way she wanted to go. "Boatman," she said, "must we travel within your craft to reach our goals?"

The archon frowned. "I know of no one who has left a boat before," he said, "but then, I have only been serving as a guide for eleven hundred years; not long at all. I am not aware that it is forbidden or impossible."

"Then I propose we each take our own way," Aliisza said. "We each believe we will find Truth where our imaginations are taking us. Let's go our separate ways and find what we seek. We can meet back at the dock when we're finished."

"I don't like it," Tauran said. "It could prove disastrous."

"Or," Kaanyr countered, "it could give us four times as much information."

"The cambion is right," Kael said. "If we each seek our own way and return with a more complete picture, won't that improve our chances of finding and stopping the priest?"

Tauran thought for a few moments more then nodded. "If each of you is even half as certain of your paths as I am of this one, then I can't see preventing you from chasing it. Go." He motioned to them. "Find what we seek, and I will see you on the dock."

Aliisza smiled and stood. "I will be the first one back." She took to the air.

As she left the boat behind, she got an even greater sense of the vastness of the cavern. It grew absolutely quiet around her, without the gentle lapping of the water against the sides of the craft. All she could hear was the faint beating of her wings. It reminded her a great deal of her time back in Amarindar, when she and Kaanyr ruled over the armies of tanarruks in that fallen dwarven city. There were quiet places in the abandoned halls there, places where she could almost hear time creeping forward.

The Eye felt like that, but there was something more there, within those caverns. A buzz pervaded everything. It was no physical sound, but rather a soft undercurrent of . . . something. An expectation, perhaps. Aliisza came to realize it was the connection between her own expectations and the knowledge the vast cavern had to offer.

As she flew, that buzz grew stronger.

The alu let that sensation guide her. She followed it like a trail, somehow sensing that she needed to travel to a small set of lights ahead and slightly above herself. It did not take her long to reach them, and when she did, she hesitated.

A great stalagmite jutted forth from the water, a towering edifice of natural stone larger than any wizard's tower. Caves riddled its surface, some very natural in shape, others looking freshly dug. A pair of torches flanked each entrance. The flames flickered and danced, but none had burned out, as far as she could tell. An idle thought swept through her about the insanity of trying to keep so many lit.

They must be magical, she decided. Perhaps they burn forever.

Shrugging off the nonsensical notion, Aliisza focused her mind once more on the quarry of knowledge. Her sense guided her to a particular cavern—one up high, near the tip of the stalagmite. She landed upon the small shelf jutting out from the cave entrance and stood there, listening.

Her wariness increased as her innate sense of danger tickled the back of her mind.

Unlike before, when she had known something threatening would be coming through the door, her sense was different, more vague. It also wasn't quite so imminent. Something about it told her that the threat came from within, a weakness of herself, rather than from some external source.

I have too many questions, she realized. About Tauran, and Kaanyr, and Kael, and how I fit into each of their lives. Put them out of your mind, Aliisza, she told herself. Don't let them distract you from finding Zasian. If you don't, you might never get out of here.

Heeding that warning, she stepped forward cautiously,

still trying to detect some noise or other evidence of something beyond. When she failed to discern anything, Aliisza took a steadying breath and stepped across the threshold.

A bombardment of thoughts assaulted her mind. She spun out of control, lost in a haze of spinning, whirling notions. Ideas cascaded one atop another, making her dizzy. She lost track of her own physical existence while caught up in the mental cacophony of concepts, images, and realizations.

Stop it! she wanted to scream, and she pressed her hands against her own ears, trying in vain to block out the crashing, relentless thoughts. Get out of my head!

But the assault did not waver, and she fell to her knees, buffeted into a stupor.

❖ ❖ ❖ ❖ ❖ ❖ ❖

The boat rocked a bit as the others pushed off and flew into the darkness. Tauran watched them go until he could no longer see any of them. Each one winged in a different direction. None was the path he would follow.

No truer, more prophetic words, he thought.

For a moment, weariness overwhelmed the angel. He couldn't fathom how he had managed to keep the disparate pieces of the group together as long as he had. Every moment, something cropped up—an argument, a scowl or brusque word, a battle of wills—that threatened all he worked for.

The world balances upon the tip of a high, steep pinnacle, in danger of tipping and falling, he thought, and Tyr cannot see it. The High Council and Micus cannot see it. Only I try to hold it in place, and my mighty army consists of three half-fiends who cannot get along. He rubbed his hands across his eyes. How did it come to this?

Each of his companions—his tools, if he was bluntly honest with himself—presented a different challenge.

Kael, he could trust. Though the champion could be headstrong and volatile at times, Tauran knew the half-drow's heart, knew that he was as dedicated to their success as the deva himself. But he was young and naïve, and Tauran had to be wary of coming to rely overly much on him for sound judgment.

He'd lay down his life defending me, but there will come a point where he might need to sacrifice me, instead. Will he know when that is? Will he understand the necessity of it? Will he do it, even if I command him to?

Vhok was precisely the opposite; he would never be trustworthy. In some ways, that made it easier. So long as the angel kept firmly in mind that the cambion served only his own interests and tried in every way imaginable to circumvent his authority, Tauran could be ready for his tricks. But it still made him dangerous. The deva had nearly slipped a few times, letting his emotions get the better of him, or he had been caught off guard, like with that sword. *Must force him to get rid of that vile thing,* he reminded himself. But each time, he had recovered. No, the danger lay not in what Vhok could do to him, but in what he could do to the other two. His actions threatened to rip the cohesion of the group apart. He required the greatest amount of attention and care.

And then there was Aliisza. She was the enigma. He had expected her to flee long before, but she had not. He wasn't certain what possessed her to continue. She showed inklings of dedication, hints of coming to understand the value of loyalty and self-sacrifice, but she was no angel, hadn't been among them nearly long enough.

Kael sees himself as one of us, even if he has no celestial blood, but Aliisza . . . I cannot see into her heart, he realized. And because of that, she is the one most likely to be my undoing.

Tauran blinked and came out of his lamentations. He remembered where he was and what he was striving to stop. Guilt forced the weariness from his thoughts and made him renew his determination. The boat sat still in the black waters of the cavern. The boatman stood just as still, waiting for him.

With a deep breath, the angel refocused. What is Zasian planning? Where will he try to lead us? How can we stop him?

The boat began to glide forward in the water.

❖ ❖ ❖ ❖ ❖ ❖ ❖ ❖

Aliisza stood in a great rotunda that was dim with the light of a few faint candles. The large, circular room echoed with the sounds of voices, but those voices were indistinct, illogical. She stood away from the center, behind a thick, ornate column.

No. I am hiding, she heard herself think.

It was not the alu's own inner voice that spoke, though. She was also someone else.

She looked through the other's eyes, peered carefully around the side of the column toward the center. She glanced down at herself and gasped.

She was a thing of shadow, midnight black and indistinguishable from all the other shadows that filled the room. Cloaked.

In the center of the room, three figures stood, deep in conversation. She could see them only indistinctly, as though they were blurred, not solid. But somehow, she knew they were gods.

They argued.

One was a woman, coldly beautiful and tall. Black flowing hair. Pale radiant skin. Imbued with magic.

Aliisza felt jealousy. She desired the end of that one.

The pale, magic-infused woman stood beside a man, elderly, wizened. His flowing white hair joined with his thick, full beard and moustache, a mantle of authority upon his shoulders. He, too, seemed the embodiment of all that was arcane.

Together, they faced the third. A thin man, emaciated, craven. His chalk white skin stood in stark contrast to his fierce black eyes. He cringed before the pair, listening as they seemed to berate him, a wisp of a secret smile on his face.

Aliisza felt drawn to him, thought him handsome.

Another figure appeared, also on the periphery of the chamber. She, too, was indistinct, a thing of shimmering light. Nearly naked, her jet black skin covered the curves and litheness of a streetwalker, a night dancer. She was beautiful.

Aliisza wanted to fall on her knees, worship the dancer, bathe in her beauty, serve her forever.

But she must not.

There was work to do. She would do her job, perform her task, and curry favor from both the dark dancer and the craven one.

Yes.

The wizened man turned to the dark dancer, seemed startled that she had appeared. The pale woman with the dark hair and radiant skin also turned, and she seemed more angry than before. She and the dark dancer confronted one another as the wizened man looked on.

It was time.

Aliisza crept out from the shadows. She glided, step by step, behind the wizened man. She was nearly within reach, standing just behind him.

No one seemed to notice.

She waited.

The dark, beautiful one danced. She moved to some unheard rhythm, gyrated to a beat that did not reverberate within the rotunda. She was awesome to behold, undulating before the wizened man and the radiant woman.

The old one's posture changed. He seemed to lose his focus, becoming enamored of the dark dancer. He leaned forward, drawn to her.

In his enthrallment, he let his staff slip from his hands.

Aliisza knew it was her moment.

She reached out, prevented the wizened one's staff from falling, kept it upright so no one would see.

She grasped it in her hands, felt its power.

Long and wooden, each end shod in iron, it pulsed with arcane energy. Runes and sigils of every type shimmered and danced along its entire length. They had life and magic of their own. At the top, a brilliant sapphire as large as Aliisza's fist pulsed and hummed, vibrating with even more energies.

The magic that coursed through the staff was almost too much to bear. She hated that magic, wanted to beat the staff against the floor, rid it of the horrible power.

But she must not.

She had another purpose. She was a tool, like the staff was a tool.

So Aliisza remained still, just behind the wizened man. She held the staff, kept it from falling.

No one noticed her, the shimmering shadow.

A commotion arose at the periphery of the rotunda, away

from Aliisza. Others had come, lesser creatures, hated creatures. Aliisza spotted the first, and though she recognized him as friend, companion, she also hated him. An angel—a fallen angel.

Tauran.

Kaanyr appeared then, and also Kael.

Aliisza knew them, wanted to go to them, but at the same time, she wanted to hurt them, to see them suffer. She hated them.

The three of them called, trying to get the attention of the wizened man and the radiant woman, but neither of them would look over, neither of them could see or hear the newcomers.

Then Tauran tried to enter the center of the rotunda, tried to go to the wizened one, but there were others there, blocking his way.

Zasian had come.

Aliisza gasped again, seeing the priest. She felt hatred, but also appreciation. Obligation. Hope.

Zasian stood before Tauran and prevented him from crossing to the gods. Tauran tried to push past him, but Micus appeared, then, and Micus took hold of Tauran, too.

Tauran struggled, fought against them both. He shouted, called to the wizened one and the radiant one.

The gods noticed. They turned toward the commotion, seeing the newcomers for the first time.

All eyes were elsewhere, watching the angels and Zasian struggle.

Very carefully, Aliisza stepped back, away from the wizened man, creeping so as not to be seen, and took the staff with her. With each step, she stopped and looked back, checking to see if the wizened man or the radiant woman had taken note of her presence.

They had not.

She turned, finally, to the chalk white man.

He smiled at her and held out his hand.

Aliisza smiled back, though she knew he could not see her face, for it was cloaked in shadow. It *was* shadow. But she smiled at him just the same, for she liked him and wanted him to be happy.

She handed him the staff.

The chalk white man raised the staff, looked at it. He nodded in approval. Then he raised it high, holding it in both hands. He stepped right behind the radiant woman, the being who embodied magic.

The chalk white man brought the staff down, slamming it on the radiant woman's head.

He struck her so hard the staff cracked.

There was blinding light.

Aliisza screamed.

❖ ❖ ❖ ❖ ❖ ❖ ❖ ❖

The alu came to, huddled in a ball within darkness. Her head throbbed, but she no longer felt the assault of knowledge upon her. She could hear herself panting, but otherwise, all was quiet. She was drenched in sweat.

The images of the rotunda, of the trickery, came back to Aliisza. She did not understand it all, wasn't even sure who it was she had witnessed, but she knew one thing: Tauran and Micus would feud, and Zasian would use it to his advantage.

And another god would die.

I have to warn Tauran!

She sat up and peered around. She was just inside the cave mouth. It was a small chamber, no larger than a couple of paces on a side. The light of the torches shone dimly from just beyond the entrance. She had no idea where it came from, but a terrible sense of urgency overcame her. She had to hurry, though she did not understand why.

Aliisza heaved herself to her feet and ran. She launched herself out of the small cave and into the air, pumping her wings as hard as she could.

There was so little time.

Please be there, she thought, imagining her companions waiting at the dock for her.

She didn't want to be the first one back. She wanted them to be finished already, to know what she knew, to be ready to go when she returned.

So little time!

Though she had lost track of the way back to the dock during their passage, she knew the direction intimately during the return trip. She kept seeing her companions standing on the dock, waiting for her, and that kept it clear in her head. She fixated on that, thought of nothing else.

Get to the docks. Warn Tauran.

She saw the dock lights from a great distance away. They were nothing but a set of tiny glowing pinpricks, but she knew without a doubt that they were her beacons. She increased her speed, flying for all she was worth. Aliisza gasped for breath, fighting the weariness in her wings. The lights grew slowly larger.

At last, she began to make out features. She saw the boats first, moored to the docks, then the docks themselves.

There was no sign of her three companions.

Where are they? she wondered in dismay. We have to hurry!

She landed upon the docks and rushed over to the hound

archon that had greeted them. It was the same one, his gray muzzle familiar.

"My companions," she gasped. "I must find them, now. Can you help me bring them back here?"

The celestial creature looked at her in surprise. "They have already gone," he said. "You have been missing for four days."

CHAPTER SIXTEEN

his is unacceptable!" Tauran shouted. "You have done nothing but throw bureaucratic barriers in front of us since we got here. It's been three days!" He jabbed a forefinger into the archon's chest to drive home his point. "Now let me speak to someone who can do something about this!"

The archon stood straighter and glared at the angel. He reached up and straightened his white tunic so that the emblem of a hand wreathed in blue fire on his chest showed a little bit more prominently. "Do not touch me again," the dog-headed creature warned. "Or I *will* call for help, and you *will* be escorted out of here."

The clerk's officious tone made Tauran want to punch him. *I've been around Vhok for too long,* the angel thought. *I'm too quick to lash out.* He took a deep, calming breath and tried again.

"I'm very sorry," he said in gentler tones. "I am weary and it has been a long, perilous journey. But I have explained my urgency to you, and you do not seem to heed it."

"As I told you three times already," the archon said, "everyone is very busy. The proper people have been notified of your request, and when one of them gets a free moment, he or she will be happy to meet with you to discuss your concerns. Until then, you . . . must . . . wait!" The archon punctuated the last three words with little jabs of his finger, though he did not touch Tauran when he did so.

The angel sighed and turned away. "This is getting us nowhere," he muttered to Kael and Vhok. "We're going to have to find another way. Come."

He led the other two out of Azuth's Hall of Petitions. He stopped when they stood upon the street running in front of it and turned to look back. The edifice was immense, filling the cavern like some monolithic mountain. Tauran swept his gaze up, taking measure of the seemingly endless levels, plazas, and towers that rose by turns toward the ceiling of the great chamber. Near the top, surrounded by walls and minarets, a very large dome sat, the most splendid part of the structure.

Right there, the angel thought. *That's where it happens. And if we could just get inside and warn someone, we could stop it. That would be it. Zasian's plot would be foiled.*

"A lot of good it did us to leave Aliisza behind," Vhok grumbled from behind the deva.

Tauran resisted the urge to whirl on the cambion and glare at him. He could feel it all crumbling apart. *We're so close, but I can't hold this together much longer. My sanity teeters on the edge of oblivion.*

Vhok had been angry about abandoning the alu since Tauran made the decision. In fact, he had refused to entertain the possibility at all when the angel suggested it. Tauran was forced to explain the direness of the situation in terms that magically coerced the half-fiend to acquiesce. Vhok had fumed for the three days since, constantly uttering disparaging remarks, often under his breath, about every move the angel made.

"No more," Tauran said to Vhok. "You made your objections clear the day we left, and I've heard enough. Keep your silence."

"What? You think I'm some child you can scold and discipline?" the cambion said. "You may compel me to assist you in stopping Zasian, but you hold no sway over what I say."

Tauran closed his eyes and swallowed. He did not open them as he spoke. "Perhaps," he explained, "but if you do not cease your complaints, it will hinder my ability to think clearly, and we might not be successful in denying the priest his scheme."

He opened his eyes again. Vhok tried to say something, but he could not form the words. The harder he worked at it, the more his eyes bulged. Veins in his neck stood out from the exertion of trying to defy the *geas* upon him. When he finally stopped, he just glared at Tauran and then moved off a few steps to pace.

"That was clever," Kael said, keeping his voice soft so that Vhok could not hear.

Tauran sighed. "I didn't even mean for it to work that way," he said. "I merely wanted him to understand how maddening his comments have become. I'm losing control, Kael. Everything is slipping through my fingers."

The knight cocked his head to one side. Tauran could see the worry in the half-drow's eyes. "You're just weary and frustrated," he said, trying to sound encouraging. "You know we're close. And I'm here to help. Just tell me what we need to do."

Tauran took another deep breath, thinking. He wanted to tell Kael that the champion's trust in him was misplaced, that he had led them all on a big, frolicking adventure to a dead end and had managed to ruin all their lives in the process. Instead, he said, "We need to find a way to get inside the rotunda." He pointed to the dome at the top of the Hall of Petitions. "That's where my vision happened. That's where Zasian and Kashada will steal Azuth's staff. You saw it, too."

Kael shook his head as if trying to shake something free. He scrubbed his hand across his face. "I saw it, too," he said. "It's just so hard to believe that such a thing could happen. As powerful as they are, there's no way that Zasian and Kashada, two mere mortals, could sneak in there and steal the Old Staff right out from beneath Azuth's nose."

"If I had told you before all this started that Tyr would slay Helm, would you have found that easy to believe?"

Kael stared at the ground. He shrugged. "No," he admitted. "It would have seemed preposterous. I suppose I just can't imagine how they're going to pull it off."

"That's not important," Tauran said, laying a hand on his companion's shoulder. "Whatever Cyric's intentions are, no good can come of it. And if we can warn Azuth—either directly or through his most trusted advisors—we may never find out what the Liar planned. But if we don't get past all this bureaucracy and actually stop him, Zasian *will* succeed."

Kael nodded. "Maybe we're going about this all wrong," he said. He turned toward Vhok. "Half-fiend, come here."

Vhok turned and frowned. "You do not give me orders, whelp," he growled.

Tauran started to intervene, but Kael held his hand for the angel to wait. "I know, but we need your expertise."

Vhok grimaced, but he rejoined the two of them. "What?"

Kael smiled. "We need to figure out how to break in

there"—he pointed to the dome—"and we figure you're just the clever fellow to come up with a plan."

Tauran tilted his head, looking appreciatively at Kael. Very good, he thought. Draw him in, get him interested again.

Vhok stared at the imposing edifice for a few moments. "Very well," he said. "What do we know about it?"

Tauran shook his head and interrupted. "Not here," he cautioned. "Let's get off the avenue and talk about this somewhere private."

The trio turned and headed away from the Hall of Petitions. They found a private spot within a stone garden and sat down together beneath a series of crystalline columns to discuss things.

"This is where that arcane magic you like to look down your nose at might just come in handy," Vhok said to Tauran as they began to plan.

❖ ❖ ❖ ❖ ❖ ❖ ❖ ❖

This isn't going to work, Kael projected. *They must have safeguards in place for tricks like this.*

Kaanyr would have smiled if he had a mouth, but he had rendered his body insubstantial and nearly invisible through the use of some of his favorite magic. In gaseous form he glided along the roof of the lowest floor of the Hall of Petitions. He angled toward a wall surrounding the next level of the edifice. Behind him, Tauran and Kael moved in similar fashion.

You'd be surprised, the cambion said. *Everyone expects the flashy magic—the teleportation, the invisibility—but no one ever thinks to watch for a near-transparent cloud of gas. Just stay low, against the surfaces, and you'll be fine.*

Kaanyr's plan had also called for them to link mentally to

one another. He needed a few simple items from a vendor in the streets to pull it off. He was proud of its simplicity.

Well, this may get us to the rotunda, but getting inside will be another matter, Kael said. *There's bound to be a whole host of protective spells there to keep us out.*

We'll deal with that when the time comes, Tauran interjected. *We only need to make them see the threat. Even if they catch us, at least we'll have gotten their attention and can explain the dire situation to them.*

A thought had been plaguing Kaanyr, one that he had stubbornly shoved to the back of his mind. He didn't want to think about it, but he could no longer ignore it. *How do we know Zasian hasn't already succeeded?* he asked.

I think we'd have noticed if something had happened, Tauran replied. His thought conveyed wry amusement. *You don't steal the Lord of Spells's staff without a bit of noticeable backlash.*

Kaanyr had to admit that would be true. *Still,* he argued, *Zasian and Kashada might already be up there, getting ready.*

Perhaps, Tauran said. *But even if that is so, we are not too late—yet.*

Recognizing the angel's sense of urgency, Kaanyr focused on getting the three of them to the dome as quickly as their magic would allow. He led them up and over the wall, where they encountered a colonnaded porch. From there, they climbed to another level and drifted past windows and balconies until they reached a great plaza that surrounded the dome.

The cambion spied sentries everywhere they moved, both archons and angels, dressed in the livery of Azuth and keeping a watchful eye on the surroundings. He led his two companions between the guards, through places where they would best blend in with the architecture. They traveled along corners, glided up columns, and at one point they even seeped through a series of cracks in the stonework, passing right between a hound archon's feet.

Kaanyr thought of Aliisza. He wondered again why she had not returned to the docks to meet them. He remembered the grizzled guide at the docks and his suggestion that some never returned from their journey.

Is that what happened? he wondered. Are you trapped there forever? The thought made him remarkably sad. He felt a brief surge of renewed anger at the angel for leaving her behind.

In his own way, Kaanyr knew he loved her. She could be insufferable at times, strong-headed and too cunning by half. But they had shared much together, and he missed her.

If you could see me now, the cambion thought wryly, helping these two like this, you'd smirk and tell me I was letting my human side get the best of me. He shrugged. Maybe I am.

The real conundrum in Vhok's mind was, he didn't know if he was doing it because Tauran had compelled him or because Aliisza would have insisted on it if she were there. Kaanyr sighed and swore yet again that, when they were finished dealing with Zasian and when the angel released him from his servitude, he would return to the Eye of Savras and find her.

What now? Kael asked, drawing Kaanyr our of his thoughts. *We're almost to the rotunda.*

Kaanyr had led them all the way to a narrow railing that encircled the great dome. Narrow windows pierced the surface of the dome at regular intervals there, too small for most creatures to fit through.

Through the gaps, Kaanyr instructed. *And we'll see what we see.*

He moved to slip through one of the windows and felt a trigger of magic. He had disturbed some arcane barrier.

Uh-oh, he projected. *I think I tripped an alarm.*

I can sense it, too, Tauran answered. *Too late to worry about now. Is something barring you?*

Kaanyr tested the window and discovered that it was not blocked. He told Tauran and Kael as much and glided through the gap.

The cambion emerged into a large, curving hallway that clearly surrounded an inner chamber within the dome. Deep azure carpet covered marble floors, and graceful sweeping arches ran from the floor to the ceiling along the outer wall in between each window. Farther down to Kaanyr's left, a set of double doors led into the interior of the dome. In the opposite direction, he could see a pair of archons and a green-skinned, bald-headed planetar approaching. They moved rapidly, clearly in a hurry.

I think they're coming to investigate us, Kaanyr projected. *Whatever we're going to do, we'd better do it fast. They won't overlook us now that they're wary.*

You two keep going, Tauran instructed. *I will confront them. I will try to stall them so you can get inside and warn someone, but whatever happens to me, don't stop.*

That's not wise, Kaanyr said. *You're an angel, more reputable than either of us in these parts. You should be the one to keep going. They'll listen to you inside. Let me hold them off. A cambion trying to sneak into Azuth's inner sanctum may seem like suicide, but it will also be a reasonable explanation for why we're sneaking in and not knocking on the front door. They won't think to look for accomplices quite as fast.*

He's right, Kael agreed. *Speak the truth, and they will listen to you. But we don't belong here.*

I can't let you do that, Tauran said. *I am the one respon—*

To the Hells with that, Kaanyr decided. He's not coming up with some coercive reason to make me obey. Before Tauran could finish, the cambion banished his spell of gaseousness and materialized in front of the oncoming celestials.

Beside Kaanyr, Kael appeared just as suddenly. *I guess we had the same idea,* he said, grinning.

You two are both fools, Tauran said.

Kaanyr smiled back at the knight as he raised his hands in supplication. *I couldn't help myself,* he answered. *It just occurred to me that it was the best chance to succeed, and it happened on its own.*

You're a liar, Vhok, Tauran said. *Thank you.*

Just go, Kael said. He, too, had his hands in the air. *Stop Zasian.*

The celestials approached the pair of half-fiends warily, their eyes wide. "Unbelievable!" the planetar said, raising his enchanted sword. "How dare you defile this holy place of magic, you fiends!"

"We surrender," Kael said. "We must spea—"

Kael's explanation got cut off as the planetar spoke an all-too-familiar word of power.

The resultant blast of holy energy knocked Kaanyr unconscious.

❖ ❖ ❖ ❖ ❖ ❖ ❖

Kael watched Vhok crumple to the floor beside him and then turned back to the planetar in disbelief.

The emerald-skinned creature watched them both, and when he realized that his divine attack had not affected Kael, he brought his sword up and began stalking forward.

"Wait!" Kael said, his hands still raised in the air. "We are surrendering!"

"You are intruders defiling the sacred inner sanctum of Azuth himself, and you shall be slain!" the planetar replied. He kept coming.

Behind him, the two archons vanished. Kael assumed they had fled to seek help.

With a growl of frustration, Kael dropped his hands and grabbed his own sword. He raised it into position and stepped in front of Vhok. "I don't want a fight, but I won't let you just cut us both down," he said.

The planetar raised his eyebrows in surprise. "You think you have a choice in the matter?" he asked. "I don't remember offering one."

The celestial swung his blade at Kael. The champion of Torm countered the stroke with his own weapon. The two swords clanged together and sent shivers down Kael's arms. Sparks flew from the grating edges. Kael grunted at the force of the blow.

The angel swung again, and it was all Kael could do to get his defenses up in time to parry the attack. The power of it forced him back. He had to mind his footwork so as not to stumble over Vhok.

Fool angel, Kael thought. As bad as Micus and the High Council. "Why won't you listen to me?" he demanded. "I am not your enemy!"

The emerald creature said nothing but continued to press his attacks.

Again and again the planetar attacked, and each time, Kael barely managed to deflect the strike. The creature was simply too strong. He would wear the knight down in only a matter of moments.

I'm not afraid to die, he thought. But this is wrong. Such a waste.

"You have the power to tell if I'm lying," Kael said. "Use it! I'm here because of a common enemy. Tell me how to prove that, how I can win your trust."

The planetar struck again, and the force of the blow knocked Kael's blade completely to the side. He was exposed. The celestial attacked once more, slicing into the half-drow's arm. The plating there split in half and the sword sliced deeply into the flesh beneath.

Kael grunted and stumbled down onto one knee. "Come now!" he shouted. "Do something smarter than just kill me, you idiot!"

But the planetar drew back for another, killing stroke.

◆ ◆ ◆ ◆ ◆ ◆ ◆ ◆

Tauran let his flowing, vaporous body drift beneath the heavy doors. The moment he got beyond the portal and into the chamber, he dismissed the magic keeping him insubstantial and returned to his solid form.

A chill went down the angel's spine.

He stood in the rotunda, the same one from his vision. It was identical in nearly every detail, only everything appeared sharper and clearer to his eyes.

A set of columns stood in a circle halfway between the surrounding wall and the center of the room, rising to the domed ceiling, which was cloaked in darkness overhead. A few candles set in holders on those columns kept the chamber dimly lit, leaving plenty of gloom around the perimeter.

The angel saw one difference between the real version and his vision. No gods stood within. He did not feel the presence of anyone. There was no staff to steal.

He had expected to find celestial beings—solars, perhaps—to convince. He had imagined the chamber serving as a council room, such as what he was used to back in the House of the Triad. But Tauran stood alone within the rotunda.

True apprehension crashed through him, one of the few times in the angel's long existence that he felt such.

Very well, he thought. I'm here. Tyr has abandoned me, and I seem to be playing right into Zasian's hands. Now what?

The deva took a few steps forward, staring into every shadow. He strained to spy what might be hiding behind the columns. He sought other doors or windows, any means at all of entering the room. No one seemed to be there, nor did it appear that they could slip in without sentries noticing.

I did it, Tauran reminded himself. But perhaps I am the first to arrive.

He walked farther into the chamber. His footsteps echoed within the confines of the round wall until he stood within the exact center, where every sound bounced back to him in perfect clarity. Even the deva's breaths returned to his ears. They sounded unduly rapid, nervous.

If someone else were there, he would hear them.

But Tauran was no fool.

"Zasian," he called. He kept his voice soft, but the word came back to him from every direction. "I know you're here. You cannot hide forever."

Tauran heard a faint rustle of cloth and turned to see a tall, handsome man dressed in black with highlights of gold in his tunic step out of the shadows beyond one of the columns. He stood a few paces away from the angel, smiling. His dark hair hung down his back past his shoulders, matching the color of his flowing moustache. A pendant hanging from a chain around his neck, a silver skull, marked him as a priest of Cyric.

Zasian Menz.

"Very good," Zasian said. "You figured out my little secret."

Another rustle, quieter than Zasian, reached the deva from his right. He spotted a form of darkness and shadows emerge. He glanced at it and confirmed that it was Kashada the Nightwraith. Her figure remained swathed in shadow, indistinct. Midnight eyes smiled at him from above her veil.

Tauran swallowed his worry. "Your welcoming party at the dryad village told me all I needed to know," he said. "But then, you knew it would, didn't you? You wanted me to figure all this out."

"Down to the last little detail," Zasian replied. "And you performed admirably."

"But why? Whatever my role is supposed to be in your plan, you cannot truly hope to steal Azuth's staff," Tauran said. "Bringing me here was a mistake. You know I will try to stop you."

"Oh, I'm counting on it," the priest said. "You'd be surprised what a little distraction will do for Kashada's chances to succeed."

As if that were a signal, Kashada stepped backward and vanished into the deeper shadows of the chamber. At the same moment, Zasian moved toward Tauran, his pendant in hand.

❖ ❖ ❖ ❖ ❖ ❖ ❖ ❖ ❖

Micus stared across the plaza at the Hall of Petitions. "You are certain?" he asked the zelekhut beside him. "Tauran is within?"

The centaurlike construct nodded. "Indeed," it said in its flat, mechanical voice. "Within that dome at the highest point." It pointed to the apex of the cavern.

Micus frowned. "Now, how did he manage to pull that off?"

"I am afraid I do not know," the zelekhut answered.

Micus dismissed the response with a wave of his hand. "No, of course not." *But I'm going to have to get inside, and that's going to be tricky.*

"I think you will have to wait for me here," the angel said. "I can move faster by myself."

"As you wish," the construct replied.

Micus strolled across the plaza to the imposing building, leaving the zelekhut behind.

I could ask for an immediate audience, the angel thought. *But would they receive me without the required notifications that I am here on official business? Probably not. The need is great, though, so perhaps . . .*

Micus paused midstep. Aliisza the alu swooped in and settled to the ground in front of the main entrance to the hall. She stood there a moment, peering up at its façade as if deep in thought.

She hasn't seen me, the angel realized. *She can be my bargaining chip.*

Micus moved toward the half-fiend, careful to remain quiet. He longed for his mace. He felt naked without his weapon, but that wretch Tauran had taken it.

He had other options.

"Well met, Aliisza," he said quietly.

The alu gasped and whirled to face him. She staggered back and reached for the hilt of her sword.

Before she could take hold of it, though, Micus uttered a word of power.

The half-fiend tumbled backward as if he had slammed into her with a battering ram. She crumpled to the paving stones of the avenue and lay still. A few passersby stopped and stared.

"Escaped fugitive," Micus explained. The onlookers shrugged or muttered and went on their way.

Micus quickly disarmed Aliisza and motioned for the zelekhut to assist him. The construct approached.

"Watch her," the angel said, gesturing. "She is slippery. Secure her for me and be ready for her tricks."

The zelekhut nodded and extended its chains from its forearms. It wrapped them around the alu and made her immobile.

Micus sorely wished that he had the dimensional shackles with him, but they, like everything else, had returned to the House of the Triad with Garin. Micus should have gone, too, but he had refused Garin's urgings.

I *will* catch him, the angel vowed. This will end. Tyr's laws *will* be upheld.

Aliisza stirred. She blinked a few times and groaned. She tried to sit up, pulling against her bonds.

"Don't," Micus warned. "Or I will scour you with the wrath of Tyr again."

She froze and looked at him, grimacing. She sank back down. "Listen to me," she said, her voice filled with desperation. "I know you think you've got to stop Tauran, but if you do this thing, something terrible is going to happen."

"Hush," Micus said. "Enough of your lies. I have a single

task before me, and that is to bring Tauran to justice."

Aliisza rolled her eyes. "You're unbelievable," she said, but there was no admiration in her tone. "You have the power to see if I am truthful, and you're so full of pride that you won't use it."

"Where is he?" Micus asked.

She said nothing, but her eyes betrayed her thoughts as they flicked toward the building behind her.

"I know he's in there," Micus said, "but what is he doing?"

"Trying to stop Cyric from stealing Azuth's staff. Because if Cyric does, another god is going to die," she said. "It's what I'm trying to tell you, and if you weren't such a bull-headed fool, you'd know that!"

For a moment, Micus could only gape. That was not possible. Cyric was a cowardly, craven worm. Micus shook his head, dismissing the thought.

"You lie," he said. "Once more, and I will ask Tyr to send you to oblivion. Now, what is truly happening?"

"I speak the truth," she said. "I saw it. In the Eye of Savras. Zasian and Kashada are there, too, trying to steal Azuth's staff. All they need is a distraction, and you and Tauran are going to provide it for them if you storm in there and try to subdue him. I think Cyric means to kill Mystra with it. What can I do to prove it to you?"

Micus blinked. What she claimed was preposterous. Mortals, stealing the cherished possessions of gods? Still, he sensed that she believed it.

"Azuth's host will stop them," he said. "They do not need my help to deal with this."

"Oh, yes," Aliisza said. "Just like all of you did such a good job stopping them in the House."

Micus mused for a moment. Then inspiration struck. "If what you say is true, then this crime cannot be committed if Tauran and I do not battle. True?"

Aliisza nodded. "Yes. That's what I saw. Tauran tries to stop Zasian, and you try to stop him. Kashada steals the staff during the commotion."

"Then come with me," Micus said. "Convince Tauran to surrender without a fight."

Aliisza's eyes widened. "You're asking me to betray him?"

"If you believe your own vision, then you are actually saving him." *And he's already betrayed himself, and you, in so many ways you can't imagine,* he thought. *It's hardly the worst thing that will befall him, believe me.*

The alu bit her lip. "I can't," she said. "I can't do that to him."

"You'd rather see him bring about this terrible crime? That's almost like aiding Cyric yourself. You'd be no better than Zasian and Kashada." He felt a tinge of guilt at suggesting that, but she had to see the consequences of her choices. "Is that what you want?"

"Of course not!"

"Then do this. For him, as well as for me. You have to know that I will take Tauran eventually, even without your help."

Aliisza groaned.

Micus knew he had her then.

❖ ❖ ❖ ❖ ❖ ❖ ❖ ❖

Kaanyr groaned and became aware. The sound of battle filled his ears, but in his groggy state, it didn't make sense at first. He rolled over, blinking to clear the cobwebs from his mind, and peered in the direction of the fight.

Kael faced off with the planetar. The two exchanged blows, their swords ringing like hammers on an anvil with each strike. It appeared to Vhok that the celestial was getting the better of the half-drow.

I must help him, the cambion thought. He struggled to rise, but his limbs felt like jelly. Get up, Vhok. Stand and fight!

"You have the power to tell if I'm lying," Kael said, frantically deflecting a series of vicious attacks. "Use it! I'm here because of a common enemy. Tell me how to prove that—how I can win your trust."

The planetar's next swing opened Kael's defenses wide. The celestial brought his blade down again, and Kael grunted and crumpled down before the onslaught.

Rage boiled in Kaanyr. Old hatred bubbled up, disdain and spite for the rigid, holier-than-thou attitudes of cursed celestials. He rose to his knees.

"Come!" The knight shouted. "Do something smarter than just kill me, you idiot!"

Kaanyr slid his own blade free of its scabbard.

The planetar raised his sword to finish Kael off.

Kaanyr jumped, drawing on every bit of his reserves of strength. It was a weak attack, a pitiful display. But the sword dug into the planetar's back, and black, malevolent energy crackled over the celestial.

The planetar roared in pain and staggered. His killing blow went astray enough that Kael rolled to the side to avoid it. Kaanyr fell forward to his hands and knees. The planetar pitched off balance and took three stumbling steps until he careened off the wall and sprawled.

Kael climbed to his feet, and Kaanyr noted that the

half-drow's arm was a mangled, bloody mess. He could only drag his sword with his good hand, but he came to the cambion and proffered it as a brace. "Get up," Kael said.

Kaanyr eyed him, but the planetar was already rising. Vhok grabbed the hilt of Kael's sword and dragged himself to his feet. Together, they turned to the planetar.

"Since you're too thick-headed to listen," Kaanyr said to the emerald-skinned being, "it's time for you to—"

Kael! Vhok! Aid me!

The desperation in Tauran's mental message slammed into Kaanyr. The cambion wanted to resist, wanted to finish off the planetar, but Tauran's insistence was clear.

Vhok had no choice.

Together, he and Kael lumbered forward. As they reached the celestial just rising to his feet, they slammed their shoulders into him and knocked him into the wall again. Then they aided each other down the curved hallway toward the door to the rotunda.

CHAPTER SEVENTEEN

V ery well," Aliisza said, her voice choked with guilt. "I'll help you."

I hate you, she thought, glaring at Micus.

The angel did not notice, or if he did, he did not react. He nodded curtly, acknowledging her acquiescence, but otherwise, he showed no emotion.

For some odd reason, Aliisza had expected him to gloat.

"Release her," Micus commanded, and the centaurlike construct loosened the chains around her and retracted them. "One false step, one shout of warning to try to allow Tauran to flee, and I will make certain you spend the rest of your days in a gray void, with no contact with anyone, ever again." The angel gave Aliisza a hard stare. "Do you understand?"

"Yes," the alu snapped. "Now hurry!"

She prepared to open a dimensional portal.

"Stop," Micus warned. "Not like that. We must follow protocol, procedure. We may not trespass on this sacred place."

"There's no time!" Aliisza snarled. "We have to reach him right now. Do you want my help?"

"I've already secured it," Micus answered. "Would you back out of our agreement already?"

"If you don't listen to me, yes," the alu said. "I am not bound by your myopic sense of law. For once, you're going to have to bend the rules a bit for the greater good."

Micus stared at her, considering.

"Which is the bigger problem?" she demanded, "violating protocol or letting Tauran slip away again?"

Micus's frown deepened, but he nodded. "Do it," he said. "I will face the consequences later."

Relieved, Aliisza opened her doorway. She nearly ran through the thing to get to Tauran.

On the other side of the portal, the alu found herself standing in the very same chamber she had seen in her vision. Everything, from the columns to the shadows, matched her memory of the place. Only the gods seemed to be missing.

Tauran crossed the middle of the chamber, bloody and panting. His mace hung from one hand, nearly dragging on the ground. One wing sat cocked at a wrong angle, and his tunic was blackened and smoking.

Across from him, Zasian Menz retreated. He limped slightly, and one arm hung uselessly at his side, but the other hand held a pendant aloft, and a faint smile shone in his eyes as he chanted. A shimmering glow of amber light radiated around him, a magical barrier of protection.

Tauran tried to close the gap. He hefted his mace with both hands to strike at the priest. The weapon wobbled unsteadily in the air.

"No!" Aliisza shouted. "Tauran, stop!"

The alu felt Micus step through the door behind her. She released the doorway and ran to Tauran. "Don't fight him!" she pleaded as she reached the angel's side. "It's what he wants." She reached for his arm and tried to force him to lower his mace. "He needs to steal the staff."

Across from her, Zasian completed his spell, and the amber glow expanded, became a sphere of energy that surrounded him.

"I know," Tauran gasped, "and I have to stop him."

"No, Tauran," Micus said from behind them. "It's not your task. Listen to her. Surrender and come back with me."

Tauran had been staring at Zasian, grim determination on his countenance, but at the sound of the other angel's voice, he turned to Aliisza.

The hurt and anguish in his eyes bore into her. "You brought him?" he asked.

"Please," Aliisza said, hating herself. "I know it seems like I betrayed you, but my vision . . . I know what happens if you resist. Don't do this! Step back, walk away. Please," she pleaded, still holding his arm. She felt him sag, all the will to keep fighting leaving him.

Zasian chuckled. "Well played, Aliisza. But it won't make any difference. What's done is done."

Aliisza ignored the priest and watched Tauran's face. He just stood there, looking deeply into her eyes as if searching for some form of understanding. "I knew it would be you," he mumbled. "Kael and Vhok, I understand their hearts. But you . . ."

Please don't do this, Aliisza thought desperately. Please understand why.

The door to the chamber slammed open. Aliisza looked over Tauran's shoulder and spotted Kael and Kaanyr staggering in. Her son's arm hung bloody and useless, and the cambion had a glazed look in his eyes. They propped one another up like two sailors after a long and boisterous night at the taproom.

"Trouble on our heels," Kael said as he guided Kaanyr to Aliisza and Tauran. When he saw Zasian and Micus both in the chamber, the champion of Torm slowed. "Looks like trouble in here, too. Vhok, it's time to swing that sword of yours."

"No!" Aliisza shouted. "Don't engage them. That's what Zasian wants."

"Don't listen to her," Tauran said. "She's betrayed us, brought Micus here with her." With that, the angel shoved Aliisza away and limped toward Zasian.

The alu fell to the ground. "Stop!" Aliisza pleaded. "This is just what he wants!"

But none of her three companions paid any attention to her at all.

Kael gave her a single searing glance, then began chanting as he made a line for Micus. The knight's expression sent a stab of pain through Aliisza's heart.

My son, she thought. He hates me.

As Kael closed with Micus, his arm began to function normally again. He brought his sword up. "Help us or stay out of the way," he said.

Micus frowned. "It's time I teach you a proper lesson in respect for your superiors," he said without any eagerness at all. He still held the sword he had taken from Aliisza earlier. He swished it in the air a couple of times to get a feel for the blade, then turned his full attention to Kael.

Aliisza turned to Kaanyr. "Wait," she said to him. "Let me explain. You're playing right into Zasian's hands!"

Kaanyr gave Aliisza one brief, puzzled stare, then shook his head in consternation and hefted his sword. Clearer eyed than he had been before, he followed after Tauran, moving so as to circle around and flank the priest of Cyric.

Him, too, Aliisza realized, devastated. They all believe I betrayed them. And I did, she admitted. Guilt and anger washed over her. Despite her foreknowledge, despite all her efforts, everything was playing out just as it had in the vision.

A hint of movement caught Aliisza's eye. It came from several feet up, a figure drifting out of the shadows right at Kaanyr, from behind him where he couldn't see. The thing looked like a bluish hobgoblin with dragon wings, and it held a massive war axe in its hands.

Myshik, Aliisza realized.

She opened her mouth to shout a warning to Kaanyr, but the creature reached the cambion just as she blurted, "Watch out!" and drove the blade hard into her lover's back.

Kaanyr grunted and staggered forward as blood sprayed everywhere.

Myshik settled to the ground and plodded after the cambion.

No, Aliisza thought helplessly. Don't kill him! She staggered to her feet.

Tauran swung his mace at Zasian with both hands, but the weapon bounced harmlessly off the amber barrier surrounding the priest. The countershock sent the angel teetering backward, off-balance.

Zasian raised his hand and gestured. A column of pale yellow flame erupted around Tauran, scouring him. Aliisza could see the angel flinch in anguish and drop his mace.

Stop, she silently pleaded, tears welling in her eyes. Don't do this.

Behind the alu, Kael screamed.

Aliisza whirled around to see Micus driving the blade—her

blade—through the knight's gut. The angel pushed Kael backward, using Aliisza's weapon to guide him against a column. When the half-drow struck it with his back, Micus shoved the sword in deeper.

My son! Tears streamed down her face. Don't kill my son, she pleaded.

Zasian stood over Tauran's still form and chuckled. "Now do you see the power of the lie?" he asked Aliisza. "Now, when you've been a party to the betrayal, do you understand the triumph of deceit?" The priest gestured around the room. "This is it. This is Cyric's moment. And you played your role O, so well, Aliisza."

The alu glared at Zasian through her tears. She wanted to claw his eyes out. She took a single step forward. "Burn in the Nine Hells for eternity, you—"

Zasian gasped and his eyes went wide. He staggered forward, his arms flailing. He seemed to be trying to reach behind him, but his arms wouldn't work right. He fell to one knee, his eyes rolling up in his head.

Behind the priest, a woman stood there, indistinct and cloaked in shadow. Only her eyes appeared real, and they glittered with delight. She held a black dagger in her hand, dripping with Zasian's blood.

Kashada, Aliisza realized.

Zasian began to shake. He looked back over his shoulder as his body slumped. He fell to the stones of the floor, twitching, staring at the shadow-shrouded woman. "You!" he said hoarsely. "What have you done?"

Kashada giggled. "Cyric sends his regards," she said to Zasian. Her voice was husky with allure. "He thanks you for your service. The betrayal is now complete." Then she looked up and stared at Aliisza.

Aliisza didn't know what possessed her to do it, but at that moment, she drew on the magic of Pharaun's ring. Kashada became clear and solid to her.

Where a shadow-image of mysterious beauty once existed, a decrepit woman stood, garbed in simple robes. The woman's homely, wrinkled face smirked, and her graying hair hung down in limp strands behind her back. A nimbus surrounded the old woman. Aliisza could see it as a larger figure, a beautiful black-skinned creature of lithe grace and dangerous cunning.

The raven beauty from her vision.

Shar.

The nimbus of Shar held a large staff in one hand like a walking stick.

The alu understood, and she wanted to retch.

Kashada and Shar were connected. Kashada *was* Shar—or a tiny piece of her. The shadow-mystic had been made, a creature to serve but one purpose, so that Shar could be in two worlds at once and steal a staff. Everything else was just one more lie, one more betrayal. Zasian had been told the biggest lie of all, by his own god.

The realization that some small part of Shar stood in that room with her made Aliisza tremble. She wanted to throw herself prostrate on the floor, to hide her eyes. But she could not tear her gaze away.

The nimbus and the old woman smiled together, but it was not a warm expression. There was cold satisfaction there, and hatred. Hatred for all things living.

The pair of them disappeared, leaving only a swirl of shadows.

"No!" Aliisza screamed into the darkness.

Myshik stepped out of the shadows to one side.

"Please," he said, lifting his bloody axe and coming toward Aliisza. "Don't do that. It hurts my ears."

Aliisza sobbed. "But I saw it," she said, looking at him plaintively. "I saw him kill her, with the staff."

The half-dragon smirked and opened his mouth to say something in reply, but the words never came.

Aliisza felt a ripple of something pass through her. It was magic, pure, undiluted. A bubble. It crashed into the alu, through her.

Everything around her shimmered with the ripple's passing. It looked different afterward, for the heartbeat that she could take it all in.

Then the fabric of reality imploded.

FORGOTTEN REALMS®

They were built to display might.
They were built to hold secrets.
They will still stand while their builders fall.

THE CITADELS

NEVERSFALL
ED GENTRY
It was supposed to be Estagund's stronghold in monster-ridden Veldorn, an unassailable citadel to protect the southern lands ... until the regiment holding Neversfall disappeared, leaving no hint of what took them.

OBSIDIAN RIDGE
JESS LEBOW
Looming like a storm cloud, the Obsidian Ridge appears silently and without warning over the kingdom of Erlkazar, prepared to destroy everything in its reach, unless its master gets what he wants.

THE SHIELD OF WEEPING GHOSTS
JAMES P. DAVIS
Frozen Shandaular fell to invaders over two thousand years ago, its ruins protected by the ghosts and undead that haunt the ancient citadel. But to anyone who can evade the weeping dead, the northwest tower holds a deadly secret.

SENTINELSPIRE
MARK SEHESTEDT
The ancient fortress of Sentinelspire draws strength from the portals that feed its fires and pools, as well as the assassins that call it home. Both promise great power to those dangerous enough to seize them.

Stand-alone novels that can be read in any order!

From acclaimed author and award-winning
game designer James Wyatt, an adventure
that will shake the world of EBERRON
to its core.

THE DRACONIC PROPHECIES

were old when humans first began to forge their civilization.
They give meaning to the past, guidance in the present, and
predict the future—a future of the world's remaking. And now,
one facet of the prophecies is being set in motion, and all of
it revolves around Gaven, exiled from his house, thrown into
prison, and in the grips of a terrible madness.

Book One
Storm Dragon

Book Two
Dragon Forge

Book Three
Dragon War

And don't miss James Wyatt's first EBERRON novel
In the Claws of the Tiger
Janik barely survived his last expedition to the dark continent,
but when he finds himself embroiled in a plot involving the
lost wonders of Xen'drik, his one hope at redemption is to
return and face the horrors that once almost destroyed him.